I0562484

ACKNOWLEDGEMENTS

Nearly all of the material regarding pioneer life along the Big and Little Sewickley Creeks came from a pamphlet entitled *History of Sewickley Township*, compiled by John J. Wilson in 1962. It is a collection of stories and photos submitted by people who grew up in the area and were knowledgeable of historical events. The photographs on the front and back covers of the book came from that pamphlet. The Westmoreland Coal photo was originally provided by Herman Brown. Other information was obtained through interviews, internet research and personal experience.

Historical information on the Shawnee and Cherokee Indians was obtained from Lee Sultzman's website www.tolatsga.org, the Museum of the Cherokee Indian and the Oconaluftee Indian Village in Cherokee, NC and from other books and articles of history too numerous to list.

Data on the Hessians came from *Hessian (soldiers) – Wikipedia*. A recount of Pittsburgh's early history was obtained from Stefan Lorant's *Pittsburgh – The Story of an American City (1975)*. The photos of Running Creek, Moon Shadow and Rilla came from the Cherokee Museum in Cherokee, NC. I acquired the photo of Ear Flop viz. a greeting card produced by leanintreemuseum.com (original art work by Russ Docken).

Virtually all of the information on the coal mining history and operations came from Historian and Editor Raymond A. Washlaski's *The Old Miner, (website:patheoldminer.rootsweb.ancestry.com.)* Added credit goes to Kurt Kragness, who posted the memoirs of Frank Dushack and to Marjorie Wertz, staff writer, Tribune-Review, Greensburg, Pa., for her description of life at the mines in Hahntown. The photo of Miss Welty was provided by Rawn Hutchinson (Weed), an early schoolyard friend who still attends his high school reunions.

I credit Wikipedia for its detailed narrative on the Westmoreland County Coal Strike of 1910-1911, the life of Porky Chedwick and the history of rock and roll, including the stories of Pat Boone, Little Richard and others.

The passages describing the overseas events of World War II, including the 28th Infantry Division and the 101st Airborne came from Lone Sentry at www.lonesentry.com. The names of the Rillton war veterans can be found in a pamphlet entitled *Rillton In World War II* (undated).

A special thank you goes to my old friend and former high school football quarterback Leo Vozel who reminded me of the Gardner point system and the incredible coaching record of John C. Bruno.

Finally, my dependence and appreciation of Jenine, my niece and voluntary editor, cannot be adequately expressed. Without her help, I would have suffered for months on end, trying to piece together a message that made sense. To her I owe my deepest gratitude.

AUTHOR'S NOTE

My story about Rillton, while partly true, is largely fictional. I hope the reader will not only enjoy my version of the events but will remember, or perhaps identify with, some of the people who grew up there. Because Rillton is a real place with its own roots and unique history, retelling the story from my own memory and limited research is a formidable task that I trust will always cause me to wonder, "Did I get it right?"

My days of growing up in Rillton ended in 1961 when I ran off to college, got married and settled down in the Midwest. There I spent the better part of my adult life, though I did manage to visit family back home each year during the holidays. In spite of my life away from Rillton, I have revisited my youthful days there many times in thought. Eventually enough memories were stirred up, along with Rillton's history, to create a story. Regrettably, the story ends in the mid-1960s, when I felt as though I had lost touch with current events in and around what I call my hometown.

RILLTON
A NOVEL

TOM ZIMMERS

The old forget,
The young don't know.
Japanese Proverb

PROLOGUE

Three hundred million years ago the earth was a steamy, hot jungle. Massive ferns 50 feet tall and trees 200 feet high with 30 inch leaves stretched across a great swamp. Over time, the dead trees and plants sunk to the bottom of the swamp, accumulating layer after layer of a soggy, carbon-rich material known as peat. A million years of floods deposited sand and mud over the peat, burying it deeper and deeper into the soil, compressing it twenty-fold and squeezing water from it before eventually transforming it into coal.

Later on, whole continents collided together, uplifting the flat land of Pennsylvania into jagged rows of mountains reaching 16,000 feet. They slanted like table tops, the high ends facing northeast, the low ends facing southwest. Instead of running horizontally beneath the earth's surface, the compressed peat material was pushed about and re-shaped into V-formations, running up and down the newly created hills near the mountains. A few of these coal seams measured only a few inches thick. A large number of them extended some ten or twelve feet thick. Other vanes of unknown depth and thickness still remain buried deep in the earth.

A series of ice ages followed, eroding whole mountain tops to only a third of their original height. As the ice began to melt, huge depressions formed the Great Lakes in addition to many other lakes. Water gushed down the mountainside via numerous rills, carving out new valleys. At the bottom of the mountains, newly formed rivers flowed in all directions.

Following the last ice age (10,000 years ago) the land of western Pennsylvania, with its eroded mountains, slowly developed new-growth forests, thick with trees. Rocky hills nearby became grassy knolls. Vast numbers of four-legged, furry animals which had previously adapted to the arctic environment began roaming the hills - elk, moose, deer, beaver, otter, bear, muskrat, raccoon, squirrel, bison.

There was plenty of meat to supplement the diet of the Monongahela Indians who tried to farm the rocky hilltops as early as 880 BC. They lived in shacks, shaped like beehives, arranged in a circle and protected by a stockade[1]. Aside from the presence of these early Indians and a few other tribes which arrived after 1400 AD, such as the Shawnee, the

[1] There is evidence of a Monongahela Circular Village near Shaner.

pristine landscape of western Pennsylvania remained essentially undisturbed.

But two great waves of change occurred within a 150-year period beginning around 1760. The first wave began when the Commonwealth of Pennsylvania opened up new land for the new English colonists because of their military service out of Ft. Pitt. The rush for land sent native Indians west, though not without conflict. Land was sectioned off, boundaries were marked, fields were plowed, fences constructed and trees cut down. Logs used for building materials and charcoal were hauled by flatboat down the three navigable rivers to Pittsburgh and points beyond.

The second wave came when Pittsburghers decided to manufacture their own goods due to the high cost of transportation from Philadelphia and other cities along the eastern seaboard. Though many industries did well, iron and steel became the frontrunners. The work required a vast supply of coal, which was abundant in the tri-county area. Mining operations dotted the hillsides. Railroads connected the dots so that shortly after the turn of the century, the Industrial Revolution had reached its full impact. Pittsburgh was producing half of the nation's iron and steel. Dust and dirt filled the air in the process. Pittsburgh became the smoky city, and the areas around it weren't much better. Rillton was one of those areas.

PART I

THE LAND OF SEWICKLEY

(Before Rillton)

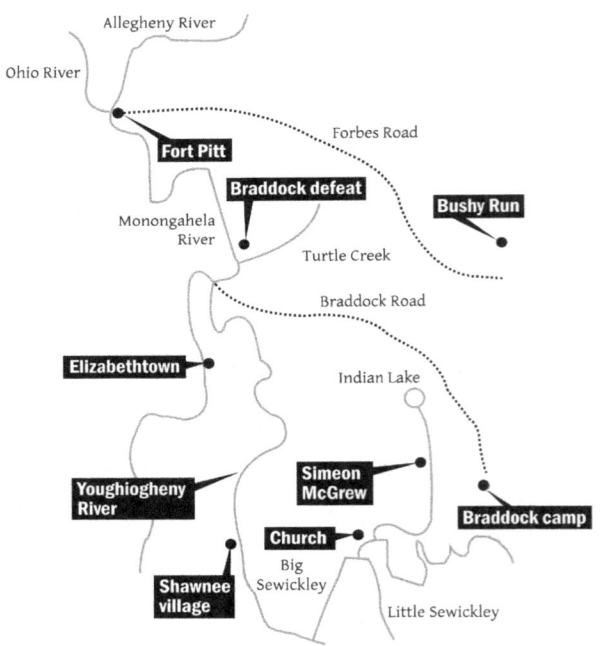

1

THE SHAWNEE

In the year 1630, the Shawnee in the Ohio Valley numbered somewhere around 6000. Shawnee comes from the Algonquin word *shawun* meaning "southerner," the southern area being the Ohio Valley. It included all of southwestern Pennsylvania below the area of the Great Lakes, which everyone called the Land of the Kickapoo.

That year marked the beginning of the Beaver Wars. Beaver pelts were prized trading items, especially with the French. Competition for these furs led to an all out 70-year Indian war. The Shawnee battled not only the Great Lakes tribes from the north but also the Iroquois, whose muskets acquired from the British and whose great numbers all but conquered the remaining Indian tribes in that area. By 1700, only a handful of Shawnee stayed. The rest had scattered in all directions.

RILLTON

Of the five Shawnee sub-nations, one joined the Susquehannocks in the east. Another tribe joined the Cherokee in the Carolinas. A third group settled with the Creek Indians in Georgia, referred to as the Savannahs (present day Savannah, Ga). The 4th group, the Chillicothe, fled west to the Cumberland Basin and later joined forces with the Miami in Ohio and continued to fight for land rights 100 years later. The final group, The Thaweglia, huddled along the Youghiogheny River and held their ground for as long as possible before finally being ousted by the ruthless Iroquois.

The custom of the Shawnee was to name their villages after the sub-nation of which they were a part. Thus, the Thaweglia called their village Thaweglia (Sewickley) as well as the 2 creeks nearby, the Big and Little Sewickley. Alas, following a fierce battle with the Iroquois, the tribe was forced to migrate some 35 miles in search of a new village. Meanwhile, white settlers continued to call the old abandoned village, Sewickley Old Town.

Following the conquest of their enemies, the Iroquois never occupied the land of western Pennsylvania but continued to use it as their prime hunting territory. For practical purposes, the land was uninhabited except for a few Mingo hunting camps located along the upper Ohio River. The Mingo, descendants of the Iroquois, permitted the Sewickley refugees to camp there as well. In time the camp became permanent. It soon became known as

Sewickley Village. Encouraged by the friendly interactions of the Mingo, the Shawnee invited the Delaware to set up their camps too so that by 1748 the population of the Mingo, Shawnee and Delaware approached 10,000 souls, or 2000 warriors. Thereafter, the Sewickley tribe began drifting back to the old camp near the Little Sewickley Creek where they encountered trouble, not with the Iroquois as they might have expected but with the new white settlers along the three rivers known as the Forks of the Ohio. Because of the continued encroachment by these settlers, the Indians periodically conducted raids to drive them out.

The raids consisted of mostly the trashing and burning of farmer crops, the tearing down of fences and an occasional fire to a shed or a barn. This did not deter settlers from cutting down more trees and sectioning off even more land. A build-up of hostilities would lead to skirmishes along this new frontier.

2
THE HESSIAN

During the French and Indian War, volunteers of the British military were offered as a reward for their services 50 acres of land. Most of the volunteers were farmers or artisans from the newly formed colonies. However, roughly 25 percent of them were Germans who came from a principality called Hesse-Kassel. These were the Hessians. Thousands of Hessian troops arrived in the 13 colonies and fought in almost every battle. Among them was Johann Bachman.

Bachman got to know the land near the Youghiogheny River very well. It reminded him of Bavaria. That was his home until age 17 when he was forced to leave the city because of the horrific economic conditions. The core problem there was overpopulation which led to a housing shortage. All over the Rhineland people young and old lived in crowded houses. One in three could not find work, especially young, inexperienced workers. Most of them lived with their parents or on the streets. Ironically, young Bachman led a comparatively stable life while living and working on his uncle's farm. Still, he was frustrated with the crowded conditions and the bleak economy. There were rumors of a better world outside of Deutschland and ideas began to play on his mind. One day he went to an old school teacher for advice.

Hans Gunter, retired language instructor and now a printer of maps, had always encouraged his students to listen. "Listen and learn," he used to say. Gunter, a short-bearded, round-shouldered man with wide suspenders that made his belly protrude, had just finished his second helping of lamb stew when he spotted the young Bachman through the window walking up the steps. He recognized the lad immediately, jumped up and met him halfway to the door.

Gunter: Mein Gott! Vat a delightful surprise to see you. I vonder vether I vould see you again.

Johann smiled: But of course. You are busy wis maps.

Gunter: The world is changing as you know.

Johann: Yah. And because of dat, I thinks I must change too.

Gunter: Aha, so now you come to me and vonder how that can be done?

13

Johann: (eyes widened) How could you know dis?

Gunter: It vas da look on your face. I can tell you one thing for sure. Der changes vill not come so easy if you stay in Bavaria, or any other city here in da Fatherland. Germany is not ready to change from da inside. Der changes must come from da outside.

Gunter looked up at the taller boy and smiled, waiting for a response.

Johann: It is vhat I thought, too. But vhere should I go?

Gunter: Da colonies of New England. Pennsylvania! Dat is the place you must go to. It is za most friendly and za most like Germany. Und it offers the best chance to own land. Some say for free, provided you are villing to vork. Free land? Free land! With that thought in mind, Johann was off, creating dreams of a new life ahead.

In the days that followed, Johann worked feverishly at the farm of his uncle. He pitch-forked hay from the barn with more energy, whistled as he milked the cows, helped deliver two newborn calves (something that he normally avoided), plowed new fields with a vengeance and, in the evenings, mended his torn shirts, socks and other garments. Knowing the boy had made up his mind to leave the farm, Uncle Alfred said little. He saw it coming weeks ago when the boy started yelling at the chickens, swatting the horses for no apparent reason, brooding at night after dinner, staring into the fireplace and just not saying anything. Yes, he knew it was coming. The boy was not happy. Someday soon he would leave the farm. And now the time had come. But would the boy have a change of heart? After all, he seemed happier today, and yesterday, and the day before that. The answer to that question was quickly resolved the next evening at dinner when Johann said, "I need to ask a favor."

"Vhat is it?" asked Gertrude, Alfred's wife. She too knew something was up. Normally, she would not be the one to jump into a   conversation. Her husband, the head of the household, should do the talking. Whatever she had to say could wait until later, when she and Alfred were alone. That was the custom. But somehow she felt compelled to blurt out the question, though she immediately felt embarrassed for doing so. Alfred said nothing.

"Dere is no future in Bavaria, much less Nuremberg, for young males like me," Johann began.

The next morning he was out the door with his travel bag – plus a hundred borrowed marks, courtesy of his uncle – and a feeling of confidence that he had made the correct decision. He spent little time with farewells once the tears begin to swell in his eyes.

Like many young men, Johann went to Hesse-Kassel and quickly joined the volunteer army. A week later he found himself on a boat headed up the Rhein River to Holland. From there he was placed on a ship to Staten Island to fight on the side of the

British. The trip took 29 days. It was the second year of the French and Indian War.

The war began when the British attempted to construct a blockhouse at the Forks of the Ohio. The French destroyed it and proceeded to build Ft. Duquesne in its place. In an effort to recapture the fort, General Braddock with 1400 troops cut a new trail from Ft. Carlisle beginning in July 1755.

It was slow going. Six weeks later, they rested near Simeon McGrew's cabin near the Little Sewickley. During this time, a young soldier accidentally shot and killed the son of the Iroquois Indian guide, Monacutucca. A week later, absent a guide, the inexperienced troops continued four miles up an old Shawnee Indian path until Braddock's troops lost their way on a muddy hill. Braddock decided to hack a new trail along the Youghiogheny which required crossing the Monongahela River[2] twice before setting up camp near Turtle Creek. The troops were exhausted

The next morning advance troops from Braddock's army accidentally bumped into French forces and quickly ran back to the Braddock camp via a narrow path. They collided into the main body of their own men where chaos and disorder followed..

---

[2] Monongahela is an Indian word meaning Falling Banks.

GREAT LAKES WARRIOR

The French and about 300 Great Lakes Indians were able to regroup, mount a coordinated attack and shoot Braddock from his horse. With his troops now cut in half, Braddock was forced to retreat to a campsite 20 miles away. There he died.

A second attempt to capture the fort did not come until 3 years later. It was at this time that Private Bachman, under the direction of a land surveyor named Simeon McGrew, was assigned to cut trees and clear fields for a new road in order to transport an army of 600 men from Ft. Bedford. The creation of this new Forbes Road and the construction of two forts took six months. By September, General Forbes's army was 50 miles from Ft. Duquesne.

Everyone expected an assault the following spring. But instead of fortifying his troops and hunkering down for the winter, Forbes decided to attack at once. When the French commander learned of Forbes' surprise move, he set fire to the fort and retreated north towards Canada. Not a shot was fired. Soon the remaining French traders along the three rivers followed. The area, now secured by Forbes and free of the French nemesis, allowed more English settlers to infiltrate the new land near the Forks.

At the time of the reconstruction of the new British fort, Indian slaves did most of the heavy work. But following an exchange of prisoners, the Hessian soldiers took over those duties. It was during this time that Bachman learned a great deal about carpentry. Once the fort was completed, he was reassigned duties of husbandry, including the complete care of all of the horses. Even though Hessians comprised roughly 25 percent of the militia, neither Bachman nor any of his companions were properly trained in artillery, such as the shooting muskets, howitzers or canons. This was mainly because of British arrogance and feelings of superiority over other Europeans. The British also had suspicions of mercenaries turning into traitors. Nonetheless, Bachman did at least learn how to pack and fire a musket and this would work to his advantage in the months ahead.

With the war ended and the signing of the Easton Treaty, which renounced the claim of territory west of the 3 rivers, the Shawnee expected the families of the British military to leave. But after the completion of Ft. Pitt in 1759, squatters began settling nearby which was in violation of the treaty. In another unexpected and unexplained move, General Forbes suddenly cut off all trading. The Indians felt betrayed. This action literally forced many tribes along the Ohio River to reform alliances with the French. The French were only interested in trading whereas the English had an insatiable hunger for land.

After receiving no response to their many complaints about land violations to British authorities, some of the Indians simply packed up and headed further west to the Ohio Valley. Others – The Delaware, Seneca, Mingo and Shawnee – decided to get rid of the settlements,

In June 1763, Seneca warriors attacked Ft. Pitt. During the month-long siege, 650 settlers sought refuge within the fort. A fur trader, without authority, removed contaminated blankets from the smallpox hospital and traded them to two Delaware Indians. An epidemic spread quickly among the Delaware, then to the Shawnee and other tribes. Hostilities increased. The Delaware and Shawnee burned homesteads, took captives and murdered soldiers and civilians. British soldiers retaliated. Western Pennsylvania had become a killing ground.

3

MOON SHADOW

In the summer of 1749, a forty-six-year-old squaw named Tashonna gave birth to a tiny papoose during a full lunar eclipse. The newborn had a round face, round eyes and round cheeks. Everything about her looked round. It was a sign, Too Sweet thought. They named her Moon Shadow.

Moon Shadow was not a typical little girl in that, despite her cute physical appearance, she displayed many kinds of unusual behavior. Tashonna once found a rat in her baby's bed, squeezed to death by the hands of little Moon Shadow, less than a year old. At age 3, she could arm wrestle boys 4 and 5 years old. At age 6, she spent more and more of her free time playing with boys — chasing turtles, throwing spears, catching toads, squishing mud between her toes as she hunted crayfish, making up new rules for the kickball game which, until now, had been a game for boys only. At age 8, she used her voice to chase away a pack of wolves that had surrounded a small doe across the meadow. "It was her eerie scream that frightened them," a young brave recounted.

Moon Shadow was fascinated with beavers and spent hours watching them construct their stick teepees. Whenever a hunting party gathered, she insisted on tagging along, not because of her interest in killing game, but rather protecting those magnificent creatures with the chiseling teeth. On more than one occasion she would crack a stick or accidentally cough or otherwise find some means to warn the beaver of danger.

On a very hot, sticky day in July when the hunt was not going well and the mood of the hunters was not good for such tactics, Moon Shadow once again made an unnecessary noise as the hunters approached a beaver dam. She was severely reprimanded by the lead scout and ordered back to the village. Disappointed, she dilly-dallied her way along the old deer path and then sat down to rest on a fallen log. She heard a threatening rattle and looked down to see that a coiled serpent was about to strike. Out of fear, she fell backward off the log but quickly gathered her wits and grabbed a sizeable tree limb to club the head of a timber rattlesnake with such force that the snake stood straight up out of its coil before collapsing to the ground. The rattling had stopped. Apparently it was dead.

When Moon Shadow got back to the camp with the 6-foot rattler dragging behind her, Tashonna nearly fainted. Other squaws began to talk. Did the moon event cause this? Why did the moon try to hide its face at the time of the girl's birth? Maybe the moon was ashamed. "The girl was supposed to be a boy," said one squaw.

As the days passed, there was more and more pressure on Toshanna to "do something" about the strange ways of the moon girl, and so Toshanna went to see chief Too Sweet. The chief recommended the child's duties be limited to the agricultural ways of the Cherokee women, for it was their place to tend to domesticated affairs, such as farming and tending to the animals. From now on, only the braves would do the hunting and Moon Shadow would learn squaw work. Toshanna did her best to re-educate the wayward girl. Not an easy task, given Toshanna's weak physical condition caused by whooping cough that tormented her over the last year and given the diffidence of the squaws in the village.

At age 11, when she began showing physical changes, the moon girl displayed yet another new behavior. No longer did she allow young braves to touch, much less pull, her braided hair. And there were other demands: no more wrestling; no more watching her bathe in the lake; no more name calling. She hated the nickname Rattlesnake and severely scolded anyone still calling her by that name.

Too Sweet understood the changes in the young maiden. For reasons he could not fully explain, he had tolerated her rebellious ways more than he did with the other children. Initially, Moon Shadow despised the mandates inflicted upon her and at times argued with the other squaws as to how best to wash the clay pots, pick berries, clean fish or even prepare meals. Later on, she softened her approach and made a valiant effort, it seemed to Too Sweet, to regain respect, to no avail. Why was this child different?

Was it because she had no father to teach her discipline? Was it the recent death of her mother? Maybe it was the moon. The unusual appearance of the moon on the night of her birth surely was some kind of sign. Even so, did not the great Horned Owl appear soon after her delivery, make the moon full and bright again and scare away the crow to save our corn? And did not Father Sun hide his face and allow the rain gods to fill the ponds with fresh water during the long drought?

The child was special. She deserved more leeway, Too Sweet told himself.

Beginning in the fall of 1761, a series of skirmishes with the Chickasaw deep in the Blue Ridge Mountains took place which would eventually force the tribe to migrate north. The Chickasaw, new allies of the British, were given the task of finding an alternative route to the Forks of the Ohio through Virginia territory. Doing so would enable the Ohio Company of Virginia to lay claim to the territory west of the Appalachians.

The feud began with a stolen horse. A party of 20 Cherokee braves set out to retrieve the horse and punish the thieves but they were out-gunned by a small band of Chickasaw who saw the Cherokee advancing. The raiding party waited behind some large rocks high on a ridge and, at the right moment, fired their weapons. All but three of the Cherokee braves were killed. In retaliation, the Cherokee raided two villages, shooting flaming arrows into tents and stealing several horses. The Chickasaw responded by setting fires to Cherokee villages at night as well as trashing their corn crops. There was death and destruction on both sides. As the raids continued, it was clear that the Cherokee tomahawks were no match to the firepower of the long-knives used by their adversary. By springtime the Cherokee had lost nearly all of its 70 warriors, including the war chief who masterminded the ill-advised attacks. It was time to leave.

With now only a small numbers of braves to hunt for food, much less to protect the village from raids and with the squaws now outnumbering the men by nearly three to one, it would have been logical, indeed perfectly natural, for Moon Shadow to once again perform the duties of a brave. Instead she constructed several barrows made of pinewood poles tied together with grass so that the older squaws, many now widowed, could drag their personal goods on the long trek north. Because of this act, Moon Shadow, in a time of crisis, had finally earned the respect of her peers.

By early March 1763, the Cherokee tribe that once numbered 500 had dwindled to 41. With no war chief, no medicine man and no horses, Chief Too Sweet, 7 braves, 13 squaws, 10 maidens, 9 children and Moon Shadow headed north towards the Youghiogheny River. After three days of travel, the tribe rested near the Ohiopyle falls where they killed some otter and caught a few trout. The numerous hills and ravines and rugged terrain made it unsuitable for farming. In addition, the 14 miles of water rapids made it nearly impossible to canoe. Too Sweet quickly led his band further north on the morning of the second day. They came upon the shallow waters of the Youghiogheny where the river extended 200 feet wide. There they spotted a small cabin halfway up a steep ridge to the west.

William Stewart, who had settled at this spot some 10 years prior, called the place Stewarts Crossing. Before that, it was a French trading post. And before that, a campground for the Catawba Indians who created a foot path from the Appalachians to the Ohio River in present day Wheeling, West Virginia.

Stewart was a likeable, friendly, unassuming chap with whom both the French and Indians traded. Unlike other settlers, he built his cabins and barn 200 yards distant from the water, which allowed for the uninterrupted crossing of the river by the Iroquois and others. Furthermore, he had no fences which otherwise might impede horse travelers through the nearby woodlands. In short, this particular colonial settlement in the hills of western Appalachia posed no threat.

When old man Stewart sighted the Indians, he assumed they would simply cross the river and then, like others, follow the old Catawba path north. Instead, the band stopped to look up at the cabin for an extended period. The farmer became concerned, for the Shawnee and the Delaware had issued warnings against such settlements and there was talk of recent Indian attacks at the forks of the river.

Stewart grabbed his rifle, loaded it with powder and gazed down the hill a bit longer to study the group. They did not look like either Shawnee or Delaware, as they were outfitted differently. There were more squaws than braves. No war paint. No horses and few weapons. *Are they lost? Who are these people?*

Something told Stewart to wrap a white flag over the barrel of his rifle and hop down the bank to greet the strangers before they decided to hike up the hill to meet him. Waddling down the embankment, waving the handkerchief flag side to side, bobbing his head up and down between the slippery leaves while weighing any suspicious movements by the Indians, Stewart finally presented himself at the water's edge, still huffing and puffing as overweight white men do in their unique style.

The conversation that followed between Chief Too Sweet and the odd character coming out of the woods was more comical than informative. Stewart, red in the face from sunburn and exhausted from high blood pressure, smiled a wide grin and spoke immediately.

"How!" he half-yelled. "Me Stu," he said, pointing his right thumb to his chest. "You Chief? " He flicked his index finger toward the chief.

At this point, Too Sweet was forced to take a step back because Stewart's foul breath was so grotesque that the chief could not focus on the conversation without first taking in some fresh air. It was the first of several backward steps he would take during the conversation.

Hardly a moment passed following the short meeting before the Indians began heading north to their new destination. Stu now knew for sure these were Cherokee not looking for trouble. He still had his gun, his cabin and his life.

Too Sweet learned that all of the French traders had gone north. The only traders left were a few isolated British settlers along the three rivers. Stewart advised the chief to take the new, hardly used Braddock trail and to avoid the difficult hills along the Youghiogheny. Taking the old man's advice, Too Sweet followed the old Catawba path that led to the Braddock trail, crossed several streams including the

RILLTON

Little Sewickley and finally settled at Indian Lake. As he lay on his blanket inside his makeshift teepee, Too Sweet could see the full moon and swear the man on it was the same one with the bad breath and stinky clothes.

Moon Shadow lay in her bed too, tired and weary but relieved of only two Cherokee deaths during the four day journey. She thought about the events of the last year — the Chickasaw war, the killings, the sickness, the struggling widows, the French traders forced out of the area, the white settlers invading Indian lands. Where next would they be forced to go? If the Indian could speak the language of the white man, would that make a difference? There seemed to be a thousand unanswered questions going through her head as she dozed off to sleep.

That night the face of a white man appeared in her dream. The face was in the middle of the full moon and was smiling down at her. She tried to speak but could only stammer. She sat up from her bed, now fully awake and nearly out of breath. One day she must learn the white man's language, she vowed.

4

THE CREEK RUNNER

Shawnee boys were taught to be self-reliant and underwent a physical test of endurance at around age 10. They took daily jumps in the river, even during the winter months when it was necessary to break the ice beforehand. With their faces blackened with charcoal, a sign that others were not to help them, they were sent into the woods with bows and arrows and told not to return until they shot something to eat.

A young, wiry brave named Running Creek loved the water and had no problem swimming the frozen waters of the Big Sewickley Creek. He even learned how to catch fish with his bare hands. His greatest challenge was spending 3 days in the woods, fighting hunger and exhaustion that left him too weak to shoot straight. But by the next day, he entered the camp with a young elk draped over his shoulders. That day he became a man.

While most Shawnee, like other Indians, used

well-trodden paths, Running Creek continually searched for alternate passages which were shorter or safer for travel through unknown territory, particularly during winter snows and the early spring, when trails turned to mud, when rocks and trees slid down mountains and blocked passage. He used the sun or moon to guide him. On cloudy days he would look at the moss on the trees, knowing that it nearly always grew on the north side. He was very good at painting pictograph messages on trees, stripped of bark, advising others which Indians were in the area, who the leader was and how many were in the war party, how many prisoners were taken and how many were captured, killed or wounded. All Indians, regardless of the tribe, could read and understand these messages. By age 13, everyone in the village – and all of the other villages nearby - knew that Running Creek would one day become the lead scout.

Running Creek was among the small band of Shawnee refugees living along the Big and Little Sewickley Creeks. In 1762, they were a tribe of more than 200. A year later, the numbers had dwindled to 46, mostly because of the Smallpox viciously spread from the blankets of the red coats. On his dying day, the old grandfather encouraged Running Creek to find a way to increase the village population. But with no other Shawnee clans left in the area, Running Creek asked, "How can we do this?" The old grandfather replied, "It is my belief that the Susquehanna tribe had never completely surrendered claim to their homeland in Sewickley. Go to Chief Bacala. Speak with him about our desire to band together again in the Sewickley village. On the next day, Running Creek journeyed 100 miles east to the Susquehanna River for a pow-wow with the chief.

Following the missionary work of the Quakers beginning in 1740, the Susquehanna Shawnee remained peaceful. But after 23 years, because of some childish dispute with the Susquehannocks involving a grasshopper, the Shawnee were now on the brink of war. Chief Bocala called for a vote but failed to get a consensus. He conferred with the medicine man. The medicine man vacillated and could not make a decision.

Chief Bocala was ill-prepared to speak with the young scout from Sewickley the day he rode into camp. Move the tribe at a critical time of war? Impossible! But the medicine man thought that the sudden appearance of the messenger from Sewickley was a sign, perhaps a sign of peace.

Chief Bocala and the young scout Running Creek were the only two on horseback as they led their Shawnee tribe out of the Susquehanna valley on a rainy morning in June 1763. A few other horses, loaded with supplies and equipment including a dugout, followed the clan of forty tribesmen trekking up and down the strenuous hills and challenging streams of the Appalachian Mountains. On the ninth day of the journey, they camped at Mt. Laurel. When the young scout reported that Ft. Ligonier lay a mere 10 miles ahead and very close to the trail, Bocala wisely chose to set up camp at a concealed spot until the night of the half moon, only three days away. He was aware of the recent Indian attacks and the edginess on the part of the guards protecting the fort. Musket fire was often unnecessary, mostly due to overreaction to unfounded fears of yet another Indian attack. It was better to travel at night, Bocala concluded.

At sunset after the third day, the tribe began the next leg of their journey. By the time they reached Ft. Ligonier it was well after dark. They edged their way past the fort, off to the side of an old Indian path known as Burnt Cabins. The path was now widened. White men called it Forbes Road. Patches of moonlight glowed like stepping stones between the shadows of the trees lined up along the road. They paraded forward undetected. After a long night of travel, they came to a small village at Indian Lake where they counted six huts made of tree saplings and thatched roofs. It was now daybreak.

In years past, the lake had been one of the camping grounds for the early Monongahela Indians. Twenty-five hundred years later, these ancient Indians fell prey to European diseases and attacks from the Iroquois until they mysteriously disappeared. Now the camp was inhabited by the Cherokee.

Chief Too Sweet, a short, happy-go-lucky man with a very round face and belly to match, had excellent communication skills and seemed to understand everything Bocala was saying. Looking upward, nodding and making hand gestures at the much taller Shawnee chief, Too Sweet welcomed the new visitors. "Shi yo," he said, which meant hello.

Using sign language, Bocala explained that his people had broken relations with the Delaware in the Tuscarawas; the long journey from the Susquehanna had exhausted his people and the horses.

It was customary for Indian tribes to share camping grounds with other Indian allies for brief periods, particularly along waterways. The Shawnee had come in peace and Too Sweet allowed them to camp at the opposite end of the lake. A short time later the Shawnee unpacked their gear and slept away the morning hours. When they awoke, the Shawnee squaws began helping Cherokee squaws weed gardens, pick berries, mend moccasins and clean fish. Men hunted the woods. Eight young Cherokee warriors demonstrated war dances, leg wrestling, tomahawk skills and scalping techniques. In the early afternoon, following a meal of cooked meat, sunfish and blackberries, Running Creek found himself looking at a Cherokee girl swimming in the lake. While other younger children, holding their noses, took turns jumping into the lake from a large oak log close to the water's edge, the young maiden dove straight into the water with grace and beauty.

She had long, black hair, muscle-toned legs, a tiny waist, and a small, shapely body. Her round face was similar to the other Cherokees but her lips were so perfectly matched, the young scout could not keep his eyes off this young princess. He knew that staring was distasteful and felt awkward about his attraction to her. He looked away, as if trying to balance the time his eyes should spend on other things. That night he could hardly sleep. Whenever he did, he experienced repeated visions of a lovely head of hair rising from the clear water...hands gliding behind delicate ears... drops of water falling from a face...dark brown eyes opening... beautiful mouth smiling...soft lips parting ...whistling sounds ...

The young scout woke up to the sound of a Whippoorwill and the smell of sassafras. The squaws across the lake were up early. One stirred a pot of boiling water. Others washed blankets, fed horses or lugged clay pots of water to the corn field. A hunting party assembled bows and arrows for hunting game in the fields. Another group set out on horseback into the woods. Young braves and maidens baited hooks made of bone, hoping to catch a Bluegill before the sun shone overhead. Where was the long-haired girl?

Running Creek spent the remainder of that morning bathing the horses at the far end of Indian Lake, taking more time than necessary to groom each one. From time to time he found himself gazing across the lake, looking for the girl who appeared in his dreams the night before. She was nowhere in sight.

Meanwhile, Shawnee boys were fishing the lake. Unlike the Cherokee who used baited hooks, they used nets. And though the lake was small, the catch surprisingly was enormous, enough to feed both camps for at least two meals. Learning this, Bocala, with a proud look on his face and a little extra bounce in his step, walked to the hut of Too Sweet and offered to share the bounty, lest the Cherokee become envious of the superior fishing skills, or even worse, think that the Shawnee people were greedy. The little Cherokee chief was elated. Soon young girls along both sides of the lake began cleaning the many Bluegill, sunfish and speckled trout from the nets of the Shawnee braves. Surely the lovely maiden would appear by now, thought the young scout. Still she was nowhere to be seen.

Alas, the scout was irritated, frustrated and also bewildered. He wanted her to notice his horse, which was really a pony but one worth showing off. And he wanted her to know that he was the best scout in the tribe. But the opportunity did not come and he suddenly felt very foolish. And then he lost all thought. In a fleeting glance, he spotted her sitting down with legs crossed near one of the huts. Apparently she had been searching the bushes for blackberries. She was sorting them now, placing some in one clay pot and some in another. He watched her intently, her left arm swinging back and forth as if it were dancing. *So, she is left-handed.*

When the little, round-bellied chief struck the large drum, the tribe members assembled in a square much larger than usual, for the guests now numbered three times as many. Running Creek found his spot almost directly across from the long-haired girl. A mere seven paces away now and almost directly face to face, she could not help but to notice periodic glances from the young scout. And so the next time he looked her way, she slowly and nonchalantly turned her face toward his. But as soon as their eyes met, the young brave looked down at his meal and began boning the fish on his plate. When he glanced at her again, now she too suddenly looked away, avoiding his eyes. The pattern continued. So pre-occupied with amorous feelings, Running Creek suddenly had difficulty swallowing his food and felt frozen in time. *This game of game of cat and mouse is getting absurd.*

A short time later – although it seemed like forever – he looked at her directly and purposefully. This time, her eyes were waiting. She smiled. He smiled back. It was a magic moment he knew would last in his mind forever.

That night Moon Shadow had trouble falling asleep. After tossing and turning in her bed for what seemed like half the night, one of the squaws sat up and said simply, "His name is Running Creek." Moon Shadow asked "Who?" and the squaw answered, "The boy that smiled at you, the one that looked at you all

day long by the lake. His name is Running Creek."
There was silence. "And he is leaving tomorrow to
find other Shawnee villages near the river with the
falling banks." More silence. "He is their best scout.
He rides the pony." With that information, suddenly
Moon Shadow yawned and fell right to sleep.

Just about the time the young Shawnee scout was
ready to head down the north branch of the Little
Sewickley Creek from Indian Lake, he heard a voice
calling, "Farewell, Running Creek, farewell!" And
when he turned his pony around, he saw that the voice
came from the long-haired girl standing at the edge of
the lake. She raised her right arm with closed fist,
meaning good fortune in your travels today. He in
turn raised his arm and fist to acknowledge her sign.
Then, for good measure, he pumped his arm up and
down two more times, bellowed out an E-E-E-O-O-W
and sped off.

As Running Creek headed downstream, he could
not help but revisit the events of the morning and the
previous evening. The thoughts circulated over and
over in his head - the young maiden at the lake, the
dream, the fish meal, the early morning send-off.

Shortly after his run down the north branch
of the Little Sewickley, a shallow stream with many
small to medium-sized rocks, Running Creek
dismounted the pony and started running through the
water. He went slowly at first, then went faster and
faster, whooping and hollering and stomping his feet.

RILLTON

Water splashed, skippers zigzagged, crayfish scuttled, frogs jumped, squirrels scampered, robins fluttered and crows cawed as he reveled in a feeling he had not experienced before. Suddenly he stopped midstream, water dripping from his hair. *How did she know my name?* And then a few steps later, *she likes me.* He lifted his head skyward and began to laugh. It was the best feeling he had experienced in his whole life.

Before the sun passed overhead, he reached the Little Sewickley which was bordered by tall trees with three lobbed leaves. The Shawnee had named them Seweekly trees. White settlers called them Sugar Maples. The pleasant fragrance in the air surrounded him as he followed an old footpath alongside of the stream. A short time later, Running Creek reported the news of Chief Bocala'a arrival at Indian Lake and his eagerness to join the Sewickley tribe. Young braves immediately began to celebrate, throwing tree limbs onto a great bonfire while dancing and yelling. Joyous tears flowed in the eyes of the squaws, as they rushed to Running Creek, wanting to know more tales about their brothers and sisters from the land of Susquehanna.

Before the celebration had ended, Chief Long Tooth summoned Running Creek to his tent. And while the chief seemed calm enough on the outside, Running Creek could tell that he was agitated, preoccupied in deep thought. A series of smoke signals from the Delaware camp had been spotted over the last few days. It was a clear meaning of war. But where and when and with whom, Long Tooth could not be sure. He was depending on Running Creek to find out the answers. No one in his clan could understand the Delaware language better, nor interpret the exact messages contained in the smoke signals than Running Creek. He was the only good scout left in the clan.

At sunrise, Running Creek headed down the Big Sewickley. He smelled smoke near the confluence of the Youghiogheny River. It was coming from the remains of a small English trading post, now reduced to ashes. A white settler lay near the ashes, absent his musket and his scalp. Was this incident, in fact, the war Long Tooth wondered about? He continued down river. About 2 miles short of the Monongahela, he rode into the Delaware Indian camp.

The camp was nearly devoid of braves and Running Creek saw only squaws initially. He edged his way to the west end of the camp while holding his right hand in the air, a sign of peace and a custom among Indian tribes as far back as the 1400s. Yellow Wolf, age 10, was the first to greet him. But his two older brothers, with painted faces, were right behind him and carrying long spears. Running Creek introduced himself, saying, "I am Running Creek from the Shawnee tribe. I come from the land of Sewickley."

The boys looked at each other, unsure of what to say or who should speak. After a few moments of dead silence, Running Creek began to repeat his words in broken Delaware dialect but was interrupted by the oldest brave who threw up his hand – stop speaking. Then, turning toward the camp, he yelled, "Tiki Bola!" Soon 70-year-old Tall Bear, a former chieftain, came to the aid of the young braves. He too had stripes of black and red painted over the cheeks of his face, having just participated in a war dance that morning. Standing together, the old man and the three boys looked ready to defend the camp with force if necessary. But they relaxed their guard once Tall Bear repeated the questions of Running Creek to the others in more understandable Delaware language. At this point, Tall Bear gestured for Running Creek to dismount his horse. And once he did so, the chief spoke in broken Shawnee, explaining that after the French had moved north to the land of the Kickapoo five summer moons ago, the white faces of the English took over the trading posts but refuse to trade with the Indian. Meanwhile, white settlers are destroying our hunting grounds. This violates the treaty.

Tall Bear continued. War parties of the Delaware and the Seneca have gathered to fight the white man near Turtle Creek. Warriors are needed to fight the red coats and drive them from the fort at the three rivers.

Chief Long Tooth was somewhat surprised, though not entirely, hearing about the developments at Turtle Creek. Regrettably, the planned attack could not have come at a worse time for the two Shawnee

sub-nations for they were just now getting back together after a 100 year separation. But at least, Long Tooth thought, his tribe would have new warrior blood – the Susquehannocks – to help fight the red coats.

5
BUSHY RUN

$\mathbf{A}$t Ft. Pitt General Forbes, concerned of the escalating Indian attacks, sent Lieutenant Johann Bachman on a mission for help from Ft. Carlisle.

There were two reasons why Forbes chose to send Bachman. First, he was an excellent horseman. Having worked his uncle's farm ever since he was a small boy and having cared for the animals at the fort, he had developed an uncanny ability to work a horse, getting it to turn this way and that, to avoid low hanging branches and step ever so gently over slippery rocks mid-stream. He got the horses to climb impossible muddy hillsides when other trainers could not do so. Yet he knew a horse's limitations. One afternoon when a sergeant thought he heard young Bachman talking to the horses in German, he ordered him to cease and desist. General Forbes reversed the order. Bachman was to talk to the horses whenever was necessary. Especially in German!

A more important reason for sending Bachman on the mission was because of his sense of direction and awareness of time, a gift few people possessed. One day Bachman returned to camp from the woods moments before the dinner bell sounded. "I swear that man has a clock ticking inside his head," growled the sergeant.

Just before the break of dawn in mid-July 1763, Bachman headed east toward Ft. Carlisle, using not the Forbes Road where many Shawnee and Delaware had frequently waited in ambush, but the old Braddock trail which had been all but abandoned by the British army eight years prior.

Bachman crossed Turtle Creek at a spot between two Indian villages just before sunrise, then headed southeast, going up and down hills and gullies that lined the east side of the Youghiogheny. When he passed within 150 yards of the Cherokee camp at Indian Lake, the air was thick with patches of fog, enabling him to remain undetected. A short ride later, he stopped to rest at the small cabin of Simeon McGrew, apprising McGrew of the impending danger as he fed on some blackberries. It was 7 a.m. He had a long way to go. Bachman continued down the Braddock trail, turned east on Glades Path (present day Pa route 31) to Ft. Bedford and on to Ft. Carlisle just after 5 p.m. to deliver General Forbes' message to Colonel Henry Bouquet.

RILLTON

On July 18, with 500 British soldiers, Bouquet set out to relieve Ft. Pitt via Forbes Road. By the time they got to Ft. Ligonier, the Indians already knew about the expedition. Some 400 Delaware, Mingo and Seneca, who had gathered at Turtle Creek, suddenly turned their attention to Bouquet's advancing troops in the open territory between the 2 forts.

When Running Creek reported to Bocala the location of the Shawnee tribe along the Little Sewickley and the events unfolding at Turtle Creek, Bocala decided to break camp immediately. A few minutes later, his tribe was on the trail, this time to join their Shawnee brothers. At first Moon Shadow was forlorn, thinking she might not ever see Running Creek again. But when he told her of his plan to return to the Cherokee camp once the Shawnee had settled near the Falling Banks, she rejoiced and squeezed his hand with both of hers. Her warm touch sent shivers down his neck and shoulders. His heart pounded. His eyes widened. Gentle smiles crossed their faces as they said goodbye to each other, knowing the day would soon come when they would see each other again.

The two clans of Shawnee shared the camping grounds at the Youghiogheny for three days before an Indian warrior reported the news of the plan to attack the redcoats between the forts. Bocala struggled with the critical decision of sending any of his braves into battle. None of them had been involved in any serious conflicts, having lived in peace for so many years. They had no war chief and, aside from Running Creek, Bocala was the only one who even knew how to apply war paint or conduct a war dance. Bocala held a powwow to determine what to do. There was a vote. The final count was 17 spears up and 9 down, including women who had a say-so during council meetings. Thus, the Susquehanna tribe agreed to go to war.

Chief Long Tooth beamed with joy, as he fully expected the tribe to vote for peace. His tribe too held a powwow and the vote there was 25 to 8 in favor of war. For the time being, the two Shawnee tribes, now 43 of the Sewickley and 38 of the Susquehanna would work together to rid the area of white settlers.

On Aug. 4 Bouquet pulled his column off Forbes Road to rest at a trading post called Bushy Run. On the following day at 1 p.m. the Indians attacked, killing 40 soldiers. The raids stopped after sunset but everyone knew they would continue the next morning.

After setting up a redoubt with sacks of flour the night before, Bouquet sent some of his troops running towards Ft. Ligonier, as if in retreat, soon after the morning attacks began. As the raiding Indians boldly entered the redoubt, they were confronted with musket fire from the 300 British troops which had remained behind. The warriors fled in disorganized retreat. The British lost 120; the

RILLTON

Indians more than 200, including Bocala and 3 young braves who refused to leave his side.

It was the beginning of the end for the Indians in western Pennsylvania. Within days Bouquet reached the fort without any further attacks by the Indians who were still on the run. Three weeks later the Indians sued for peace.

6
THE RE-SETTLEMENT

Bouquet's march into Ft. Pitt ended the five-year siege by the Indians, who put away their tomahawks and scalping knives. Frontiersmen were now free to leave the fort and return to their old abandoned farms and houses outside the fort. Of the 650 who found refuge within the fort, including 196 children, most survived the relentless Indian attacks, the outbreak of smallpox and an unusually cold winter in 1760. The European settlers were strong, determined people.

One of the refuges was Susan McGrew, now widowed with a 4 year old child. In September 1758, three months before General Forbes marched into Ft. Duquesne unopposed, a hard-headed officer named Grant persuaded Forbes to allow him to take 100 Highlanders from Scotland on a reconnaissance mission. Obsessed with the notion of capturing Ft.

Duquesne by himself, Grant had his drums beat the reveille just after reaching the fort. The French and Indians immediately rushed out of the fort and swarmed the entire force. All of the Highlanders were killed, some by decapitation, others burned at the stake. Among them was Tim McGrew, married to Susan who was 16 and pregnant at the time.

Though there were 146 houses and 36 huts near the fort, Susan and her daughter Linda had no place to stay. As the widow of the Highlander Tim McGrew, she could have inherited some 50 acres of property by way of survivorship. However, she had no money to build a cabin or even enough to get back to Scotland, thoughts that preoccupied her mind for several months. Even if she did go back, the economic conditions there were too dismal to consider as an option. Susan found herself working long hours during the day and sleeping in a makeshift lean-to at night inside of the now peaceful Ft. Pitt. It had changed from a military post to a trading post. There, Susan McGrew began a new life.

During the time she worked at the trading post, Susan had numerous opportunities to re- marry. After a year of mourning, there were three marriage proposals. She was a small-boned freckle-faced woman with rather long, curly red hair that at times seemed to engulf her worn-out bonnet. Her energy and bright smile, along with her friendly manner, pleased both her customers as well as her boss. But her charming demeanor was somewhat deceptive, for whenever the cleverest of frontiersmen fell short of negotiating in good faith an exchange of merchandise, she would squint her eyes in such a way as if to say, "I know exactly what you're up to and I don't like it." When it came to customers trying to chisel, Susan was her own trial judge and jury. She taught Linda the same code of ethics and fairness in dealing with the public, Indians included. People marveled at the way Susan and little Linda ran that store in Pittsboro. It was the best trading post west of the Appalachian Mountains, they said.

In honor of the English Prime Minister William Pitt, General Forbes renamed the settlement Pittsboro, later to be called Pittsburg, and finally Pittsburgh. By 1768 more than 2,000 pioneers had settled near the fort, many of them along the Youghiogheny and Monongahela rivers. The following year the Penn Land Company had turned over a million acres of farmland. Applicants received between 50 to 300 acres provided they were willing to work the soil. Two years later the population exploded to 5,000. And over the next five years, 10 times that number.

In 1774 former Captain Johann Bachman of the British army went to the Penn Land Company and applied for some farmland at a time when there were rumblings of a revolution. He, like many of the Hessians, had deserted the British and joined the colonists after being promised 50 acres of land and permanent residency. The area's population soared even more as 5000 additional Hessian soldiers settled in towns along the three rivers.

Bachman, however, chose an unusual spot. A good ways inland from any of the rivers stood a parcel of land located on a hillside, partly wooded, partly grassy, along a small stream near the old Braddock trail. He remembered this tranquil place while running a mission to Ft. Carlisle before the battle of Bushy Run. He remembered the blackberries in the fields surrounding Simeon McGrew's cabin, the easy horseback ride over the rolling hills, and the many small lakes and streams dotting the landscape. It reminded him of his uncle's farm in Bavaria.

The chosen parcel did not appear on any map but Simeon McGrew, the land surveyor, agreed to spot mark it on his surveying map. Afterwards, Bachman stepped off the property and marked the boundary as he best he could. He did so on a warm, windy day.

At the far corner of the property, Bachman noticed a small black bear in the meadow toying with a dead squirrel, repeatedly tossing it in the air. Fascinated with the bear's behavior, the inattentive Bachman did not see the young bear's mother. Out of nowhere it came, rushing full speed toward him with teeth snarling. His horse reared up and began running away, but not before the beast swiped its ferocious claw across the hindquarter of the horse. The horse bolted over the hill. Somehow Bachman managed to fire his musket, felling the bear. In the aftermath, the hapless cub, confused and unsure of what to do, stood nearby and bellowed nearly all day and night over the fate of its mother. By morning the cub was gone, never to be seen again.

When Running Creek heard the musket fire, he thought it must have come from a Cherokee hunter. He continued up the creek heading to the Cherokee camp. A short while later, he saw the young bluecoat tending to the wounded horse at the edge of the creek. Running Creek froze momentarily when he noted blood pouring out of the horse's leg. For unexplained reasons, he found himself dismounting his horse and walking toward the strange white man in order to help prepare a mud pack. Bachman had encountered only Indian prisoners in the last nine years, none face-to-face in the wild except for the skirmish at Bushy Run. Yet he sensed no danger. When the wound was under control, Running Creek and Bachman stood silent, looking at one another without muttering a word. Then Running Creek mounted his horse and continued on his journey upstream.

Running Creek married Moon Shadow the night she turned 15, the same night a shining star appeared near the tip of the crescent moon. It was a sign that an infant papoose would come from her womb and keep the village in harmony with nature, she said. Months, then years passed. And when the infant never appeared, Moon Shadow became heartsick. She prayed to the Moon god but her prayers were left unanswered. *Did the Sun god take it away? Why did you try to hide me when I was born? Are you also trying to hide my papoose?* Within a few short years she was beginning to look much older than her 24 years, and though she continued to pray, she had all but given up on a family.

Running Creek prepared to run the creek, once more, to the Little Sewickley, to the Big Sewickley, to the Youghiogheny, across the Monongahela and now across the Ohio en route to his old Shawnee tribe, which had recently re-settled a good distance to the west. Cornstalk, a dominant Shawnee chief, had signed a peace treaty relinquishing land south of the Ohio River. Consequently, some of the Shawnee moved to Alabama, some to Missouri and some, like the Sewickley, north of the Ohio. Now Running Creek's tribe was so far removed to the northwest that this was too great a distance for him to travel. It would be his last trip.

Bachman staked out his property in late August and had cut most of the timber needed for his small hut. He had as his tools, a saw, an axe, one shovel and a flat stone, which acted as a hammer. By mid-October, he had pieced together somewhat of a rough-sawn shack, including a corner-stone fireplace. The room offered little comfort, as it was drafty and very smoky. The bearskin rug on the dirt floor bred fleas. At night rats and snakes crawled across the floor.

His hunting skills were less than spectacular and oftentimes he mishandled his musket. Twice he forgot to load the shot after packing the powder. In another instance the gun misfired and came close to taking off his left foot. He dug out two pieces of shot from his Achilles heel and limped for a day or two. Several times he completely missed the intended target at close range. Other times he hit pigeons with such force that they were blown apart with little left to eat. Given the enormity of errors on these hunting ventures, he was lucky that the black bear went down on one shot. The meat from the bear was enough to gorge on for weeks.

From time to time young Cherokees spied the activities of the new settler over the hill and reported the progress to the tribe at Indian Lake. Periodically, Bachman heard chants from the camp as the Indians danced to the Sun god. Moon Shadow pondered the life of the new settler and how long it would be before other white settlers would come to drive her people away.

About 90 percent of the early pioneers were farmers going through the same challenges as Bachman. Money was almost non-existent. Most essentials were acquired by trade. "We eat what the Lord provided — game from the forests, birds or fish from the streams, berries, nuts and crabapples," said one frontiersman. The men built houses, plows, buckets, tubs and tankards. Women spun flax, wove linen, cut and sowed clothes for the family and maintained the gardens. Seldom did they get any bread but there was always cornmeal johnnycake made from Indian corn. Without a woman to help, Bachman had his work cut out.

On a cold day in December, after completing the construction of his cabin, Bachman headed for the trading post to exchange his many skins for winter supplies. Linda McGrew, age 16, worked the store that morning and she recognized Bachman right off. He was the British messenger, the one with the German accent who had trouble speaking English. Somehow he looked different, wearing the blue coat instead of the red one. His face had matured and there was a touch of grey in his hair near the temples. He was a handsome man, she thought.

"G'morning, Mr. Bachman," Linda said cheerfully. He looked over his shoulder, saw the brown-eyed petite girl looking directly at him, tipped his hat and smiled. "Goot mornink, fraulein." "I'm Linda," she said as she walked over and extended her hand.

"Linda. It is a nice name. Und you can call me Johann." Her hand was soft and dainty; his, rugged but warm despite the freezing temperatures outside.

Johann plopped down 6 male deerskins, 3 fox, 7 raccoon, 3 beaver, 2 wolf, 1 panther and several muskrat pelts. Exchange prices were reckoned in bucks. One buck was equal to one male deerskin or the equivalent, such as 2 does, 6 raccoons or 4 foxes. For his six bucks, Johann got a wool blanket and a tin kettle. For the cat, a month's supply of powder and shot and for the remaining items, a small container of tea, a mirror, salt, butter and nails.

Notwithstanding the many hunting mishaps, Johann had become more skilled with the musket and was now able to bring down wild turkey, grouse, quail, pigeon and squirrel as well as deer and other four-legged animals. What he lacked to properly run a farm were farm animals, particularly cattle for butter and dairy products. Linda knew of a farmer along the Youghiogheny who, after being flooded out twice since the great flood of 1762, was anxious to sell his entire farm lock, stock and barrel. But the question was, would he sell some of the animals and keep the farm?

In the early spring of 1775, Bachman spent 16 hours a day working the farm of Melvin Pennington along the Youghiogheny. Begrudgingly he worked the wet, clay soil for the spring planting, repaired tubs, fed and cared for the livestock, washed down the chicken coop, chopped wood, installed fences, milked cows and pitched hay. At night he hunted. By mid-May, he traded in his 42 deerskins, 2 elk, 53 squirrel, 3 bear, 24 beaver, 28 raccoon, 12 otter and 16 fox furs in exchange for one ox, 3 cows, 2 heifers, 1 bull, 5 chickens, 1 rooster, 4 pigs and 1 harness. Old man Pennington was a happy man. The farm was every bit as good as it used to be. He had fewer animals, of course, but the farm was once again viable.

And Bachman now had enough animals for a small farm of his own. He spent the remainder of that summer caring for them and tending to his own crops — pumpkin, squash, beans, potatoes, cabbage, turnips, watermelon, maize, wheat, rye, oats, barley and hay. He made more tools — axes, hoes and plows of wood — built sheds and a fence to hold in the pigs that kept running into forest. One never came back. By late fall, four of the 50 acres of land had changed from a weedy, rocky meadow to a tiny spec of pastureland, snuggled next to the virgin forest.

One day Bachman decided to visit the Cherokee village, perhaps out of loneliness or perhaps because he had too many eggs to eat that day. In any event, he rode to the village mid-morning with a sack full of eggs and three huge heads of cabbage, enough to feed the whole camp. Chief Too Sweet, unsure if the white settler wanted to trade the items for something in return, offered Bachman an old peace pipe and a container of tobacco leaves. When it became clear Bachman was there to present a gift and not to trade, Too Sweet then re-presented the pipe and tobacco as a gift.

Thinking the chief wanted him to try the tobacco, Bachman popped some leaves in his mouth and began chewing as he had seen other soldiers do at

Ft. Carlisle. He immediately started to gag and choke on the putrid stuff. Children started to laugh, as did some of the squaws. Too Sweet, wide-eyed and dumbstruck, hardly knew what to say, which was rare. He then showed the new white settler how to pack the pipe and draw smoke. Bachman tried to do the same, inhaling a huge amount of smoke into his lungs, and choked again, his white face turning even whiter. This time everyone laughed, including Bachman.

The days following this short visit were less intense between Bachman and his Indian neighbors. Instead of spying, young braves would walk onto the property and pet the heifers. Whenever Bachman ventured to the trading post at Pittsboro, he would swing by the camp and wave, holding his rifle high in the air. The clan would wave back. Spring arrived early that year and the newborn calves became a source of entertainment for the young boys, and now the girls too. Some offered to help gather eggs and feed the chickens. If the squaws back at camp were concerned over these increased visits by the young braves and maidens, they didn't show it. It was a peaceful time. Bachman was a little less lonely.

War was in the air once again. Pennsylvania first got news of the events of Lexington and Concord on May 16, 1776. The people of Pittsboro adopted resolutions pledging their assistance with military help. Soon new companies formed along the Monongahela and Youghiogheny and vowed to march to the relief of

Boston. Most of the volunteers, however, were not eager to travel long distances and found themselves participating in short battles closer to home, after which they would return to work their farms. Enough battles ensued right in their own backyards to keep them occupied for several years.

In 1777, the British launched a major offensive from Canada, recruiting and arming Indian war parties to raid American settlements. After hundreds were killed in Kentucky, West Virginia and Pennsylvania, many settlers appealed to the Continental Congress for protection. The forts were too spread out to stop the slaughter. The Indians simply bypassed the forts and continued with the raids. Congress agreed to build Ft. Laurens on the Indian side of the Ohio, but they were not able to provide enough manpower for any offensive operations against the British. It was abandoned within a year.

Bachman spent nearly three weeks at Ft. Laurens cutting logs. While no attacks came to the fort, there were stories of attacks all over the Ohio frontier — women taken as prisoners, men tortured before being burned at the stake, and one disheartening story of militiamen from Ft. Pitt attacking and killing peaceful Delaware Indians, mostly women and children. This took place days after the troop's unsuccessful battle with the Mingo along the Cuyahoga River. When it became clear Ft. Laurens could not be properly manned, Bachman and others left to tend to their crops. Much to Bachman's surprise, his hut was broken into. His belongings were scattered all over and most of his food was gone. Fortunately, all of the tools in the shed were still there. He spent the next two days hunting and the next week ridding weeds from the hard clay fields, a venture he thought surely would one day break his back. It was not exactly like this in Germany, he muttered.

Before winter set in, Bachman was able to dig a pond large enough to scoop whole buckets full of water. This attracted two playful otters that greatly amused him each evening as he sat down on his little wood stool outside his hut. He thought about shooting them for skins but changed his mind. Neither one of these delightful creatures deserved that kind of fate after displaying this wonderful show of acrobatics. What joyful surprises lay in these quiet woods of Pennsylvania, he mused.

On his second trip to the trading post, Bachman was sure Linda McGrew was making eyes at him. She was unusually friendly that day, touching his arm twice during a conversation about the new bees wax candles, which Bachman didn't think he needed particularly but which he purchased anyway since she seemed excited about them. And when James McCarty entered the store and smiled his wide grin at Linda, much more than was necessary, for the first time in his life Bachman felt a twinge of jealousy. On the fourth trip back to the post, he asked for her hand in marriage. He half-expected her to reject the proposal. After all, his English was not good and Linda, who had spent nearly 20 years of her life working the store, had no experience working a farm. All of her friends and acquaintances lived in Pittsboro. He was, therefore, taken aback when she replied, "Of course I will. Why did it take you so long to ask?"

What started out as a small wedding became a much larger one. Everyone in the Pittsboro area knew Linda, having seen her on many occasions working the store. At that time, Pittsboro had two doctors, one lawyer, one Baptist minister and one Presbyterian minister. No priests and no Quakers. Nearly all the rest were farmers. Some 240 people crowded the trading post at the time of the ceremony, which was conducted by the Presbyterian minister. Everyone was happy, everyone except Brennan.

George Brennan, owner of the Pittsboro trading post and several others in the Ohio valley, was upset. Not only was Linda leaving but now Susan had given him unpleasant news in that she was pregnant. She was sure. Brennan was a playboy and knew everyone would pinpoint him as the father, rightfully so. "Did ye tell anyone about this?" Brennan asked. She shook her head, no. Brennan, a former peacemaker for the British army as well as trader, had at one time set out on several expeditions since 1767 to disperse the new settlers since this violated the peace treaty. His efforts, of course, were in vain. The tides of settlement were too great. Now, having heard the disturbing news, ironically and contrary to his previous position of dispersing settlers, he instead proposed a plan to have one of his own employees settle in a new place outside of Pittsboro and furthermore run a new trading post.

"And just where might that be?" Susan asked.

"Kentucky," he stated, explaining where it was and how a plot of land lay adjacent to the post. She was entitled to the land from inheritance, he reminded her. And he promised to build her a cabin and generally provide for her and the child until she could find a husband.

A husband! She nearly choked. Susan had no interest in a husband, especially if that man were anything like the flirting George Brennan. "Of course, I've never seen Kentucky. And what if I don't like it there and decide to move back to Pittsboro?" she replied.

"Oh no! You mustn't do that, ever," exclaimed Brennan.

"Ever!" Susan looked skyward, giving the impression she was deeply thinking over her options. "Supposin' I was to stay with me daughter near the Little Sewickley and set up a new trading post there and vow not to come back here. What would you say about that, Mister Brennan?" looking directly into his eyes.

"Where the devil is Little Sewickley?" he asked. And after she told him, he snorted, "Well, I don't imagine there will be much tradin' at a place like that."

"On the contrary, there are lots of Indian tribes in them hunting grounds with enough skins to buy out anything you can supply," she snapped. Brennan looked at her suspiciously and said nothing. "And besides, even if the tradin' was not as good as I proclaim, at least I'd be happy living near me daughter. And the name Brennan would never be mentioned," she added with a note of finality.

The next morning Susan went to the Penn Land Company to claim a 50-acre plot along the north branch of the Little Sewickley Creek and next to the x-marked property of Johann Bachman. At the same time, Brennan took the Braddock trail to the site of the new trading post, looked around and became disenchanted. He doubted if a single clay pot could be sold in *those Godforsaken hills*, as there were no Indians in the immediate area, except for the pitiful Cherokee campsite upstream with only six mud huts.

By the time he got back to Ft. Pitt he was fuming. Susan was overjoyed but was careful not to show it for fear of unraveling the deal. When Brennan proposed to set up a household only and not the post, Susan threatened to set up her own post anyway and added, "Who's to say that once the MacDonalds and the MacGregors find out that Susan McGrew has her own store that they won't come to me own place for their tradin', discover me pregnancy and then go tell the others in Pittsboro? But if the name Brennan is on the building, they won't know who's workin' the store. Now would they, Mister Brennan?"

And with that argument, a deal was struck. Brennan would build the post with sleeping rooms in the back and supply all of the provisions. McGrew would keep her mouth shut about family matters.

After a rough start in life, theft and burglary became a natural part of the little bear's life. Survival skills were taught to him by his mother following the sudden disappearance of his father. Together they would go hunting and fishing and oftentimes forage for berries or nuts. One day the youngster was confronted by a panther that growled and flashed its teeth and stared directly into his face while he was cornered against a tree. He stared right back and held steady for a full minute until his mother scared the panther away. Life was hard when he was growing up.

But then one day his whole life changed when his mother was shot and killed by a white settler. Her body hung from a tree for days, a sight he would never forget. He tried to live with relatives but was snubbed. Though food was plentiful, seldom did they share any of it with him. An uncle beat him severely for no apparent reason. He found himself living alone, sneaking around at night, breaking and entering buildings and stealing food. It wasn't the life he had envisioned but when he got hungry, it was a way to survive.

RILLTON

On three separate occasions he was able to break into Bachman's cabin and steal food. On the third trip, he also stole the bearskin rug that smelled so much like his mother. He carried it off to his den and lay next to it as he prepared to hibernate during the long, cold winter.

7
THE LITTLE SEWICKLEY

A few miles east of the Youghiogheny River, maple trees lined the banks of a small stream which the Indians named Sweet-water. Early settlers called it the Little Sewickley. Susan McGrew chose to set up her trading post at the edge of her 50-acre plot of land roughly two miles away, between the properties of her brother-in-law Simeon McGrew and Johann Bachman.

The post had little impact on the people living in the area. A few curious visitors from Indian Lake popped in from time to time but actual trading with them was minimal, mostly blankets for winter, which was fast approaching, and glass beads from Spain. The Indians could not resist the beads and these became the most popular items. Other items offered for exchange included the following:

1 pistol = 20 deerskin or 120 bushels of corn
1 pair scissors = 1 deerskin or 6 bushels of corn
1 petticoat = 14 deerskin or 84 bushels of corn
1 broad hoe = 5 deerskin or 30 bushels of corn
1 hatchet = 3 deerskin or 18 bushels of corn

Except for a few hatchets, hardly any of these items were sold. George Brennan was right. Business at the trading post was woeful. There was, however, a young Indian woman who was quite attractive, radiantly beautiful in fact, who seemed genuinely interested in the pots and pans displayed on the shelves. She looked at them for three days straight and for an unusually long time. Susan, suspicious of Indians, was starting to get antsy. But toward the end of the third visit, Moon Shadow began communicating with Linda McGrew, using hand signals at first and coughing up the few English words she had picked up from

Johann. Soon they were both repeating each other's words in a focused attempt to understand one another. Occasionally, the Indian woman smiled. The smile was genuine. For Linda, it was a refreshing sign.

One day, Moon Shadow dropped by the post, not to purchase goods but just to chat with Linda. At times the conversation got to be hilarious. Moon Shadow said, Goot Mournink, just as Johann might say it. Linda phrased it differently: Gid Marening. And so, Moon Shadow, thinking that each had special meaning, repeated one phrase while holding up a finger, then repeating the other phrase while holding up another. What is the difference, she was asking? This chatter spent on such trivial matters somehow had transformed their acquaintance into a friendship within the week. As the winter months passed and as Susan's belly grew larger, Linda spent more hours at the trading post and became Moon Shadow's only English speaking friend.

By early April, Linda was once again working full time at the store, filling in for Susan, and became acquainted with Running Creek. Running Creek was eager to trade a new bear skin for a large cast iron pot. Johann had talked many times about the bearskin rug he lost and Linda thought now would be a good time to replace it. When Moon Shadow found out about the bearskin rug birthday surprise for Bachman, she decided to throw in a gift of her own. It was a beaded belt with a rather appropriate design — a bear at one end of the belt and a bull at the other with a creek running beneath. It was symbolic in that it linked their two ways of life — both hunting and farming alongside the creek.

At age 43, Johann Bachman was the happiest he had ever been. He had four new calves, a new bearskin rug, a beautiful, loving wife, and an unusual but sentimental gift from his new Cherokee neighbors. He still vividly remembered the day when he met Running Creek at the creek, the day his horse was wounded. He was happy he had a trading post next door to him. He had more tools in his shed than he could have imagined a few short years ago (including a new cross cut saw that enabled him to build a log house with a second bedroom). And finally, much to his amazement, there had been no Indian attacks.

Susan gave birth to a 6 pound boy with a full head of strawberry blond hair and green eyes. It was a relatively easy delivery compared to the feisty and contrary Linda McGrew who came 20 years earlier. Little Timmy was a good baby, hardly noticeable in the corner of the trading post during store hours. He slept well, ate well and smiled as if he had not a care in the world. He was with his mama every day and night, fascinated by the sound of the doorbell jangling whenever customers entered the store and curious about the sights and sounds of the wrens nesting between the logs near the corner of the building. By the time Linda delivered her own 5-pound son who literally kicked his way into the world, Susan's little Timmy was already crawling across the floor.

Before the Revolutionary war had ended, six-year-old Timmy McGrew was playing with five-year-old Hans Bachman on a regular basis. Johann used his new scythe to cut a special playing field on the far side of the chicken coop for the children. The piles of hay attracted other Cherokee children to the field where they enjoyed hay fights, held shooting contests with bows and arrows and played stickball. Hans was learning to use an atlatl (pronounced at'-LAT-ul) a spear launching device which greatly increased the speed and force with which a spear could be thrown. More importantly, Hans was learning to talk the Cherokee language. By age 7, he could out leg-wrestle most of the Cherokee boys ages 8 and 9. He could swim long distances under water and catch fish, using nets or baited poles. One day Hans and Timmy decided to run the creek. Later that day, Linda asked Hans why he spent all day in the creek. He replied, "We wanted to see where it would go."

There is an old saying: everything comes in threes. The prayers of Moon Shadow had finally been answered. On the night of the new moon, Dec. 11, 1783 — the day Congress declared an end to the Revolutionary War — Moon Shadow delivered a child. They called her Wet Foot. Wet Foot was unlike her mother in that she shied away from water, usually sticking one foot in the water to test the temperature, only to withdraw it moments later. She was not shy, however, when it came to playing games with the boys. In that regard she was very much like her mother.

Despite her tomboyish ways, Wet Foot was strikingly attractive, even at an early age. She had her mother's radiant smile, a perfectly shaped body, long legs and a charm unmatched by other children in the tribe. Never was there a hint of jealously among the other girls for Wet Foot would listen to their stories with great intensity and would oftentimes giggle with such sincerity that they felt she was their best friend. When the squaws needed help, they called for Wet Foot, who helped them string beads, gently braid their hair with her soft little fingers and generally make them feel important. Whenever Hans taught her a new English word, she was quick to share it with the others. And when Too Sweet was feeling sick, she brought him water and would pray for his health to return.

If Wet Foot wasn't helping other squaws or tending to Too Sweet or playing with Hans or teaching English to children or fishing the lake with young braves, she was headed down the creek on a pony with Running Creek, for her father had hopes of teaching her the way of the Shawnee as well as the Cherokee. Occasionally she would tease the hair on top of her head, looking very Shawnee-like, while the rest of her long, black hair flowed across her shoulders and down her back, like her Cherokee mother. When Moon Shadow braided Wet Foot's hair, everyone noticed her unusually long neck. It made her look much taller. Adolescent boys pulled her pigtails, teasing but secretly wishing she were but a few years older than her six winter moons.

Because business at the trading post had gotten worse, Brennan suggested that Susan start a distillery to sell whiskey. Rye, from which whiskey is made, grew aplenty in the fields of Johann Bachman. A bushel of rye sold for 30 cents but a gallon of whiskey (a bushel and a half of rye) yielded a dollar. Not only was the profit larger, but whiskey was much easier to transport.

Thanks to Brennan, the store began showing a profit within a year. With the extra money Brennan brought in new merchandise — soap, copper kettles, small barrels, clocks, men's and ladies shoes and a piccolo. And from the farmers along the Little Sewickley creek came fresh maple syrup. Bachman purchased a posthole digger and began putting up a fence. Frontier life in this little corner of the world had improved.

8

THE NEW NEIGHBORS

Just two days after George Brennan restocked the trading post, the Cherokee started their summer solstice celebration. No customers entered the trading post that week. Wet Foot, now age 8, took an active part in the sacred dances, which meant that Hans spent the week without her companionship or any of his other Indian friends.

The biggest part of the celebration came on June 20. The braves carefully selected a tree with a "fork" at the top. In the old days, to fell a tree, the braves would pack the tree with clay, then burn the base of the trunk. It took several days. Nowadays the senior leaders could cut down the tree with new iron hatchets, after which they dragged it back to camp, treating it like a fallen enemy. Squaws stripped the branches while other braves prepared to fill the fork with brush, deer hide and other suitable gifts to the sun god. Using the new metal hatchets instead of tomahawks, they carved an eagle's head at the top of the pole, for the eagle was seen as courageous, swift and strong. That evening the sun pole was raised during the lighting of a great bonfire. Chanting followed and continued well into the night.

At sunrise on the longest day of the year, with the sun pole facing the eastern horizon, there was more chanting. Occasionally a horn would sound. But mostly it was a day of dancing and chanting, as much as the day before. Hans and Timmy were lured to the edge of the camp, close enough to witness some of the events of the Cherokee Sun Dance celebration but sagaciously did not enter the camp. At age 13, Hans was intrigued. So was Timmy.

Johann and Linda never understood the importance of this religious ceremony but always respected the tribe's right to worship whatever god they believed in. They tolerated the activities much better than Susan. After awhile, what started out as senseless noise was now sounding more and more like music. In fact, Hans had been doing his version of a Rain Dance in the dry, dusty cornfield just the other day.

To Susan, the nightly sounds were eerie, if not a nuisance. Susan, a confirmed Presbyterian, felt very differently and in fact belittled the ceremony as nothing short of sacrilege. To her the whole affair sounded like some kind of war dance. "Nothing religious about it, if you ask me," she snorted.

Other dances were held throughout the summer — The Grass Dance, the Fancy Shawl Dance and the Crow Hop, all of which were sacred to the tribe. One day Wet Foot asked Moon Shadow if she could invite Hans to the Potato Dance, which was a social dance and open to anyone who wanted to participate. That afternoon, Moon Shadow went to see Linda, extending the invitation to her and Johann…and Timmy and Susan too. Understandably, Susan declined the offer and refused to allow Timmy to attend the ceremony for fear that the savage ways of the Indian would interfere with his Christian upbringing. "What Christian upbringing?" Linda argued. But Susan was adamant and stayed at the post with Timmy at her side.

The Bachmans showed up at the dance sporting regalia typically worn at such celebrations. Hans wore a breastplate made of bones; Linda, a plain buckskin dress, which she picked up at the trading post; and Johann, a simple pair of moccasins and the peace pipe, the one that Too Sweet gave him many summers ago. The Cherokee were mildly amused. Moon Shadow tugged on Wet Foot's hair to get her to stop giggling. Too Sweet was happy to see that Johann brought the peace pipe and appeared with his son at his side eager to learn the ways of the Cherokee. *If only other white men could be like him.*

The Potato Dance is a simple matter of two partners holding onto a potato between their foreheads while dancing within a designated square. The partners are required to dance to the beat of the drum. When the drum stops, every several seconds, the dancing stops. If the potato dislodges, the couple is out of the contest. The last couple standing wins.

Johann and Linda did not perform well. Johann blamed it on the moccasins. But Hans and Wet Foot looked as if they would end up winning, with their little heads turning this way and that and all the time the potato hardly moving. Only Running Creek and Moon Shadow stood in their way. Young braves began heckling the older couple in an effort to distract them so that their favored Wet Foot could claim the win. But as the drum beat got faster and faster, Hans got his legs tangled and stumbled sideways, causing his head to roll over the potato, which ended up near his right temple. Now the youngsters were in a precarious position. Hans tried to reposition the potato by turning his head but lost his balance when the music suddenly stopped. He started falling backward. Wet Foot lunged forward to keep the potato from squirting away. They both landed in the dirt, foreheads still touching but absent one potato.

There was much laughter, followed by cheers, as Wet Foot lay on top of Hans with her cheek now pressed against Hans' mouth. He kissed her gently but then blushed immediately after doing so. It was not something he had planned, especially in front of a crowd of 40 people. He got up and began walking away. Wet Foot also stood up, grabbed his hand and pulled him toward her parents, gesturing to them a sign of congratulations but at the same time rejoicing in her first kiss and holding hands with her special friend. The little smile on her face would not go away.

Johann and Linda talked about the celebration for several days afterward. One night they decided to open a jug of new rye whiskey and gaze at the full moon. With her face beaming and her eyes surveying the lunar object above them, Linda quipped, "Is this why they call it Moonshine?" Then she cackled with laughter until tears flooded her eyes. A little while later, the couple danced to the beat of an imaginary drum, kicking up dust near the pea patch and having not a care in the world. Cows were mooing. Pigs were snorting. Hans was laughing his head off. "Is that your idea of a Cherokee dance?" he taunted. Susan heard the commotion, looked across the meadow and thought they were going crazy. *They'll all burn in hell.*

Once again Susan found herself stewing. Initially, she was upset at her daughter for dancing amongst heathen Indians but tried to ignore it. But then Linda had also challenged her omission of Christian upbringing with regards to Timmy. And tonight Linda was drinking and carrying on in front of her own son. The thoughts kept resurfacing in her head. The more she thought about it, the more determined she was to do something about it. Tim was 14 years old and had never been to a church. *Neither had Linda.*

Susan went to her brother-in-law Simeon McGrew for advice. McGrew lived only half a mile away, but he had become a Quaker and as such lived in a closed society, almost completely ignoring the lives of the settlers around him. Simeon was not eager to have either Susan or young Tim join his church, the key reason being the sale of liquor at the trading post. He told them so. But when Simeon saw that look of desperation on Susan's face, he offered some hope. "I hear talk about a new Presbytery near the mouth of the Little Sewickley," he began.

Several of the Scotch Irish families settling near the Big and Little Sewickley Creeks had petitioned for a minister, pledging 40 pounds. They had been unable to secure a pastor since 1776. The problem was the selection of a site for a church. The usual meeting place was a tent setting, an outdoor arrangement with a platform for the minister and logs used for pews. It wasn't until 1808 that the first building of logs and dirt floor was erected. Meanwhile, Leland Lash acted as minister for these tent gatherings near his grist mill along the Little Sewickley.

The mill was a two-story affair with the lower part made of stone and the upper part wood. Water from the creek powered the wheel, which turned the millstones and ground flour from grain. Leland was getting older now and needed help. So when Susan McGrew and Timmy showed up three Sundays in a row for church services, he offered the lad a job. Timmy worked five days a week in exchange for free flour and horse transportation to and from his home, a mere three miles distant.

By springtime, Susan had more sacks of flour than she could possibly use or sell. So Timmy would detour his route over the "knob" on the hill and exchange flour for sugar maple syrup from the MacDonald's homestead before heading home. Soon Lash gave him another job, hauling sacked flour by raft down the Big Sewickley to the boat yards along the Youghiogheny. After several runs, a man at the yard offered 15-year-old Tim McGrew a chance to earn real wages by hauling shipments of flour, maple syrup, and various forged products by flatboat to Pittsboro.

After the adoption of the U.S. Constitution on Sept. 17, 1787, a great wave of immigration swept over the land of the Northwest Territory. Money from these immigrants presented a large source of cash to boat builders. Most of them stopped at Pittsboro, where they either bought or built flat boats to head further down the Ohio River. With the flurry of activity, the people were tired of traveling to Greensburg, some 30 miles in the center of Westmoreland County in order to conduct business. They wanted a county seat closer to home and so the following year, the Commonwealth of Pennsylvania carved out a section of Westmoreland County and called it Allegheny County. Pittsboro was now called Pittsburg with a total population of 376. Philadelphia at that time had a population of 42,000.

The boatyard along the Youghiogheny crafted three kinds of vessels: flatboats, keelboats and barges. The most convenient and inexpensive way to transport goods downstream was by flatboat. A 20' x 12" flat boat cost $20, including one steering, four rowing oars and a rudder. It could carry tons of merchandise. At the end of the trip, the boat was dismantled and the lumber was sold in the city where it was badly needed.

While downstream traffic was done by flatboats, keelboats were used for the upstream hauls. These were long, narrow boats with running boards on which the boatman walked from bow to stern, jabbing long poles against the bottom of the river, enabling the craft to move against the current. A trip from Pittsburgh to Cincinnati by flatboat took a week. The return trip by keelboat took a month.

By age 16, Tim McGrew helped steer a flatboat down the Ohio River from Pittsboro to Cincinnati and earned more money than most merchants in either of the two cities. It was an uneventful journey, save for the adventure of spotting wildlife, enjoying scenic vistas or feeling the breeze cool his face from the summer heat. When they reached the Queen City of Cincinnati, dock hands quickly unloaded the merchandise — whiskey, tobacco and maple syrup; forged implements such as sickles, shovels, hoes, axes, knives, frying pans and huge sugar kettles; and glass items, including window panes. Carpenters disassembled the flatboat and hauled away their new building materials.

The trip up river was not so joyful, for the three crew members had to walk all the way back to Pittsburg. "From now on, I say we take the keelboat," complained a burly oarsman named Maloney. By the seventh day, the complaints from Maloney became unbearable, and not because McGrew and Rooney necessarily disagreed with the boisterous Maloney. The problem was the drinking, the tobacco chewing and the farting that went along with the complaints. Mostly though, it was the snoring. McGrew and Rooney had gotten such little sleep for three straight nights that they were too exhausted to climb the muddy hills of eastern Ohio, much less the rugged mountains of Virginia territory that lie ahead.

As soon as the boatmen set up camp near Point Pleasant, a few miles short of the notorious Shawnee camp of chief Blue Jacket, Rooney plopped down without a word said and fell fast asleep. After building a fire, Tim fished along the Ohio and caught an oversized Pike, enough to feed a crew of 10. Maloney finished off the last of the moonshine from his first jug and popped the cork on jug number two. When dinner was over, Tim fell asleep halfway through one of Maloney's long diatribes but was rudely awakened by a loud belch, from Maloney of course, followed by hiccups.

On his third attempt to get his badly needed rest, Tim felt raindrops on his head. Maloney barked, "God-damnit!" Tim got up, grabbed a heavy log from a brush pile, walked up behind Maloney and clubbed him squarely on top of the head, after which Maloney fell over sideways from his sitting position and lay silent, not snoring, not complaining, not farting nor belching for the entire night.

The next morning, well after sunrise, Tim poked Maloney in the ribs. Maloney sat up, felt the large knot on his head and growled, "Who in hell hit me on the head?" to which Tim replied, "It must have been the bear."

"What bear? I ain't seen no bear."

"It was the bear that stole the fish. I tried to chase him away with this here club but I imagine he musta used it on you."

The burly oarsman stood up and pushed his face toward Tim and said in a low, commanding voice, "Iffin there was a bear, like you says there was, then why didn't it hit you? Why didn't it hit Rooney?" At this point, Rooney shoved his face into Maloney's and said, "Iffin McGrew says there was a bar, then there twas a bar, and that's that!" Maloney had nothing further to say.

Later that day, Rooney pulled Tim aside and asked, "Why'd you club Maloney anyway?" Tim smiled, knowing Rooney did not buy into that bear story from the get-go. Then he looked Rooney squarely in the eye and said, "It was the cussin'. I can

tolerate usin' the word, damnit, but not God damnit.
That's takin' the Lord's name in vain."

For the remainder of the trip, Maloney
continued to drink, spit tobacco, belch and complain
about the heat and bugs and whatever else annoyed
him. However, he did not snore at night, for whenever
Maloney tried to lay on his back, either Rooney or
McGrew would roll him over to the side, thus assuring
that everyone would have a good night's sleep.

9

WHISKEY REBELLION

The debt of the US from the Revolutionary War exceeded $54,000,000. In order to pay for it, Congress imposed an excise tax on distilled liquors. The people around Pittsburg were furious. About one in five farmers had stills. For them, whiskey was not only a drink or a medicine for ills but a bartering agent. Money was hard to come by. The average farmer never laid out more than $10 per year. While money was short in supply for farmers, whiskey was plentiful and easy to exchange for needed goods. The problem was how to pay the tax with so little cash.

Farming communities held one protest meeting after another, adopted resolutions and signed petitions, but all of these efforts failed. In September 1791, a gang of sixteen assaulted a tax collector for Allegheny County. They cut his hair, tarred and feathered him and demanded his resignation. Later they set fire to the tax collector's mansion. Another whiskey insurrection took place in Westmoreland County. When an excise collector named Graham was driven out of Greensburg, a second collector, John Wells, was kidnapped and taken to the county line. The Pittsburg Gazette called it a "whiskey rebellion."

A concerned George Washington arranged to have the Secretary of War call up 13,000 militiamen to march against the Monongahela farmers. As they advanced, commissioners offered pardons for those taking an oath of submission. The troops ended up arresting only a few who took part in the burning of the mansion. The prisoners were forced to march by foot all the way to Philadelphia. At the trials, all of them were acquitted. The Whiskey Rebellion ended in February 1795. It was the first attempt on the part of the people to disobey the national authority.

A few years later, the farmers, peaceful but still dissatisfied, drummed up enough votes to send Thomas Jefferson to the White House, after which the excise tax was repealed. But until then, because of the tax, whiskey profits plummeted.

During the summer of 1793, Brennen had come to a final decision. "I'm closing the store," he announced to Susan. When Susan objected, a heated argument followed, but it was in vain. Brennan was a determined man and won the argument, at least for the moment.

It was a hot, muggy day in June when Brennan pulled up his wagon and team of horses to load up the merchandise. As he started to load, Susan made a final proposal. She would purchase the inventory, at wholesale price of course, and run the store under her own name. "Impossible," Brennan retorted. "And how on God's earth would you come up with the money even if I did agree to sell?" he added with a tight-lipped grin.

"With me own money. That's how, Mister Brennan. Doncha think I knew the day would come would come when you'd do the very thing you're doing right now?"

"Oh? And what exactly is that, Mrs. McGrew?"

" Turnin' you back on the one chance to make up for the mistake you made a long time ago. Turnin' your back on your own son. Doncha think he should get the chance to make something of himself?"

Brennan was infuriated and about to challenge these old accusations since there never was actual proof that he was the true father. But he held his tongue. After all, he was a businessman and the debate at hand involved a business deal. "Tell you what I'll do," he began.

The deal with Brennan was as follows: McGrew would purchase all inventory at 10 cents on the dollar, which came to $55. She was short $5 but made up the difference by giving up a tallow chandelier, which she figured she could not sell in any event. At the end of the day, McGrew had a trading post, almost fully stocked, but no money to pay the liquor tax. Brennan had, by agreement, wiped his hands of any future allegations of bastardry, had 50 dollars in his pocket and a chandelier that jingled and jangled in his wagon over the bumpy road back to Pittsburg.

In early October 1796, Hans and Wet Foot were holding hands while walking along the shores of Indian Lake and heard honking-like noises overhead. Moments later a large flock of birds in a V formation flew over the lake with such noisy chatter that everyone stopped to look. "What kind of birds are those?" a young brave asked. No one knew except Too Sweet, who said, "Those are the cackling geese from lands far away," as he pointed north. "It is not a good sign," he added.

Normally a flock of Canadian geese would migrate a good distance to the west, stopping to rest just north of Cincinnati. But this flock suddenly changed direction when a strong, cold wind blew them off course. Instead of heading due south — which had always been the case — the leader directed them southeast, maintaining a speed of 60 mph and continuing in that direction nonstop until they were 250 miles away from the normal route.

At three in the afternoon on the following day, a great wind struck the Indian camp, knocking down trees, toppling over huts and generally causing havoc within the tribe. Hans ran home to tend to the horses and cattle amidst bellowing sounds of distress. Wet Foot ran too, her hair streaming from her head as she scrambled to help retrieve her mother's house tumbling towards the woods. By sundown, the wind had shifted to the northwest. The temperature plummeted to 15 degrees, then 5 degrees. The horizontal rains turned to stinging ice crystals, then to swirling flakes of snow, which soon covered the landscape. By the time the winds subsided, a wave of cold, bitter air had descended upon them. Indian Lake was frozen solid before midnight. It was -17 degrees with the temperature still dropping.

Despite the many blankets spread out on the ground in front of a great bonfire, three Cherokee froze to death including Chief Too Sweet. The Alberta Clipper storm lasted 30 hours before the weather warmed. But it was too late. For the tribe at Indian Lake, it was a disaster. All but two horses died and many inhabitants were frostbitten. Great quantities of maize and squash were wiped out.   Bachman lost nearly all of his crops and although the oxen and the chickens did well, other animals did not. Saddened and depressed with the loss of cattle and horses, he thought about giving up farm work. Perhaps working at one of the forging mills or the boatyard would be better. These of course were silly ideas and on the next day, Johann and Linda Bachman began the tedious work of cleaning up the wind debris, mending fences, re-nailing the wind-damaged buildings and preparing for the cold days ahead.

For the remainder of the winter, which was much longer and colder than usual, the Bachmans and their Indian neighbors fed off remains of the frozen animals from the farm and from the forest. Fallen deer and other four-legged critters dotted the terrain along the Little Sewickley Creek.

Following the death of Too Sweet, things were in turmoil at the Cherokee village for an extended period. Several days after his burial, a group of elders called a powwow to select a new chief. No one wanted the job at a time when settlers were forcing Indians from their sacred lands. Who would lead them to the next place? And just what place would that be, was the tormenting question.

Many Cherokee settled in Kentucky, Carolina, Georgia or Tennessee. But white men were invading those areas too, the same way they were invading the Ohio Valley. There was as much discussion about the land problem as there was about replacing the chief. The vacillation continued for weeks. No decisions were made. They struggled with the severe cold throughout the winter and continued to feed off frozen carcasses. The tribe celebrated the winter solstice and mourned the loss of Chief Too Sweet, yet still avoided the selection of a chief. The procrastination, however, ultimately worked to their advantage.

Shortly after Thomas Jefferson became president, the whiskey tax was repealed. Susan was elated. Beginning with the bad winter of 1796 and the five years that followed, the trade business had tumbled to a new low. She was behind on her taxes, as she had no money to pay them. No one had money it seemed, except for Tim. But she promised herself she would not have her son paying for any of the expenses at the store, especially the taxes, which were improperly levied to begin with. She was getting older now but held onto her hope that Tim would one day take over the business.

It was not meant to be. For the last five years, Tim continued working the Ohio River as an oarsman, earning huge sums of money while ferrying keelboats to Cincinnati and places beyond. His latest run was by barge all the way to New Orleans, which left him away from home for months. Although he was quite capable of running a small trading post, he was no longer interested in doing so. He was spending more and more of his free time in Cincinnati. A girl named Molly Roush had caught his eye, and word on the street was, they would be married before the year was out.

10
THE WEDDING

With fewer animals to feed, Johann began re-shaping his farm, utilizing sheds for the distilling and storage of more and more whiskey. He too was getting older and had planned to pass the farm on to his son, now age 22. He was not surprised to learn that Hans had given Running Creek a wampum belt with many colors of beaded glass and shells as a dowry to marry Wet Foot. He was taken aback, however, when Hans announced that he planned to build a hut within the Cherokee village and live his life according to the teachings of the Cherokee nation. Linda, sick with emotion, moped around the house for weeks, regretting she had never taken the time to baptize Hans at the Presbyterian Church. Susan was beside herself, unable to comprehend why anyone, especially Hans, would make such a grave mistake. *He will burn in hell.*

Several weeks before the wedding, Linda made great efforts to persuade Susan to participate in the ceremony at Indian Lake. But each time, Linda would walk away from these conversations feeling guilty for not insisting on a church wedding. Meanwhile, Johann made the argument that the Presbytery would not allow non-whites into the church, much less oversee a marriage between Hans, a non-member, and an Indian. Therefore, a wedding at the Indian camp was the only viable alternative. Still, Susan refused to attend on the grounds that it would not be an official wedding in the eyes of the church.

When Moon Shadow learned of the dilemma, she went to see the Rev. Mungo Dick, the new Presbyterian minister along the Little Sewickley. The reverend, suspicious during the first several minutes of the meeting, was fascinated with the woman's mastery of the English language and allowed her to continue to speak for a much longer time than was needed to answer her basic questions: *Are non-whites excluded from the church? No. Was it possible for him to marry non--members? Yes, but 30 days notice must be given. Must the wedding take place at the church? No, but the arrangements must conform to Christian practices.*

Rev. Dick also advised that both the bride and groom would be expected to attend church and undergo counseling for two months. Furthermore, no alcoholic beverages would be permitted before or during the ceremony or at the reception. The reverend was so impressed with Moon Shadow's purity that he insisted on meeting Hans and Wet Foot the very next day at the Bachman farm.

The counseling went rather well and soon Hans, Wet Foot and Susan were attending church on a regular basis. Most of the Cherokee went along with the wedding plan, which was to take place at the Bachman's instead of Indian Lake the week before the fall harvest.

A number of the church members, like the Scotch-Irish family of Covenanter Seceder, grew to like the charming, yet humble Wet Foot who sat on the dirt floor of the little church so that others could sit on the logs used for pews. These members were eager to attend the inspirational, albeit unusual, wedding ceremony. Others were leery, questioning whether the event might prompt too many other Indians to attend church and crowd out the regulars with too many savages. Even worse, they could spring an attack. Indeed, many had no idea there was even an Indian village only three miles upstream. "I thought they all went west," one member commented.

The entire Cherokee tribe came to the wedding and seemed to be in awe with the fancy dresses, hats and boots worn by the church people. Little boys and girls of different origin, ages 2 and 3, looked at each other with great fascination and seemed a lot more curious than fearful. They stared at beaded head bands with feathers sticking out, colorful shawls, white cotton dresses, shiny shoes, vests with buttons, blond hair and blue eyes.

Wet Foot, wearing an extremely ornate Regalia multi-beaded buckskin dress with lots of fringe, introduced her wedding party to all of the Presbyterians who came to honor her. After hiding several gallons of Kentucky whiskey in the trading post, Tim spent considerable time talking with his girlfriend Molly.

WEDDING DRESS

Susan seemed extraordinarily happy that morning, especially when Hans removed his Indian apparel. He fit so nicely in the new suit she ordered from Pittsburg.

Linda and Moon Shadow worked feverishly in the kitchen, assorting plates and bowls, stacking up utensils, all the while chattering and laughing out loud like 5-year-olds. Squaws busied themselves cutting up the vegetables and refueling the fire pits. Young braves hauled in fish and slabs of meat. Reverend Dick was all over the place, taking time to get to know all of the guests in attendance, while his wife and six children stood dutifully to the side, not getting in the way.

RILLTON

The day of the wedding was a joyous affair, women saying this or that about the handsome the groom and how lovely the bride looked. *How did they meet? How did she get the name Wet Foot?* At high noon, a semi-circle of Indian drummers beat their decorated drums in unison exactly every two seconds so that several drums sounded as one. After 30 booming sounds, the drums stopped, at which point Rev. Mungo Dick stepped onto a small makeshift platform. With the bride and groom and a crowd of 70 people facing him, the reverend in his resonant voice began reading passages from his raggedy Bible. Three little Cherokee girls stood wide-eyed off to the side, holding hands as they might at any other ceremony. A fourth girl from the Dick family joined them and this did not go unnoticed by Rev. Dick. He paused for a moment and smiled (...*these are God's children*...) and then he continued.

"Do thee Hans Bachman take thee Wet Foot for his lawful wedded wife, to have and to hold, for better, for worse..."

His voice is powerful, like a drum, thought Running Creek.

"...for richer, for poorer... "

Molly Roush thought, T*his is the right minister for my wedding.*

"...in sickness and in health ..."

Susan McGrew's mind flashed back to the sickness she felt in her stomach over the last several days but dismissed it as simple nervousness about the wedding.

"...to love and honor from this day forward until death to thee part?"

"I DO!" Hans said it clearly and without hesitation. Then, after repeating the words to the bride, Wet Foot said, "I DO TOO!"

"You may now kiss...

Hans planted a huge kiss on Wet Foot's cheek, the wonderful cheek he recalled so vividly at the Potato Dance.

...the bride!"

Wet foot turned Han's face to her waiting lips. Her kiss was warm and soft, luscious and sweet tasting. Hans thought he smelled iron, like the iron in a hatchet but with cherries mixed in.

The whooping and hollering that followed the vows came not from the Indians but rather the churchgoers. Irish whiskey appeared out of nowhere, as did a fiddle. Men were doing the Irish jig. There was more hooting. Before the first song had ended, the Dick family had disappeared into the woods. In the middle of his third kiss with his new bride, Hans was snatched away and carried off to a stretched-out blanket and tossed high into the air several times. Someone grabbed Wet Foot and spun her round and round. Before the pig roast began, Tim had uncorked two more whiskey jugs from the trading post. The noise got louder. The Indians stood silent with puzzled looks on their faces

RILLTON

Susan, overjoyed with emotion throughout the day, was again experiencing left-sided abdominal pain. She went home to rest at sundown. Most of the guests had gone home by then. By the time she got there, she felt bloated and was short of breath. She tried to void, noticed blood and became nauseous. She wolfed down a shot of whiskey and went straight to bed. She was pleased that the ceremony went so well, that Moon Shadow had the courage to seek the advice and counsel of Reverend Dick, that the reverend was strong-minded enough to conduct an unorthodox yet gracious wedding in the presence of the very Indians she judged to be savage when, in fact, they were simply uninformed human beings and not so very different from her neighbors back in Scotland. She was happy that her grandson Hans and his lovely wife Wet Foot had come to see the light of religion in their lives. Susan McGrew, age 63, died in her sleep thinking about the light in heaven, unaware she would never again see light on earth.

11
A JOURNEY UNKNOWN

Under Napoleon Bonaparte, France became a world power in 1800. After acquiring the Louisiana territory from Spain, they turned around and sold the 800,000 square miles of property to the United States for $15,000,000 in 1803 in order to fund the Napoleonic wars. The territory extended from the Mississippi River to the Rocky Mountains, including Arkansas, where the two Cherokee nations came to re-settle.

The pro-French Western Cherokee had already settled in northwestern Arkansas in 1763. Twenty years later, they were joined by the pro-English Cherokee from the East, whose numbers increased to 14,000. By 1803, the two nations of the Cherokee became a formidable threat to the Osage who originally claimed the territory long before the Louisiana Purchase.

But there was tension between the two groups as well. The Eastern Cherokee, who considered themselves superior, tried to set up an elaborate government, including a court system with three chiefs and a written constitution. The other group insisted on having one chief and no written laws. The dispute led to civil war over borders and jurisdiction. The dissidence continued all the way up until the American Civil War when an Eastern group of 3,000 sided with the Confederates. A Western group of 1,000 signed up for the Union. Regardless of which side they were on, after the war both groups were forced out of Arkansas and sent west to Oklahoma.

Some tribes proclaimed not to be a part of either the Western or Eastern Cherokee Nations. It didn't matter. Clans were driven out of the Tennessee Mountains, the fields of Alabama and from the hills of Georgia where gold was discovered. The legislatures simply divided up the Cherokee lands by lottery and stripped the Cherokee of legal protection. However, one clan of 1600 was allowed to stay, according to North Carolina state law. By no means did this prevent the U.S. army or the Tennessee militia from trying to capture and imprison them as fugitives. To be safe, many Indians ran off and hid in the mountains for some for 25 years before the army finally gave up the chase.

After the great Shawnee chief Tecumseh lost his final battle for the Ohio Valley at Ft. Greenville in 1811, many Shawnee migrated westward to a place called Shawnee Mission, Kansas. There was no one left to fight for these Indian lands. Tribes that did not leave voluntarily were harassed, if not attacked by frontiersmen.

When the news of Tecumseh's defeat hit the Cherokee camp at Indian Lake, once again the topic of relocation came up. Running Creek, the new chief, made great efforts to motivate members of the tribe to arrive at some kind of decision. Oftentimes he would emulate the unforgettable Rev. Mungo Dick, though his voice was rather tinny-sounding in comparison. Even so, many of his arguments were at least thought-provoking, and this was enough to persuade people to vote for his ideas.

Running Creek wanted to lead his tribe down the great Mississippi River and re-settle in the area of northwest Arkansas. He learned of this Cherokee settlement from Tim McGrew who became familiar with the boatmen traveling up and down the Mississippi. At first Tim was not eager to share this information with his friends and relatives at Indian Lake. He truly did not want to see them go. But he also knew pressure from the white settlers would one day force their departure and so he secretly planned to transport them down river by flatboat. He could get a cheap craft from his friend, Stephen Seymour, who worked at the boat yard.

William Guffey emigrated from Scotland in 1738 and fought for the British when he was 18 years old. He was a Highlander and became acquainted with Tim McGrew, Sr. (killed at Ft. Duquesne), Simeon McGrew (Tim's older brother and now a Quaker) and Johann Bachman (the scout General Forbes sent to Ft. Carlisle seeking help from Colonel Bouquet). All of these men served under General Forbes and later took advantage of the free land offer following their military service.

Guffey was awarded 300 acres of land in 1769. His son James purchased next to it several hundred more acres along the Youghiogheny and had a total of five children. His first son, John, admired his grandfather William who told stories of the Indian battles all over Ohio and Kentucky.

Old man Guffey had the extraordinary ability to not only obtain first-hand information on the many recent wars but also remember vivid details of each and every battle. For example, Guffey knew that Daniel Boone's son was killed by Shawnee in 1773 and that it was the Cherokee who tried to warn Boone of the attack. He knew of the massacre of a peaceful band of Mingo at Yellow Creek. The Mingo retaliated by burning down Hannastown, which led to the construction of a new county seat at Greensburg in 1781. The U.S. Army retaliated by slaughtering unprotected Delaware women and children. In return the Delaware Indians captured Colonel William

Crawford, a friend of George Washington, and burned him at the stake.

"When tensions are high, hatred always seemed to target the peaceful villages," he told his grandson. "Men in the position of leadership should look at the eagle which symbolizes our Constitution. In his left talon the eagle carries 13 arrows but in the right, an olive branch. The eagle first looks to the right, towards the olive branch. We should do the same."

Word got out that farmers from North Huntington intended to destroy the village at Indian Lake. John Guffey, now justice of the peace, felt it necessary to forewarn the Cherokee, just as the Cherokee had forewarned Daniel Boone of his son's killing. First, he went to the Bachman farm but was surprised to see Bachman ailing in bed. "Just a touch of the flu," Johann remarked. Guffey snarled at the discouraging news and then proceeded to the trading post where he warned Linda of the planned attack. Guffey did not realize that Bachman's son was living at the Indian camp until after speaking with Chief Running Creek.

Two days later, a mysterious grass fire damaged crops in the field and a nearby hut. The next week, the perpetrators fired rifle shots into the new winter solstice totem pole and ran off two horses. Several days later, on a cold night, a young brave was tarred and feathered and tied to a tree outside of camp. Running Creek held a powwow and asked for a vote to relocate to Arkansas via Tim McGrew's flatboat. The vote was 20 to 6 in favor of the move, including Hans. Moon Shadow and Wet Foot voted nay. Johann and Linda were gravely disappointed in the decision to leave. They feared they might not ever again see their trusted friends and neighbors Running Creek and Moon Shadow. More importantly, they feared for the safety of their family — Hans, the beloved Wet Foot and the grandchildren, Poki and Little Creek.

12
POKI AND LITTLE CREEK

Following the funeral of Susan McGrew, everyone thought Tim would give up his riverboat business and run the trading post. And he did so, but for only a short time. It was boring, lonely work. After a month, he asked Linda to help. She agreed to mind the store for a short while, until after Tim's wedding at which time Molly Roush McGrew was supposed to live at the post and manage the store, the same way Susan did.

But Molly had a change of heart and preferred to remain in Cincinnati, a paradox that left Tim waning in his decision to marry at all. Meanwhile, Wet Foot helped Linda transport syrup, flour, whiskey and other items of trade up and down the Little Sewickley. She quickly learned the business well enough to run it herself. Except that now Wet Foot was expectant.

Poki came first, a chubby infant until age two when he suddenly grew tall and slim. He was always poking things, first with his index finger, then later with a stick. When squaws bent over to pull weeds from the field of corn, beans and squash, he'd poke them in the butt with a stick. He poked in holes to see what kind of critter lived there. He had all kinds of sticks in different shapes and sizes apparently designed to poke at different objects. By age five, he was an excellent fisherman, using his special spear of course. He planted beans with the bean stick, scraped birch bark with the serrated edged oak stick and flung crab apples with his apple-piercing stick. Once he tried to use a stick to play kickball but was tossed out of the game by the older boys.

Little Creek came a year later. They named the girl Little Creek because, more than anything else, she loved playing in the creek. She knew which rocks hid the salamanders. Each salamander was given a name, based on its color or personality. She would reprimand the crayfish for coming too close to her salamander friends. At age five she would carry toads to the creek to meet the frogs, which she caught easily, placing them in the little pond she created. The next day she would, once again, catch the same toads along the bank and take them back to the pond for another powwow. She was multi-lingual. Frogs spoke in German, salamanders in Cherokee, toads in Shawnee.

She herself spoke in English, of course. This was the most important of all the languages, according to her mother.

One Sunday, Wet Foot led the family to the church of Rev. Dick so that Poki and Little Creek could be baptized. Before agreeing, the reverend suggested that both names be "Christianized" so as to avoid questions of legitimacy. Poki was renamed Paul. And Little Creek, Rilla.

"Rilla? How did you come up with that name?" Hans asked his father, Johann.

"In German, it means a little creek," he replied.

After the baptism, everyone at church referred to their new members as Paul and Rilla. At Indian Lake, they were called Poki and Little Creek.

The day after the ceremony, someone set fire to the maize field. As villagers explored the damages, Little Creek smelled a foul odor. At the edge of the woods appeared a severely burnt body of an animal. Poki poked it with a stick and heard a squeaky sound. It startled them. *Is it still alive?* They backed away and heard the sound again. It was more like a whimper.

As they began to walk away, they heard the sound again. It was coming from beneath the dead animal. Poki flipped it over with his stick, exposing four dead pups in the dug-out hole beneath. But there was a fifth pup still alive. The hair on the top of the body was singed and the left ear was bent down over its forehead. But the face was clearly that of a young wolf, curled up in a ball with its eyes closed, trembling. As Little Creek stroked his forehead with her middle finger, the pup tried to lift its head but could not. With one swift move, Little Creek picked up the pathetic critter and whisked it away from the dreadful pit of ashes that surrounded the remains of its mother and the other little ones that did not survive the fire.

Little Creek fed the animal milk at Bachman's cabin and wrapped it in a blanket. Johann was not happy about having a wolf in his house and kept thinking about the welfare of his chickens once the wolf was old enough to hunt. Nor was Linda happy. She agreed to help care for the wolf temporarily until it could find its way back to the woods where it would be "happy." Wet Foot had no problem with the new pet. One day it might warn them, even protect them, from intruders. Running Creek thought the appearance of the wolf might be a sign of good fortune.

Rilla Bachman, aka Little Creek, was 8 years old when she boarded the 20-foot long flatboat at Stephen Seymour's boat yard. She carried with her one small basket in which her puppy named Ear Flop lay curled up and fast asleep. Thirty-six others in her tribe climbed on board, carrying with them only the bare essentials plus a rooster and two chickens.

Tim McGrew was surprised but happy that his friend had pieced together a great-looking raft made of oak, the best wood available. He handed Seymour $25 in cash plus a small jug of whiskey and said, "To the best boats on the three rivers." Seymour replied, "But not for long. They tell me Fulton is building a new steamboat in the Pittsburg yard. Named it the *New Orleans*. I may not be in business by the time you get back."

Tim McGrew's flatboat, with a cargo of 20 sacks of flour, 37 Indians, rooster, 2 hens and one wolf-dog shoved off down the Monongahela in late October 1811. Half way to Cincinnati, a rugged-looking oarsman aboard a keelboat headed upriver began shooting pea gravel from his slingshot into the crowd of Indians on McGrew's flatboat. McGrew grabbed his musket and yelled, "You wanna trade lead for them rocks, fella!" The tobacco-chewing keelboat captain recognized the voice of his old friend from their previous runs down the Ohio and barked out, "McGrew, you old bear chasin' sonsabitch. I see you're still runnin' flatboats," And then he grabbed the free oar and whacked it across the backside of the young, stone-throwing troublemaker, knocking him overboard into the river. The current was too swift, even for the strongest of swimmers to negotiate. Soon the man was overcome with exhaustion and forced to dog-paddle to the slippery mud bank of the Ohio as best he could.

McGrew: I thank thee, Mister Maloney, for your exercise in good judgment.

Maloney: And I thank you McGrew for chasin' that bar awhile back. Iffin I see you in hell, I'll put in a good word.

With that, McGrew and his crew of Cherokee were off once again down river without further incident. When they reached the Queen City, being somewhat apprehensive of white men in a strange place, the Indians were at first reluctant to disembark. But the dock workers were always eager to see new faces, Indians or not, for here lay the opportunity for the great swindlers to fatten their wallets.   Vendors along the dock tried to sell whiskey under the mistaken belief that all Indians loved firewater. When this failed, they displayed beaded glass and other shiny objects, none of which surpassed the quality of goods sold at the trading post near Indian Lake. In town there were specialty shops for dresses, belts, hats, buttons and cups made of tin or brass. Under normal circumstances, the Indians probably would have traded a few items, but their primary concern was hanging onto their essentials

There were card games of which the Cherokee knew nothing about, magic tricks and ball tossing games. Poki and Little Creek got caught up in the shell game.

A man with a tall black hat and broad smile would continually ask the question: Is the hand faster than the eye? And with that introduction, he would crisscross the three walnut shells with his hands moving just fast enough to entice patrons into betting money on the correct shell hiding a pea. Little Creek managed to pick the right shell several times in a row, much to the chagrin of the shell man. But when he figured out that she was using the wolf dog to smell out the pea, he became irate and ordered her out of the tent. A short time later, Hans and Wet Foot confronted the man, Wet Foot doing most of the talking. She spoke perfectly good English, reminding the man of the possible loss of his "good reputation" and so the shell man relented, handing back the money as well as the claimed prizes.

Tim spent that afternoon with Molly discussing future wedding plans, which were tentative at best. He was uncertain when he would return from his trip south. It was the first time he was uncertain about anything, Molly thought. After steering the flatboat down river, well away from Cincinnati where pick-pockets tended to roam after sundown, the boatload of Indians camped along the shores of the Ohio under a bright moon. Gone were the noises of the city. In the quiet of the night, everyone was asleep. All except Ear Flop.

Johann and Linda did not sleep for several weeks after the Indians left the village at Indian Lake. Johann had not been feeling well even before the loneliness at night time afflicted him. At age 71, he was losing his will to work the farm. Linda tried to keep busy just to avoid her loneliness but with no one around the trading post to talk or gossip her way through the day, she too felt depressed. She especially missed Poki and Little Creek.

During the winter of 1812, Stephen Seymour's worries about the business mounted. More and more flatboats were taking over the river as people had acquired better saws and could construct their own rafts and barges. No one wanted to spend money for a product that they could now make with their own hands. Like other family-run businesses, Seymour had planned for his three sons to take over once he retired. But now he questioned whether this would ever come to pass. He worried about the steamboats. And he worried about the welfare of his three sons, especially the middle son, Charles, who had little interest in working the yards. Charles would spend his days helping the women tend the gardens or take long walks in the woods watching the animals. He loved horses and would talk to them like they were his friends.

One evening at dinner, out of the blue, Seymour said, "McGrew says Johann Bachman on the Little Sewickley needs help on the farm. Maybe you oughten get into boat building. Maybe farmin' work is better." And he looked straight into the face of Charles.

At age 15, Charles began working the Bachman farm. He spent long hours plowing the fields, sowing rye and other crops and tending to the farm animals. That was his favorite part. Johann seemed to get a kick out of the young lad as he talked to the horses the same way Johann did when training horses at Ft. Pitt. On Easter Sunday, Charles painted eggs and arranged them in a fancy bowl. Charles especially liked Linda, the way she smiled at him with her glowing eyes and spoke to him with that Scottish accent. And Johann was so patient yet so precise in explaining exactly what needed to be done each day. They were nothing like his parents, blurting out commands without much thought and then changing their minds minutes later. It was a match made in heaven. The Bachmans needed a hard worker and a companion to take away the loneliness. Charles needed that farm. It was his lifeline.

13

A TRAIL TO NOWHERE

What led to the war of 1812 was not only the reluctance by the English to surrender their claim to the northwest territory. It was the additional measure of blocking the passage of the U.S. trading ships headed for France. The blockade caused a re-routing of goods along the eastern seaboard of the Atlantic Ocean to the Mississippi River at New Orleans. From there, steam vessels hauled European merchandise all the way to Pittsburg. At the docks in Pittsburg, boatloads of cannon balls were sent down river to Andrew Jackson's army to fight the British. During this time McGrew's raft landed at Arkansas where the Indian lake Cherokee set upa new camp next to the Eastern Cherokee Nation in northeast Arkansas. It was a mistake.

The highly organized and rule-oriented Eastern Cherokee would not recognize Running Chief as an official leader. His tribe was directed to the bottom of the hill. They were asked to pay taxes, a portion of their farm produce, even though the new tribe had no produce with them from the long trip. In addition, the young braves were expected to protect the camp from Osage attacks which were frequent and vicious. Before the end of the day, they felt like second-class citizens.

Moon Shadow's communication skills had always been superb. Within a month she learned that Jackson's army needed Indian guides to spy on the British near the Mississippi delta. Not only would these guides earn Continental currency but would they have land set aside in neighboring Georgia for resettlement purposes. Two days later Running Creek and Hans floated a makeshift raft down river and signed up with the army at New Orleans.

The duo had carried out several missions before a key battle took place 12 miles south of the city on the east bank of the Mississippi near Pea Island. Jackson himself led the charge in a three-pronged attack which kept the British at bay for 12 hours. During this time, Running Creek, using his atlatl, killed a British soldier yards away from Jackson, saving Jackson's life. In the aftermath, Running Creek was honored by those serving under Jackson, though Jackson himself never acknowledged the life-saving incident. Before the battle ended, the British lost 46 men. The Americans lost 24, including

Running Creek and other Indians sent to the front lines.

At the end of the war, Hans had roughly $400 in Continental currency. He had planned to spend the money on tools, supplies and transportation to his free land in Georgia. Unfortunately, the Georgia legislature enacted laws prohibiting Indians settlement rights in the lands previously designated. And when he appealed to Jackson directly, Jackson had no alternative plan and refused to discuss the matter further. Hans was livid. He had lost his father-in-law, chief Running Creek, during what was supposed to be a worthy cause, only to see his fortunes fold and turn to ruin.

With the loss of her husband, Moon Shadow was in deep mourning. Her desire to relocate from the despicable camp at Arkansas had faded. She acted as if she didn't care. Meanwhile, Tim McGrew, who had signed up for the war, learned of the events of the battle at New Orleans while doing cannonball runs to that city. He went to see his nephew Hans. Having learned of the precarious situation inside the camp at Arkansas, Tim conspired to move the tribe, this time to North Carolina.

As the tribe began preparing for their departure, in a great show of protest, the Eastern Cherokee chiefs blocked the main passage out of the camp. At this point, McGrew cocked his new rifle and pointed it directly at the head chief while motioning for his clan to continue with their exit. The showdown was in truth not as serious as it seemed. In fact, all three chiefs were glad to see them go.

The clan from Indian Lake seldom participated in the formal powwows at the main camp. They preferred their own ancient celebrations and undisciplined dances. "They planted only enough crops to feed their own people, never enough to pay for their fair share of taxes," a chief bemoaned. "None of them have enough warrior blood in them to defend attacks from the Osage," said another. And that dog, or wolf, or whatever it was, kept everyone up at night with its incessant howling, in between chewing up moccasins and urinating on blankets. In short, the blockage was nothing more than an overt display of force, a political move, designed to discourage others in the camp from leaving.

Tim's steam-propelled boat could travel upstream with the same ease as any flatboat could downstream. It was not the flowery, floating palace that people oftentimes envision. Rather, a small, plain-looking tow boat with ropes and anchors and wads of cloth nailed to the sides. Regardless of the type of steamboat navigating the Mississippi, travel was dangerous. Many hidden tree stumps and sunken boats could rip open a boat hull like a can opener, causing the boat to sink. About 21 percent of the boats were lost from boiler explosions caused by too much pressure in the boilers. Tim had narrowly escaped injury from such an explosion on his first trip up river two years before.

The clan shoved off on a bright, clear morning in early May 1815. By afternoon, it was hot and muggy. The passengers scooped up buckets of river water to drink and cool off. Conditions worsened on the second day. The temperature hit 90 degrees before noon and continued to rise throughout the afternoon. Hans kept watch of the boiler pressure inside the boiler room where it was 120 degrees. Twice he nearly passed out.

At four o'clock in the afternoon, just as they reached the land between the lakes, strong winds from the southwest literally blew the boat to the north shore of the Tennessee River. Great swales of water crashed into the rear paddles of the boat. The engine stalled. The craft bobbed up and down like a cork. It took Tim all he could do to keep the boat steady as they unloaded the passengers. Some tried to jump onto a bank where they could hold onto bushes. Others jumped into the water and formed a human chain to help debilitated passengers get to safety.

Hans and Wet Foot, the last ones on board, had just finished helping Tim secure the last anchor and tie off the boat when an enormous wave, propelled by a huge gust of wind, knocked Hans sideways into the center post. He smashed his head and slid across the deck into the choppy waters. Without hesitation, Wet Foot dove into the water, latched on to Hans and tried to pull him back ashore.

Suddenly, Ear Flop took off down the embankment like a lightning bolt, flung himself into the river and paddled his way to the couple screaming for help. Meanwhile, Tim threw the one and only life preserver on board. It fell short, the wind continually blowing it back to the vessel. He tried again and again as wind and rain pounded his face. The victims were unable to overcome the strong undertow. After going under the third time, they were swept away by the current heading away from the boat. As the winds picked up and the heavy rains poured down on the hapless Indians along the isolated bank, Moon Shadow cried out in agonizing pain as others had not heard before. Little Creek snuggled at her side and tried her best to comfort the torn woman. But she too sobbed heavily from a broken heart.

The spring storm had created havoc up and down the Mississippi. Large numbers of shipping vessels had capsized, cargoes disappeared beneath the choppy waters and many passengers were injured if not lost. Large hailstones pounded the Ohio valley while tornados ravaged many areas of Kentucky, Indiana and northern Tennessee. The muddy waters of the Mississippi flooded just about every village along its banks. For two weeks, river traffic had come to a complete standstill.

Despite the incalculable damages in the surrounding areas, Tim's steamboat was still operable. Within a week, the calm waters of the Tennessee

River began to reappear. The small group of Cherokee, imprisoned on the land between the lakes, had somehow survived. The next day they headed east, up that long, winding river that would take them to their new homeland somewhere in the hills of the Great Smoky Mountains.

At age 18, Charles Seymour knew everything about running a farm except distilling whiskey. That had always been Mr. Bachman's job. But now Bachman had medical problems. It started with his rib — at least that's what it felt like. And then the day after his 80th birthday, he struggled with his breathing, felt light-headed and complained of numbness in his fingers. His feet were always getting cold. He'd take a shot of whiskey and sleep for hours at a time. It was time to show the boy how to make the whiskey, he decided.

The first batch of whiskey was so sour, so distasteful, that young Seymour tossed it immediately. None of the farm animals would come near it. The second batch was better — not very pleasing, but better. By the end of the summer, Linda claimed it was "darn right tasty."

So enthralled into the business of whiskey was Seymour that he even considered giving up the farm. He changed his mind the next day after crunching the numbers under more sober conditions. Still, Seymour was now able to run the entire farm on his own, which to him was an enormously proud feeling as well as a blessing for the Bachmans.

In the wee hours of daybreak as the roosters began crowing, Johann Bachman gasped his last breath in the arms of his wife Linda. She lay in bed at his side, silently wiping away her tears.

The trip to the land of the Smokys took nearly three weeks. Twice McGrew had to stop for wood to feed the boiler. The wood, not being seasoned, caused unnecessary smoke and led to unwanted attention from nosy settlers in the hills of Tennessee and Alabama. For a time, they were followed up river by three canoes, but the steamed vessel was too swift and the pursuit ended quickly. In another instance, sinister-looking riverboat men on a flimsy raft headed downstream grinned into the faces of the squaws and then made awkward faces to one another, as if they were sharing some kind of inside joke.

When the steamboat reached the foothills, everyone disembarked but did not know where to go. Moon Shadow knew. She knew from her many conversations with the Chattanooga Cherokee at the Arkansas camp. She pointed to the south end of the highest mountain and then announced that she was separating from the tribe. She decided to take Poki and Little Creek back to the land of Indian Lake in order to be with their grandmother. Moon Shadow, getting older and feeling weaker, also knew that she herself would soon perish and pass on to the happy hunting ground. And when that happened, Linda McGrew Bachman would be the only living relative capable of securing their future. Poki refused to go back. He tried to convince Moon Shadow that he could take care of Little Creek too. But her mind was set. In the end, she and Little Creek headed north while Poki remained in the mountains of North Carolina.

Following the war, manufactured goods taken to New Orleans, Boston, Philadelphia and New York were being re-routed up and down the Atlantic coast without interference from British war ships. This meant fewer boats on the Mississippi. The idle traffic worked to the advantage of Moon Shadow and Little Creek as they navigated their way back home since there were now fewer patrol boats to stop and question their travel plans.

Nevertheless, two days into the trip, Tennessee militia ordered McGrew's boat to stop for an inspection of the merchandise on board. They were mainly looking for moonshine, which was subject to the new state tax. When the captain was assured there was no liquor on board, he began his exit but noticed the two Indians crouching down near the bow of the craft. He looked at McGrew with raised eyebrows.

Inspector: Who are those people?

McGrew: My niece and her grandmother.

Inspector: Why are they wearing Indian clothes?

Moon Shadow: We lost our clothes when the river flooded. This is all we have now.

Inspector: Why were you crouching down?

Moon Shadow: (In perfectly good English) We were doing our morning prayers. That's what Presbyterians do on Sunday mornings. Do you not pray on Sunday, captain?

Inspector: Beggin' your pardon, ma'am. 'Course I pray on Sunday. I was just trying to do my job. Colonel Guffey gave strict orders…

McGrew: Guffey? I know Guffey. Did cannonball runs with the man during the war. Ain't no better man alive than ol' Guf.

Inspector: Well, I declare. I thought I'd seen you somewhere before. Glad to see you back on the river, McGrew. Need anything special?

McGrew: We could use some firewood, sir.

Inspector: Private Buford! See to it that this man gets some fuel.

In less than a minute, Buford had delivered a crateful of coal, which in fact came from the Guffey coal mine that opened in 1806. It was enough to get McGrew's steamboat all the way to Cincinnati. And with that, the ship inspector signaled Buford to rev up the engines of the patrol boat. Moments later he sped off and headed the opposite direction, down river. During the weeklong trip up the Mississippi and Ohio Rivers, Moon Shadow volunteered to keep an eye on the boiler located inside the very hot, humid shelter. She didn't seem to mind. For her it was an ideal place for mourning, which began with the death of Running Creek and was exacerbated following the drowning of her only daughter and delightful son-in-law, Hans. The combination of events proved too difficult for her to absorb all at once. She needed isolation. The boiler room was her place to spend time alone.

Occasionally Moon Shadow would try to focus on positive thoughts out of the past — tickling Running Creek's nose with a goose feather as he slept, swimming under water and grabbing his ankles in surprise, galloping around camp acting like a horse with Wet Foot riding on her shoulders, watching Hans fall down out of the corner of her eye at the potato dance. But then the sad thoughts came — the Chickasaw raids, the fallen braves in the Blue Ridge Mountains, the many funerals that followed, the last days of Too Sweet and the deep depression she suffered for weeks. But with the latest events, her sadness sank to a new low. At times the pain stuck clear to the bone, and when it did, she could not stop sobbing. A vicious cycle of moods crashed like waves in her head — sad, happy, sad, angry, helpless, restless, tired, exhausted. It haunted her day and night. When would it end?

Meanwhile, Little Creek, whom Tim called Rilla, spent the week chatting with her uncle during the day and did her mourning at night. Tim had somehow become a source of amusement that kept her out of the doldrums. He had a knack of making simple jokes out of life's ordinary events. On this day, Tim had mimicked the inspector and private Buford. "Who ARE those people?" he blurted. Rilla laughed. The day before, they recounted the trip downstream when Maloney whacked the backside of the young sailor and knocked him overboard. It was serious then. But Tim had a way of re-telling the story to make it humorous. "I ever tell you about the time I clubbed Maloney on the head with a sycamore?" Tim asked. Rilla roared with laughter even before he started telling the new story. By the time they reached Cincinnati, aside from being relatives, they had become jovial buddies.

On June 20, 1815, the new band of Cherokee high in the mountains of North Carolina chopped down a suitable tree with a fork near the top. They carried it back to camp, stripped the branches, carved out an eagle and set up the new post facing east before starting the summer solstice celebration. They were a smaller group than before. Eight were killed and 12 captured by raiding mountain men who claimed to be Tennessee militia with powers to hunt fugitives. The captured, all women and children and older men, were forced to tramp all the way to Chattanooga, a distance of 150 miles over rugged terrain. There they were corralled in a prison camp before being escorted back to Arkansas, another 350 miles. For them it was a trail of tears to nowhere. Some survived. Most didn't.

The remaining Cherokee who ran to hide in the mountains were comprised of 10 braves and 4 squaws. The youngest brave, Poki, age 14, missed his sister Little Creek and hoped that one day she would return. He especially missed Ear Flop and spent months searching the woods hoping for a miracle. The tribe continued to perform dances, pray to the Sun God, tend to a small patch of crops and hunt quail, beaver, deer and other animals without much interference except for an occasional frontiersman with a rifle. They continued to live high above the white civilization that slowly crept into the valleys below them. For now, they were safe.

14

EAR FLOP

After docking the steamboat at Seymour's boat landing along the Monongahela near Elizabethtown, McGrew and his two passengers rode to the Bachman farm by horseback. For Rilla, it felt good to be on a horse again, something she hadn't done in more than four years. She could smell the sweet scent of the sugar maples as they neared the Simeon McGrew cabin and the unique smell of the creek that she so often played in, caught frogs in, chased butterflies in. It smelled like home.

Linda was ecstatic seeing her long lost friend Moon Shadow almost as much as she was seeing her granddaughter. Though Moon Shadow looked worn and pale, Rilla was cheery-eyed, bright and smiling. Within minutes of ex-changing hugs and kisses, they heard a howl outside the door of the trading post. Tim grabbed his rifle, eased open the door with his foot and walked quietly onto the front porch. In an instant, the animal bolted through the door and nearly knocked Rilla over. "Ear Flop!" screamed Rilla. Everyone's jaw suddenly dropped.

The 4-year-old wolf looked little more than skin and bones yet somehow pulled off a nearly impossible journey. It ran day and night - from the muddy, swollen waters of the Tennessee River, through the hills of Kentucky, West Virginia and western Pennsylvania, across the Youghiogheny, the Big and Little Sewickley Creeks, past Mungo Dick's church and finally up the north branch of the Little Sewickley —until it reached Indian Lake. There the wolf searched and sniffed for days in a drastic attempt to locate its master. Despite repeated efforts by Charles Seymour to shoot and kill the wolf, the animal managed to escape. When the wolf heard Little Creek's voice coming from within the walls of the trading post, it raced across the meadow to the front porch. A miracle had just happened, far beyond human comprehension.

The return of peace brought a speculative boom around the Pittsburg area. Everyone expected growth. Merchants expanded their businesses. Prices rose rapidly. But with the completion of the national road, there was competition from other cities, like Wheeling, Cincinnati, Louisville and St Louis. As a result, the stores were overstocked, as there were few buyers for the merchandise — men's coats, ladies gowns, whips and buggies. The boom went bust by 1816.

Business activity at McGrew's trading post came to a near halt. Linda and Rilla spent their days working the farm crops while merchandise in the store collected dust. Moon Shadow spent her last few months in bed with a broken hip. She lost so much weight that she looked like a different person. At age 72, she finally passed, not from physical weakness but from a broken heart, Tim said. Linda understood. She had endured the same torment watching Johann go downhill, knowing his days were numbered. When he died, she experienced the same kind of depression, spending the morning hours in bed with little motivation to get up, even to wash her face.

But nowadays life for Linda was getting better. So full of life was Rilla and her wolf that it was contagious. Ear Flop would run deep, wide circles around the two women as they worked the fields, a strange marathon that perhaps only wolves will ever understand. Linda came up with the idea of training the animal to round up the cattle at night. Her mother Susan once talked about the fact that Border collie dogs were used to round up sheep back in Scotland. They were directed by a series of whistles from the sheep herdsman. How it worked exactly, she wasn't sure. Once it was clear that neither of the two ladies could emit a decent whistle without running completely out of breath, Rilla began experimenting with a piccolo instead.

Ear Flop seemed as intrigued with the musical instrument as Linda was. Within a week, Rilla was able to flutter a series of notes, not anything like a song but rhythmic enough to catch the wolf's attention. In response, Ear Flop howled, sounding out a somewhat similar tune. The experiment continued well into the third week, when three separate and distinct sounds were played. On the high-pitched middle C note, Ear Flop was supposed to come directly home. Two high notes, E and G, meant he was supposed to half-circle the cattle and guide them to the barn. Two short F notes meant to stop circling.

They put the wolf to the test on a cool, windy evening in September. When the middle C sounded (with help from Linda saying, "Here boy") Ear Flop came running, just as planned. "Good Boy," they said over and over. The second command did not work as well. Instead of half-circling the cattle, the wolf ran complete circles around the cows to the point where a bull named Head Strong chased after the crazy animal with reckless abandon. Chaos followed. Some cows headed for the barn. Others stampeded through the cornfield, trampling the stalks. A few hid behind Head Strong, waiting for the outcome of the confrontation. There was a lot of work to be done. But Rilla had patience.

In time, the wolf learned not only to round up cattle but to run off ground hogs, squirrels and other vermin that pestered the farm. One night it tangled with a panther. So quick and daring was Ear Flop that the cat froze in its tracks only yards away from the hen house and soon gave up its quest for a quick chicken meal.

In the beginning, the relationship between Charles Seymour and Rilla (Little Creek) Bachman was tentative. He was not thrilled with an Indian — or half-Indian, or whatever she was — living on the farm. And to make matters worse, she was a relative, which meant that in time she would end up inheriting the farm, leaving him out in the cold. He tried to tell himself that only a man could handle the total responsibilities of a farm so his position was safe regardless of any change in ownership through inheritance. In the past, he and Johann had always liked and respected one another, making his life much more pleasant than it had been as of late. Yes, working the farm as a sharecropper had worked out well for both him and Johann. But what about Rilla? Would she one day share the same contempt for him as he did now for her and would that ultimately lead to his undoing?

While Charles appreciated the extra help from Rilla at harvest time, he despised her barbaric ways, particularly the pointless prayers and foolish dances around a campfire in celebration of some moon god. *If it isn't the moon god, it's the sun god, or the rain god. How many gods are there, for God's sake?*

And then there was the wolf, a pitiful excuse for a pet of any kind, much less a dog. Instead of barking, the beast would howl at all hours of the night. Still, Charles did admire the animal's instincts — the way it found its way back home through 500 miles of forestland, the quick reflexes which enabled it to run down groundhog, then grab and snap their necks with one quick shake of the wolf's head, and the impressive bravery it showed in the face of a much larger panther that night at the chicken coop.

On Christmas Eve, Linda asked Charles to accompany her and Rilla to the special Christmas program at the Presbyterian Church. Rev. Dick conducted the program and led everyone in song. Charles tried his best to read the verses and sing the notes on his song sheet but soon gave up. Instead he sat motionless, watching the choir and listening to the melodious harmony. He felt mesmerized. One of the voices came from Rilla. She had no trouble sounding out the notes, much less reading the verses. Occasionally, she'd look up, her eyes sometimes drifting to Charles and Linda who were seated near the front row.

The top of Rilla's white ruffled dress peeked through the black gown she wore. Her black hair, pulled back, exposed her round face, dark eyes and bright white teeth against her tanned skin. She looked lovely, as beautiful and elegant as Charles had ever seen her. He smiled. Rilla thought he was smiling because of the musical performance and had no idea he was in fact smiling at her. By the time the program ended, it was dark outside. Sitting near their 3 horses outside of the church was Ear Flop, who darted forward with a great yelp as Little Creek made her way to the exit. When members of the congregation saw the animal, they panicked. Women screamed. A man cursed. Another man went for his gun and ordered everyone to stand back. Once it was clear that the wild animal was in fact a pet wolf, everyone felt quite relieved, though some shuddered.

On the way back home, Charles asked Rilla, "How did you learn to sing the notes from the sheet?" to which she replied, "The piccolo and the song practice on Wednesdays at church." Rays of moonlight glimmered from the Little Sewickley creek as they headed back to the farm. Charles saw the silhouette of the little girl dressed in white transform into an adorable young woman before his very eyes.

Despite the fact that she was growing up, 13-year-old Little Creek was still somewhat of a tomboy. On a beautiful spring day in late March, she felt the urge to build a small dam a few hundred yards down from Indian Lake. Seldom did she spend any time at the lake. Whenever she did, sad memories of the old Cherokee tribe would re-surface in her head and send her home in a somber mood. She decided to construct her own swimming hole instead.

Little Creek spent the whole day scooping out mud and sand from a 12' by 12' section of the creek near the trading post, then filled up old bags made of twine. If she accidentally displaced a crayfish, she would pick it up gently and help it relocate to a new home. It took two days to dig the hole. On the third day, she lined up the 50-pound, sand-filled bags 2 deep and 4 high for a total of 48 bags. Upon completion, Little Creek could stand nearly chest deep in the middle of the dammed-up pool, deep enough to dive from the top row of bags without scraping bottom. The water at that time was nearly ice cold. Little Creek didn't care.

One day, Charles picked up the piccolo and did his best to sound out notes. The event was not left unnoticed by Ear Flop, who arose from his afternoon nap and trotted across the meadow to further investigate. Once Ear Flop started to move, all of the animals at the farm momentarily stood still. Cows slowly turned and lowered their heads while their bodies remained frozen. Gophers sat up tall, with one eye focused entirely on the movement of the beast. Head Strong stopped chewing his cud, mouth drooling. A quail fluttered across the field. When Ear Flop saw that it was the Seymour boy, not Little Creek, blowing into the wood instrument, he knew the commands were not serious. He sat down near Seymour, listening to the interesting — though not very pleasant — sounds with limited enthusiasm.

A minute or so later a wolf in the woods began to howl, then another and another, which eventually led to a cacophony of howls all around them. Ear Flop remained silent, then lay down and closed his eyes, listening to the fractured notes coming from the piccolo and the distant sounds from his long lost cousins somewhere deep in the woods. Charles, now out of breath, briefly listened to the howling wolves, then threw down the piccolo and walked away. He never tried to play it again. *Some things in the world are just not worth the effort.*

On May 1, 1816 Charles finished plowing the fields. He expected Linda and Rilla to begin transplanting the young vegetable plants and seeds from the barn the following day. On May 5, when nothing was planted, he began the planting himself but was interrupted when Rilla advised him to hold off for another five days. But Charles was not one to sit idle at any time at the farm, especially during the spring planting. He took it upon himself to set the plants and sow the beans while the weather was sunny and warm and the soil perfectly crumbly.

On May 8 a sudden hailstorm, followed by strong winds not unlike the one that tumbled huts at Indian Lake 20 years earlier, came upon the farm with great fury. Huge swirls of dust from the plowed fields climbed the purple skies. Wind sheer descended and literally uprooted trees and toppled a shed. Great waves of rain pounded the fields. Valleys of muddy water gushed down the hillside, washing away the newly planted seeds. The creek water swelled and gushed over Little Creek's dam of sand filled bags. Before the night was over, a cold, brisk wind with temperatures in the upper 20s swept through Sewickley Township. It lasted twelve hours. The next day was sunny, cold and windy. Charles tended to the animals. No one else worked the farm that day.

On May 10 Rilla planted beans, squash and corn in the muddy fields of the Bachman farm. It was a long day. The Pennsylvania wet clay took its toll on her legs and back as she did her best to re-work the mud-packed soil around the newly planted seeds. That night she lay in bed exhausted, thinking that the hard-packed clay, once dry, might choke off the delicate roots fighting for life. *Will they even survive a week?*

By mid-summer, dozens of summer squash appeared, along with towering rows of corn and handfuls of beans. It was a windfall crop unlike Charles had ever seen. From that day forward, Rilla was put in charge of all future crops, including the oats and rye. The bumper crop was so bountiful that Linda spent several days in the hot summer preserving the freshness of the vegetables in sealed glass jars.

July was unusually hot that year. One night Little Creek jumped into her homemade pool wearing not a stitch of clothing. In modern terms, she went skinny-dipping. Ear Flop stood ankle deep near the side of the dam, deep enough for him to cool off. He had no interest in what Little Creek was wearing. She was simply someone to play with at nighttime.

When Charles heard the splashing of water from the dam in the still of the night, he figured it was an otter or a raccoon. But as the splashing continued,

it sounded more human-like. He looked across the meadow through the darkness but saw nothing. He listened for more sounds but heard nothing. Finally, curiosity got the best of him. He grabbed his rifle and walked down the path toward the dam, some 200 yards away. As he neared the dam, Ear Flop, recognizing that the person approaching was Charles, darted up the muddy bank and shoved his nose into Charles's free hand. It frightened Charles, who pulled his hand away abruptly, then lost his footing on the muddy path and fell hard on his rump. He cursed, something he had not done before, at least not in front of Little Creek. Startled, Little Creek shrieked, then called out, "Charles, is that you? "

Charles, unaware he had just fractured his coccyx, tried to stand up but groaned instead. Little Creek, wet and naked, quickly made her way out of the water, scooted up the muddy hill and tried to get Charles to stand up by pulling on his right arm. "I don't think I can get up," he said. Little Creek stooped down and touched his hot face with her cool left hand. He said nothing and seemed to be gasping for air. She instructed him not to move, said she would go get Linda and be right back. She darted up the hill and in a flash was out of sight.

Charles lay in total silence waiting for help. He shivered slightly, not from the touch of Rilla's cool hand but from the sudden whiff of her sweet breath, the smell of creek water and the scent of her body which had just registered in his brain. It was a fleeting moment, and it gave him goose bumps.

During the three weeks Charles was down on his back and confined to his bed, Linda and Rilla tended not only the crops but the farm animals as well. Rilla noticed that a young calf kept following Linda around the barnyard in spite of its mother's beckoning calls to stay within the herd and as far away as possible from the annoying wolf. Within a week, the young calf became Linda's favorite pet. Since it smelled a little like barley, Linda named it just that, Barley. In no time at all, Barley grew so accustomed to Ear Flop that when Barley heard the sound of the piccolo at sundown, he stood at the cattle gate watching the roundup much like a supervisor. He would be the last one to enter the barn gate.

Once in the middle of a hot day when Ear Flop sought his afternoon nap in the shade of a tall oak tree, Barley nudged the backside of the slumbering wolf with his nose. Ear Flop raised his head momentarily, saw that it was just Barley, plopped his head back down to the ground and instantly fell asleep.

The extra farm work required of Linda and Rilla was, in a sense, therapeutic for both of them. For nearly three years, Linda sat at the trading post, isolated from society and from her family. Hans and Wet Foot had gone south, taking with them her only granddaughter. Then, once Johann fell ill, she spent her days either inside the trading post or inside the cabin that housed her bedridden spouse. They were dark days, days she seldom got to enjoy the sunshine. But her life was different now. Each day brought new joy — from Rilla, from Ear Flop and from Charles who joked about the mud on Linda's nose after a hard day's work. And from Barley, who of course was incapable of saying anything yet was able to let her know that farm life was worthwhile. How she cherished those moments, looking into the face of that little bull with those adorable eyes.

Rilla initially felt awkward catering to the needs of the incapacitated Charles. She had never tried to care for a man before, something that even at her young age she had wondered about. She discovered it did not come naturally. But soon she learned to shave his beard, cut his hair and scratch and rub his back. More importantly, she learned how to talk with him on both important subjects and trivial matters.

Charles talked to her about ways to make money, like distilling whiskey which was presently tax-free. She talked about the effects of whiskey on the Indians and the foolish things the Cherokee did because of it at the Arkansas camp, like shooting arrows into the air for no reason only to see them fall and injure innocent bystanders. For the Indians, fire water was a bad thing. He talked about how the early settlers sold England huge amounts of tobacco, a product from the Indians and the only viable commodity that held the Jamestown settlement together. She talked about the glass beads from Syria, which greatly devalued the seashells used to make wampum, thereby ruining the monetary system of the Indians. He complained about the taxes imposed on the settlers to pay for the wars waged by the British against the French and then again when the Americans waged war against the British. She complained about the forced crop-sharing by the Eastern Cherokee Nation which was essentially a tax. Mostly though, the two of them talked about the farm animals and about the stars and peaceful nights in the wooded hills of Pennsylvania. By the end of the third week, Rilla had become attracted to Charles and one night leaned her forehead against his shoulder for a moment. It was the best moment of the week.

In September, Linda secretly arranged for Tim to deliver a new white silk dress for Rilla's birthday. The day before, which was the day of the fall equinox, Little Creek wore her buckskin dress and run-down moccasins. She spent the morning creating another sundial similar to the one she made in March of that year. For the rest of the day, she prayed to the sun god and danced around a rather plain looking totem pole, poorly decorated with dyed string and twine representing an eagle's nest but without a carved eagle at the top of the pole.

When Tim presented Little Creek with the surprise birthday gift, she was thrilled with excitement and could not wait to try on her new dress. In a jiffy she was in and out of her bedroom, transforming herself once again from Little Creek into the new Rilla, dressed in white. The beautiful dress was a bit too long and loose-fitting. As Linda began smoothing down the sides of the dress, tugging on the sleeves and bunching the material together at the back where the buttons matched up, it became abundantly clear that not only did Rilla have shapely hips but a well contoured bosom. "Rilla, you're a fine young lady. You're growing up," Tim remarked. Molly, who came all the way from Cincinnati to attend the party, said, "I don't suppose it needs to fit all that tight." Charles stood tongue-tied and flushed, staring at Rilla's gorgeous slim figure. His attraction to her had reached a new high.

Rilla wore the dress to church that Sunday. A month later, she wore it to her wedding. Nearly the whole Presbyterian congregation attended the ceremony. Most of them found their way to the Bachman farm via horse and buggy, using Simeon McGrew's new road over Mars Hill.

People got drunk on barrels of rye whiskey from the Seymour distillery. Linda cried at the wedding but was in a more jovial mood at the reception. She insisted the band play the potato dance song after downing her share of the spirits. Tim told a host of river rafting stories to the kids before the moms and pops dragged them away. Old man Maloney showed up drunk and continued to imbibe, fart and belch, as usual. A ruckus ensued after Maloney grabbed Molly from behind during the Irish jig. Molly squealed, slapped his face and marched off to tell Tim. Tim marched right back to Maloney and punched him square in the jaw. "What's that fer?" he asked. "Fer arse grabbin', that's what fer!" Tim responded. A minute later, they were making another toast to the bride and groom as if nothing had happened.

Charles's younger brother Riley made it to the wedding by horse and buggy, hauling his pregnant wife Amy, his two young children and a gift from his glassworks shop — a huge champagne bottle filled with bourbon whiskey from Kentucky. He made a toast, actually several, to the bride and groom and was later seen sprawled out in the back end of the buggy with his wife driving the family back to Pittsburg.

Rilla either talked or danced with all of the guests in attendance. And all of them agreed that the young bride was very sage at age 14. The compliments came throughout the evening. *A delightful lady. Adorable and quite the conversationalist. The prettiest little girl I ever saw. The best thing that ever happened to the Seymour boy. Lots of energy in that one — got it from her mother, no doubt.*

Eventually Barley found his way out of the fenced pasture to mingle with the guests, which caused Ear Flop to immediately jump the fence and run the young bull right back to the gate. Some of the guests witnessing the "wolf attack" scrambled to safety. Afterward they commented how well the Seymour boy had managed the farm and the training of his animals, especially the wolf. Said one woman named Mrs. Newlin, "It wasn't the boy who trained that wolf. It was the girl. She did it with the piccolo."

15
SMOKY CITY

Contrary to Stephen Seymour's concerns about a downturn in the flatboat business, a demand for large barges of coal kept him busier than ever. The oldest son took over the operation in the new village of Elizabeth when Seymour fell ill. The youngest son, Riley, found employment at a glass factory along the Monongahela and learned to make glass almost overnight. Within a month, Riley married a Hessian girl from Pittsburg and began raising a family soon afterwards.

But business activity for others, generally speaking, was still slow. Pittsburg tried to strengthen its markets by linking a transportation route to Philadelphia. They called it the Pennsylvania Turnpike. Following the completion of the turnpike in 1820, former army General William Larimer and his friend John Irwin put together a new enterprise called The Conestoga Wagon System. It enabled citizens to transport goods between the two cities during the time when rivers were too difficult to navigate. Each Conestoga wagon carried as much as 4,000 pounds of goods and this greatly facilitated trade in the east for the next 30 years.

Because of the success of the turnpike, other pikes were built throughout western Pennsylvania including Sewickley Township. A new road called Clay Pike began at Larimer's Tavern (now Circleville), went southeast past the Bachman farm, over the Little Sewickley to what is now Herminie, through Madison to Waltz's Mill and then across the Big Sewickley and on to Connellsville.

The name turnpike comes from the pike or pole that was placed across the road, preventing a traveler from passing until a toll as paid at which point the pike was turned around to allow the traveler though. Farmers from the stockyards in East Liberty (Pittsburg) used the pike to drive cattle to the distilleries in the Connellsville area in order to fatten them up on the refuse. They paid tolls every 10 miles. A score of swine cost 6 cents, a score of cattle 10 cents, and a wagon per horse, 12 cents.

Toll Houses were built along the turnpike including one at Slab Town. They called it that because slabs of wood were laid on the road near the Little Sewickley to keep the road surface out of the mud, as there was no bridge at that point to cross the creek. Travelers sometimes lodged overnight. They would pack their own bedding and rent bunk space on the floor of the toll house.

Linda McGrew Bachman died at age 61 from a sudden stroke while clearing snow from the roof of the trading post. McGrew's Trading Post was still owned by Tim McGrew, even though it had been operated by Linda for years. After that, Rilla ran the store.

For 15 years before Clay Pike was built, Rilla transported whiskey and excess farm crops to either Slab Town or Larimer's Tavern which was located along the old Braddock trail 5 miles from the trading post. In exchange, she would get materials for clothing or household items from Pittsburg. Once she traded a cow for a barrel of salt.

Like other poor farmers, Charles and Rilla struggled to earn, much less save, cash. But now they were landowners through inheritance, the farm having been willed to Rilla Bachman Seymour. Soon after the pike was built, the land value had increased significantly, from 12 cents to $1.25 an acre, a tenfold increase. This was their only savings.

With the completion of Clay Pike, Charles and Rilla's social life vastly improved due to an influx of travelers. Though seldom did a Conestoga wagon appear along Clay Pike, many one-and two-horse carriages, sleighs, sleds, carts and wagons traveled up and down this road. Some of the local travelers would stop at the McGrew trading post for tea, fresh vegetables, whiskey and conversation. Artistic sketches of Ear Flop on the walls of the trading post caught the attention of many. And when they asked the cost of the sketches, Rilla informed them very simply that they were not for sale. The watercolor painting on the far wall was the one talked about most. It showed Ear Flop in a crouched position behind a herd of cows. One of the cows, standing behind the wolf, nonchalantly chewed on grass. The painting was entitled *Barley.*

Barley, a master of breaking out of the barn, or gate or wherever he was penned, lay in a rye field alongside Ear Flop the night Ear Flop died. The wolf was paralyzed from the hips for three days. For Little Creek, it was a blessing that her longtime companion would not suffer any longer. She buried Ear Flop near the old totem pole at Indian Lake, spent the week in mourning and sometimes lay awake at night listening to the wolf howls. After several nights of insomnia, she arose from her bed one early morning and did her farm chores as usual. After that, she said little or nothing about her longtime friend ever again.

Because of the 1832 flood, Tim McGrew lost his small steamboat docked along the Monongahela. Two years later in the early spring, soon after he had just purchased another steamboat, he was struck with Cholera. His timing for contacting the disease was fortuitous in that he happened to be staying in the city and was able to spend three weeks at the new, albeit primitive, Mercy Hospital. It was Pittsburg's first hospital.

Unlike hundreds of others, McGrew survived. He spent the next 10 years of his life hauling salt down the Youghiogheny from the salt wells of Alexander Guffey. Rilla lived a short hike from the salt wells and so from time to time Uncle Tim would drop by to tell jokes and reminisce about the old days.

One day out of the blue, Tim invited Rilla and Charles for a joy ride on his boat. With the responsibilities of the farm, particularly the animals, Charles initially declined the offer. But when he saw the look of disappointment on Rilla's face, he mulled things over and came up with a practical idea which he proposed to Tim. "Instead of taking a simple joy ride, why not take Rilla on a shopping trip to Pittsburg?" The gallon jugs of whiskey stored in Charles's barn were too plain and too bulky to sell at a reasonable profit to Larimer's Tavern or to the toll house at the Little Sewickley. He needed the new smaller glass bottles, a fifth of the size, the kind that could be easily poured into 6 and 8 ounce glasses at the nearby taverns. The cost of the glass bottles was less now because of the competition among the 5 glass factories around Pittsburg. Now was the time to shop, Charles stressed.

Tim hated shopping but was quick to endorse the idea. It was a chance to relive his journey up the

Mississippi with Little Creek. He vividly recalled the young girl bouncing out of her bunk in the early morning, wrinkling her cute little nose as she squinted from the sunlight. She'd whistle at the birds, trying to imitate cardinals. She'd toss her fishing line into the river with a look of confidence that she would land a fish. Whenever she did, she would shriek as the fish flopped around each time she tried to unhook it. Most of all, he remembered her innocent laughter at his dumb jokes.

Rilla and her Uncle Tim set off on horseback for Pittsburg at daybreak. They arrived at the Guffey salt works at 7 AM, loaded 12 barrels of salt onto Tim's plain-looking but sturdy steamboat and then headed down the Youghiogheny River.

As soon as they reached the Monongahela, they spotted a convoy of connected barges hauling logs, not for the building of another fort as Rilla had guessed but for the making of charcoal. Charcoal was used for the smelting of iron. "What is smelting?" asked Rilla. Tim scratched his head a moment and replied, "It's when a person bends down to take a big whiff of something metal. That's what I call smelting iron!" Rilla laughed, mostly because of the goofy look on Tim's face.

Once they got to Pittsburg, Rilla saw more houses and commercial brick buildings than she remembered on her previous trip along the river. In addition, a slew of barges passed in both directions. Church steeples peaked skyward amidst a multitude of other buildings lined up along city streets. Smoking chimneys from coal furnaces polluted the air on both sides of the river - from steamships, foundries and city dwellings. They gawked at the flood damages to the Monongahela Bridge. At the confluence of the Monongahela and the Allegheny, they counted 20 or more steamboats lined up, waiting to load passengers or cargo. A short distance up the Allegheny River another bridge-like structure, an aqueduct, enabled horses to pull keelboats over the river and through an 800-foot tunnel dug into the side of a steep mountain. Rilla was amazed.

After Tim docked his boat in the usual spot at the Monongahela Wharf near the three rivers, he and Rilla promptly disembarked and watched other passengers strolling along the wharf. Some wore fancy attire. Ladies donned wide bonnets and long, broidered dresses while men sported three-piece suits and ties and tall hats.

They walked down Water Street (now Blvd of the Allies), and passed by a horse market where men pulled on horses' tails and picked up their legs to inspect hoofs. They meandered through the fruit and vegetable stands at the Market Place and sampled chocolate at the confectionery. Rilla bit into her very first truffle and mumbled something about *heaven.* Behind the shop was Pittsburg's first courthouse. Inside, men dressed in black suits with white, ruffled shirts looked so formal and so serious.

Up the street sat the Presbyterian Church, a large brick building with glass-colored windows, perfectly balanced on both sides of the huge oak doors at the entry way. When Rilla asked the young minister if he knew Rev. Mungo Dick, he wrinkled his brow, trying to remember. Rilla was sorry she asked him that question. They strolled in front of the Drury Theatre along Fifth Street. It had fancy railings along an outside balcony where the performers could later wave to the crowds. It was one of the most elegant theaters west of the Appalachians.

A small tavern, The Falstaff House, was squeezed between the theater and a row of picture-perfect brick houses with multiple paned windows and sculptured brick lintels.

At the Exchange Hotel they scanned the Bill of Fare on the dinner menu and saw that no prices were shown for any of the entrees. The cheapest bottle of wine was $1 (a week's wages for many workers). They quickly exited the building. Apples and plums back at the Market Place suited them just fine. Tim was starting to get bored but tried not to show it.

In 1844, there were more than 20 glass factories on the south side of Pittsburg, a lot more than Charles had figured. All of them were situated on the other side of the Monongahela in a community called Birmingham. Rilla visited only three of them before stopping at the glassworks shop of Riley Seymour. His bottle prices in the shop were no less than the competition up and down the river. But Riley led them to the salvage yard where Rilla was able to buy a sack full of jugs for pennies on the dollar (the imbedded glass plugs were inadvertently stamped upside down.)

On the way back home, Tim insisted that Rilla navigate the boat on her own through the choppy waters, while he did little, other than to mind the steam gauge. And tell jokes, of course. As Rilla negotiated the vessel upstream between the many barges headed in the opposite direction, Tim puffed on a new pipe he bought at the tobacco shop. The smell was quite aromatic compared to the sooty coal fumes around the city. Rilla asked, "Hey, I didn't know you smoked? How long have you been smoking?" Her uncle responded, "Oh, about 3, maybe 4 minutes!" Rilla laughed, as usual. The bumpy ride caused the bottles in the sack on board to clink together. Tim commented, "When you get home, don't tell Charles about me tinkling along the river." Rilla laughed again.

The following year a great fire swept through Pittsburg and destroyed a thousand buildings. It began when an Irish woman lit a fire to boil water for her laundry. Fanned by high winds, the flames engulfed the shanty and spread to an adjoining ice house. Businessmen worked in a frantic effort to put out the fire but it was hopeless. Said one firefighter, "All we got was sick, muddy water coming out of the hoses." Thus, block after block fell prey to the flames. The city was rebuilt and was now called Pittsburgh. And because of its magnificent river highway, it remained the center of commerce west of the Appalachians. The great Monongahela House was rebuilt as well as 17 other hotels, 14 banks, more churches and a new Sixth Street suspension bridge. There were bigger buildings, more river traffic, more iron foundries and more smoke.

While life along the river was bustling with activity, the pace of life in the nearby hills of Sewickley Township was not. The number of cattle droves along Clay Pike nearly ended once the Connellsville distillers began sending refuse by rail to farmers near Pittsburgh. There was, however, enough traffic generated by locals to keep the pike profitable for a few more decades.

As a welcome gesture for these travelers, Charles cleared the brush around Indian Lake.

151

Farmers could stop to water their animals, wade them down the creek past the Seymour farm — which everyone stilled called the Bachman farm — and talk to Rilla at the trading post about the latest gossip. They talked a lot about the Civil War and the fact that Westmoreland County sent off more volunteer soldiers than the entire city of Philadelphia. They discussed how the Quakers at Mars Hill refused to bury the dead in their graveyard since they did not believe in wars. They lamented the widows of the soldiers who were left without pensions and forced to sell their farms. They talked about the increased prices of farmland, not because of the rich soil, rather the value of the coal hidden beneath it. They talked about the locomotives, so noisy and so dirty. People were now calling Pittsburgh the "Smoky City."

The neighborly visits had become a major part of Rilla's social life after her Uncle Tim passed away. And then a year later, Barley died. Her closest friends — a wolf, her one and only uncle and a bull— were gone from her life. So were most of the farm animals. Charles sold them to nearby neighbors once he started bottling whiskey in different bottles. The demand for cheap whiskey in expensive-looking bottles was a hit at the trading post, at Larimer's Tavern and at the Toll House in Slab Town. Even though the sale of whiskey didn't generate much income, it produced enough cash to pay for all of the supplies to keep the store open. Charles too missed his farm animals and his days and nights were sometimes lonely. But he and Rilla at least were able to enjoy the beauty of the forest and rolling hills around them where there was peace and quiet away from city life, at least for the time being.

PART II

RILLTON

(*The first 65 years*)

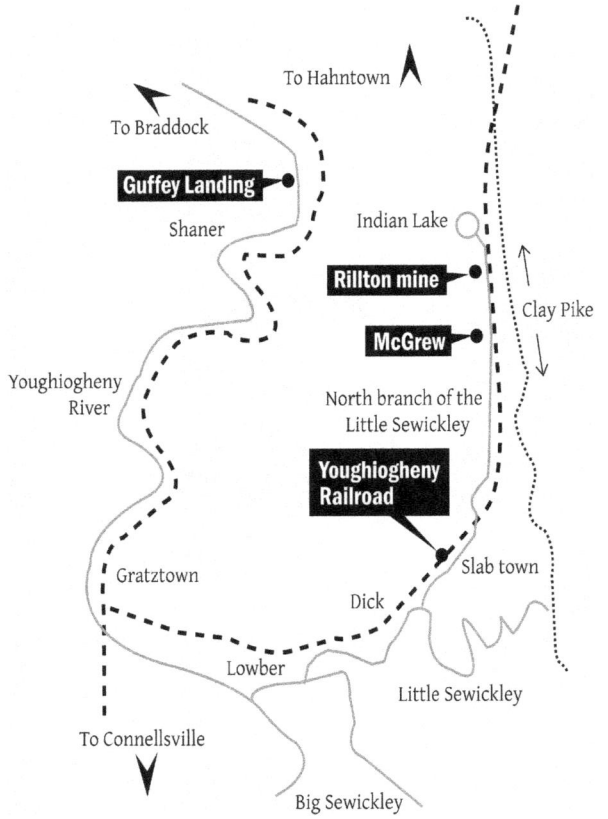

To Hahntown

To Braddock

Guffey Landing

Shaner

Indian Lake

Rillton mine

McGrew

Clay Pike

Youghiogheny
River

North branch of the
Little Sewickley

**Youghiogheny
Railroad**

Gratztown

Slab town

Dick

Lowber

Little Sewickley

To Connellsville

Big Sewickley

16
THE BEGINNING

While the Pennsylvania Turnpike facilitated the purchase of many goods from the eastern cities, transportation costs - 300 miles overland - was high. People began manufacturing their own goods. There were huge deposits of iron and an inexhaustible supply of coal in the Pittsburgh area. Iron foundries multiplied.

Before 1840, iron was smelted from charcoal since timber was abundant in the area. Then a new technique was introduced, utilizing coke instead of charcoal. Another innovation – the Bessemer process - converted iron ore into steel. By 1860, Pittsburgh was producing half of the country's iron and steel. This gave tremendous impetus to the coal industry.

RILLTON

Coal mining in western Pennsylvania began in the mid 1700's and was mainly used for domestic heating. Later, coal was needed for railroad and boat engines, artificial gas for lamps and street lighting and for making coke.

There were numerous mines in the hills near Pittsburgh but the only means of transporting coal to the market was by way of the river. The shipments were undependable because the water was often too low or too high or frozen during the winter. To make the river more navigable, dams were constructed but they only lasted until 1866 when they were destroyed by ice. Railroads solved this problem.

The railroad era began in 1851 when the first Pennsylvania Railroad train traveled to Pittsburgh from Philadelphia. Six years later a Pittsburgh-Connellsville line (P&C Rail) connected Pittsburgh to West Newton. As rails were being laid along the Youghiogheny River, coal patch towns were popping up at the station stops along the way including Scott Haven, Buena Vista, Shaner and Guffey. And as the railroads continued to expand, other coal towns emerged – Hahntown, Herminie, Keystone, Lowber, Yukon, Hutchinson, Herminie #2, Edna mines #1 and #2.

The Guffey coal mine, opened in 1806, had been shipping coal extensively down the Ohio River by flatboat to Cincinnati for a period of 20 years. With the increased demand for coal and the new train service, Guffey Station (originally called Guffey's Landing) prospered overnight. Thirty houses were built along Possum Hollow, accommodating some 300 workers. Ninety-five percent of them came from the Po River Valley in northern Italy (and were continually harassed by the Mafia attempting to extort large sums of money). Years later, the extortion problem was brought to a head. On September 17, 1901, the Newspaper Dispatch in Pittsburgh reported:

"Thirty armed men, imitating movements of the Ku Klux Klan, raided the anarchists and forced 25 families to depart the town. The raiders surrounded the houses and terrorized the anarchists by firing Winchesters and yelling like Indians ... They were to leave the vicinity of their wives, children and all their belongings before daybreak. ... Before the sun rose, every house in the settlement was deserted. The only favor they asked in return for their exodus was that their lives be spared."

With the departure of Italian Mafia, Guffey's work force was cut in half, but the community did well. A school was built. John Finch Guffey, whose father John Guffey was once sheriff of Westmoreland County, became a U.S. Senator. The two brass bands and the two string bands were reduced to one 30-member Cosmopolitan band that played for audiences all over the county. The old Italian Brotherhood Hall continued to survive without Mafia influence.

The first mineshaft was dug at the Armstrong Mine in Shaner. Five mines later, Shaner was the largest village in Sewickley Twp. with 2 saloons and a hotel. People could board the train from Shaner to Braddock and then hop the Pennsylvania RR train to get to Greensburg.

In 1860, a farmer named Hohn conducted a small mining company near Irwin. It was a slope mine where mules lugged the coal from a hillside tunnel, much like the early mine at Guffey. Two years later the Penn Gas Coal Company sunk a shaft near the slope and built a row of houses along the west side of Main Street. They called the place Hahntown.

The Ocean Coal Company opened a mine near Slab Town and called the town Herminie, named after Hermine White who owned the land. All the houses built around the mine had wood sidewalks.

Northeast of Herminie, the Pittsburgh & Baltimore Coal Company sunk a shaft at Edna No.1 mine. This town had 3 parallel streets and mostly double houses. Initially, 276 men and boys used picks and shovels to extract the coal.

Westmoreland Coal purchased a small mine from Penn Gas and re-named it the Lowber mine (John Lowber was a big company stockholder). Within 2 years the mine had 100 coke ovens.

When surveyors from the railroad hacked their way through the thick weeds along the north branch of the Little Sewickley, Charles and Rilla looked on with great interest. At first they thought someone was clearing land for a farm across the creek. A few months later, iron rails were unloaded from wagons and deposited near Indian Lake. A Penn Gas company spokesman came to the trading post and briefly explained the company's mission: the installation of the railroad and the possible digging of a mine. Then he made an offer to purchase the timber and mineral rights of the Seymour property for cash. Given the harsh financial deprivations since the Civil War, the price offered — $2.50 per acre of land — seemed like a windfall to Charles. He was tempted to agree to the deal on the spot. But Rilla held back and said she wanted to think it over.

After the meeting, Charles and Rilla engaged in a lengthy discussion. The time had come when the aging Charles, suffering from arthritis, had already thought about selling the farm. Except for the chickens and two horses, all of the animals were gone. The whiskey business was on the decline. So was business at the trading post. They needed the cash.

Rilla learned about the activities at Hahntown from gossip at the post — the cutting down of the trees, the ruined landscape, the dust and dirt that filled the air, the slate dumps heaped in piles, immigrants living in crowded rooms in makeshift houses, and the company store where the workers were forced to purchase all of their necessary goods. Rilla thought about the smoke in Pittsburgh and could not imagine living in such a place. She wanted to quash the deal, take their chances and spend the few remaining years in the virgin woods of what they called home.

Another meeting followed. Rilla began to change her thinking. Even if they remained on the farm without giving up the mineral rights, the mining operation would take place across the creek in any event. The dusty, barren landscape would stare them in the face either way. The coal company needed the Seymour farm property to construct housing for miners. If not on Seymour's property, the houses would be built along the pike opposite the mine. After the meeting, Rilla came up with the idea, *why not sell the property outright and relocate?* "Where would we go?" asked Charles. Neither one had an answer. They were stuck.

It took the company representatives several more trips to finally work out a deal, which was as follows: The coal company would purchase not just the mineral rights but the entire Seymour farm, less 6 acres in the back, or 44 acres at $6 an acre. In addition, they would purchase the McGrew post for $100 and the 50 acres Rilla inherited at $6 an acre. Total price, $664. Rilla would run the McGrew trading post which would be renamed McGrew Station.

In 1872, Penn Gas constructed the Youghiogheny Railroad. It had three-foot narrow gauge rails that offered passenger service from Irwin to Pittsburgh-

Connellsville Railroad station on the Youghiogheny River. The original stations were as follows:

1. Irwin
2. Hahntown
3. Linencross Station (now called Cereal)
4. Chambers Station (now gone)
5. McGrew Station (now Rillton)
6. Millville (now Dick Station)
7. Cowans (now Cowansburg)
8. Blackburn Station (now Lowber)
9. Sewickley Station, later called Gratztown Junction (now Gratztown)

Soon after the trains began rolling up and down the tracks, Rilla and Charles hopped aboard for a ride to Irwin. While they were excited going through the 400-foot-long Lindencross tunnel at Chambers, the slate dumps in Hahntown depressed them. They never rode the train again.

In addition to arthritis, Charles came down with Parkinson's disease. Because of the need to care for him, Rilla could no longer work the store. The coal company changed the name of the store from McGrew Station to Rillton, in honor of Rilla Bachman Seymour who had worked the store for some 70 years.

A year later Charles lay down to sleep on a rainy afternoon and never awoke. At the funeral, Charles' younger brother Riley spoke with Rilla. He had not seen Rilla since she had visited his bottle shop some

40 years prior during her shopping trip to Pittsburgh. He told Rilla that her Uncle Tim left his steamboat at the dock at Elizabeth (the old Elizabethtown) just before he died and said it was there for her whenever she wanted it. The boat was placed in storage where it sat idle for all those years. "Do you not want it?" Riley asked. Rilla replied, "I didn't know it was mine. What would I do with it?"

A few months passed. Riley reported that the old steamboat was apparently not saleable. The engine needed to be overhauled, the hull needed patching and painting and the rudders and paddles would have to be reworked. The cost to complete the repairs might exceed the value. Another option would be to junk the boat and possibly salvage the engine. "Or maybe..." Riley said with a wrinkled brow while gazing at the floor as if he were trying to collect his thoughts. "Or maybe what?" Rilla asked.

Josh Seymour, age 16, tried working at his father's glass factory, then the iron works across the river, then the shoe shop in downtown Pittsburgh. He didn't do well in any of those places. It wasn't that he was lazy or too proud to do the work. It was the smoke. There were days when the smoke and soot was so thick that the city was nearly pitch-black at 9 a.m., even in the summer. He found himself coughing uncontrollably, at times nearly choking to death. His eyes would water, his throat would burn and his head would throb.

As a young boy, he wished he could get away. Somewhere. Anywhere.

After Uncle Raymond offered him a job at the flatboat yard in Elizabeth where working conditions were much better, Josh grew to like the boat building business enough to work the long summer hours from sunup until well past sundown. Much of his work entailed repairing barges when the timber snapped from the overloaded coal. It was not unusual for him to help make emergency repairs to merchant vessels at ten o'clock at night while boat captains screamed in his ear for immediate service. One night he spent 3 hours shoveling coal from a nearly sunken barge. His nose filled with so much dust, he nearly fainted. He worked until midnight and was rewarded with a handsome tip of $2, more than a day's wages.

Joshua especially liked the old-timers who stopped by in their small flatboats just to say hello and brag about their latest ventures down river. They talked about the wild saloons in Cincinnati, the beautiful southern belles in Louisville and the ruffians in Cape Girardeau. They talked about bear attacks, giant otters, alligators, snapping turtles and sneaky buzzards. The stories fascinated Josh and caused his mind to wander. Once late in the evening he spotted a small family of Indians dressed in buckskins, drifting down river in a dug-out canoe. He had seen Indians wearing white man's clothing in Pittsburgh but never wearing rawhide in the wild. *Where on earth could they be going?*

Toward the end of the summer, when the air was thick with morning fog, when the leaves on the trees sweated oily residue and when the smoke from the factories permeated the still air, Josh began coughing and sneezing to the point where Riley had to take him to the doctor. The doctor just shook his head and stated, "You need to get this boy out of the city. The way he's going, he'll not make it through the winter."

By the time Riley had gotten through telling the story of young Josh Seymour, Rilla interrupted and said flat out, "I want that boy to fix my boat."

Riley: But as I said before, the old tub ain't worth fixin'.

Rilla: You implied that Josh could fix it up.

Riley: What I meant to say was, Josh needs that boat, to get out of the city. He doesn't have the money to buy it. Can't you just gift it to him? Maybe he can find a way to get the damned engine started and begin a new life somewhere down the Ohio, away from this hellhole. It's like a furnace without a lid around here.

Rilla sat back in her chair, looked at the far wall and studied the painting of Ear Flop. His eyes were so intent, so intelligent and so alert. They say that wolves study their environment with intensity down to the last detail and never miss a trick. Rilla could feel the wolf in that painting keeping his eye on Barley, knowing exactly where he was and what he was up to. *How is it even possible for an animal to run back to Rillton, find his way through virgin forests — places he had never seen before – cross over an unimaginable number of streams and hills and valleys and not get totally lost?*

Rilla: Has the boy ever operated a steamboat?

Riley: Well, I don't suppose he has. But…

Rilla: I can teach him.

Riley: You? (Riley started to laugh. Then Rilla started laughing too.)

Rilla: Navigating is the easy part. The hard part is feeding coal into the engine and keeping an eye on the boiler. That's where I come in.

Riley: (More laughter) Of course, once he heads off down the river, he'd be on his own. I imagine he'll just have to get used to the boiler.

Rilla: Not unless he wants to get rid of me.

Riley: (Looking puzzled) What do you mean? You're not going with him, are you?

Rilla: I aim to.

Riley: So you're not giving up the boat?

Rilla: Not until Josh gets me to the mountains.

Riley: What mountains?

Rilla: The ones behind the land between the lakes. I reckon that'll take a week or more. After that, he can have the boat. Meanwhile, here's $40 to fix up the engine. Josh can paint up the hull. When it's ready to go, let me know.

Riley: What about your house and the land?

Rilla: Don't know yet. I'm working on that.

Uncle Raymond found a steam engine repairman named Rupert who was proficient at overhauling any kind of engine or boiler. He was young, full of energy … and cheap. His normal fee was $2, though he ended up charging three times as much. The engine, as it turned out, ran just fine. It was the built-up residue in the smokestack and other corroded parts outside of the engine that needed extensive cleaning or replacement.

Finally, there was the bat problem. An enormous colony of the critters had dropped so much dung in the fire pit that firing up the engine would be a health hazard. It was the last place young Josh needed to be, given his respiratory problems. But Rupert was patient and methodical. It took two entire weeks to rid the area of bats, clean out the flue and fabricate the necessary replacement parts. It was well worth the money spent. When Riley asked Josh how the boat repairs were coming along. Josh smiled his toothy grin and said, "She shines like a whistle."

The next day, Josh launched the boat near the river landing, fired up the engine and heard loud popping sounds at the rear paddle wheel. Two of the paddles were warped and another one completely snapped off. Meanwhile, the stern-wheeler sat idle along the Monongahela for another two weeks waiting for a local carpenter to convert some scrap lumber into replacement paddles. That cost another $6.

On the last week of August, Rilla cooked up the last of the corn, beans, squash, summer apples and blackberries from the fields and stored them in wax sealed jars. She lined them up along the wall near the 40 bottles of whiskey from the distillery and the makeshift wooden cages she had pieced together to transport a few chickens. She packed and repacked her one and only trunk 3 times, substituting some items while discarding others. *What should I do with the wedding dress?* She struggled with this decision for the better part of the day. On August 31, she carried the dress, the same one she had worn to church at least 100 times, to Charles' gravesite near Indian Lake. Along the way, she collected wildflowers — goldenrods, touch-me-nots, mountain mint, purple asters and milkweed. She folded the ruffled dress, placed it on the grave and tossed the flowers, one by one on top of the dress.

Rilla walked to the edge of the lake at the south end and gazed across the pond for a last look. The water was peaceful, very calm and silent except for the little stream behind her. She heard trickling sounds as water gently tumbled over the rocks — lip, lip, aerial, lip, aerial lip, aerial oriole, lip. She listened again to the sounds of the creek and heard very clearly and distinctly *Farewell, Running Creek. Farewell.* She felt goose bumps on her arms and shivered slightly. She started walking the shallow creek, at first stepping on the tops of the dry stones. A short time later after her moccasins got wet, she walked right though the water, splashing her way downstream. For reasons she could not begin to explain, she ran.

RILLTON

Crayfish scuttled across pebbles, frogs hopped over rocks, minnows zig-zagged across the ponds and dragonflies hovered, waiting for smaller flies to escape the chaos. For a few fleeting moments, the 86-year-old named Rilla had turned into an 8-year-old child whom everyone called Little Creek.

The next morning Rilla hitched up her two horses, loaded up the buggy and headed south on Clay Pike. Her first stop was the Toll House. Because the Possum Hollow Rye Company in Guffey had gone out of business earlier that year, she was able to get a higher price for her whiskey at $1 per bottle. The next stop was the Dick Station, where she arranged to donate the buggy and horses. The money from the rummage sale would help maintain the brick church which was 50 years old and in need of repairs. The congregation had lost membership to West Newton and Madison around 1860 after Rev. Mungo Dick died. The third and final stop was Elizabeth where she met the Seymour boy for the long journey south.

The refurbished steamer was loaded and seemed ready for departure. When Josh fired up the boiler, a giant cloud of grey-black smoke puffed out of the stack, followed by hundreds of bats moments later. Apparently, no one thought the critters would return in the two weeks the boat sat idle. Within a minute, the smoke appeared a little less black and the two passengers breathed a sigh of relief.

They arrived at Pittsburgh around noon. The buildings were taller, the bridges more plentiful and there were barges piggybacked one after another on both sides of the three rivers. More passenger steamboats than ever before lined the wharfs of the Allegheny and the Monongahela. But one thing had not changed, and that was the smoke and soot that covered the city in black. In spite of the horrible smoke, many Pittsburghers loved the city and would not move to any other place on earth. At least they had good jobs, they argued. But for others, living near the city of Pittsburgh was just not meant to be.

17
THE MINE AT RILLTON

You load 16 tons, what do you get
Another day older and deeper in debt
St. Peter don't you call me 'cause I can't go
I owe my soul to the company store
    (Song sung by Tennessee Ernie Ford)

At the turn of the century, there were hundreds of coal mines in Westmoreland County. Thirty-eight of them were inside Sewickley Twp. The coal mined in Sewickley for the most part was unsuitable for use as coke but was ideal for conversion into coal gas. For this reason, the Penn Gas Coal Company dominated mine operations in this area until 1902 when customers began using natural gas. At this point, Penn sold their interests to Westmoreland Coal, a more diversified company which is still operating today.

The Seymour farm with its berry bushes and wildflowers and fields of grain would become transformed into a small village where rows of double houses lined two muddy roads across the creek from a dusty mine.

Rillton was built on the side of a hill along the north branch of the Little Sewickley Creek. It was a coal patch and like other towns scattered in the hills of Appalachia, it faced hard economic times for nearly half a century.

It began when Westmoreland Coal dug a 350-foot mineshaft east of the tracks from McGrew Station. Along with it came a large brick building housing 3 air compressors and a hoisting engine next to the 68-foot tall tipple. Nearby were four other buildings of common brick — a boiler house, a repair shop, a bathhouse and a mule barn They called it the Criterion Mine because the extracted coal was used to demonstrate the quality of the product. The word *criterion* means "sample." The coal company constructed more than fifty single and double-family dwellings with clapboard siding and hollow clay-tile foundations. Families got their water from drilled wells and cisterns. Indoor bathrooms were non-existent.

When the Criterion Mine opened on Dec. 17, 1904, workers lined up for whatever jobs were offered, signing *yellow dog* contracts which was written in language completely foreign to them. They signed the papers anyway, sometimes applying their properly witnessed "X." The fine print contained language similar to the following:

> *He will not stop work, join any strike, or combination, for the purpose of obtaining or causing the company to pay the miners in advance of wages or pay beyond what is specified in this contract, nor will he in any way aid, abet, or countenance any strike, combination, or scheme, for any purpose whatever, during the time specified.*

Most of the workers came from southern and eastern Europe. Irish and Anglo-Saxon workers referred to them as *Hunkies* — a descriptive term that included not only Hungarians but Slavs, Croats, Greeks, Poles, Bohemians, Russians and others. They got all of their food and supplies from the company store. In Europe the same people had earned roughly 25 cents a day. In the mines at Sewickley Twp., they could earn seven times that amount and were content with what they considered a large income. Meanwhile, many of the native English, Irish and Scots gradually gave up their jobs, not because of the newcomers but because of the harsh conditions. They were able to make a better living taking on jobs in other industries.

Shaft mining involves the removal of coal in a four-step process — undercutting, drilling, blasting and loading. First, miners used picks to carve a 4-foot wedge into the lower part of the coal seam. Next, they drilled holes in the coal face with an auger and blasted the coal with small powder charges placed in the holes. After the blast, they shoveled the lumps of coal into cars, each car having a one or two-ton capacity. Mules pulled 5 or 10 of the loaded cars along the tracks to a point where cables hoisted the cars up to the mine entrance. At the "tipple," each car was weighed and credited tonnage to the respective miners below. Screen shakers then separated the large lumps of coal from the medium. Nut-size coal was separated from the slack coal.

The life of the coal miners and their families was cold, dark and dusty, as tough as life can get. One miner described it as being the meanest life in the world. Another said, "Home is just a place where I eat and sleep. I live in the mine." Underground work was dangerous, dirty and damp. The ceilings inside the tunnels were so low that miners could not stand up straight. They picked and shoveled coal for 10 hours or more a day, usually on their knees or lying on their sides. For the entire shift, miners breathed stale dusty air. They used lumber to prop up the roof in the area they worked, but often huge rocks would fall, trapping, injuring or killing them. Some were killed by explosive gas, some crushed by runaway coal cars, and some drowned from large amounts of water that suddenly poured into the mine.

The coal company owned the land and built the houses that workers rented or bought. If a miner quit work or went on strike, the company evicted the worker from his home. Workers were forced to buy at the company store. Credit was available but prices were steep. Sometimes the company paid in scrip (play money) which was redeemable only at the company store. Miners were paid monthly, with two weeks wages withheld. That way, miners who quit often lost two weeks pay. Miners bought their own oil for their underground lamps, sharpened their own tools and, for the most part, paid for them as well — shovels, pry bars, saws, axes, tamping bars and blasting powder.

If the miner were married, the needs of a growing family usually outstripped his ability to provide for them on the wages earned, thus most miners were perpetually in debt to the company store. Nearly all of the miners maintained small gardens to supplement their meals. If a family member became ill, the company doctor was called in and the expense deducted from the wages. The sons of miners would often tag along with the fathers to help pay off the debt. It was not uncommon to see them injured or killed in the same mining accident.

Miners were paid by the ton. The coal operators often cheated the miners, claiming too many rocks, clay and slate were mixed in with the loaded coal. The coal was dumped over screens. The miners were paid only for the large pieces above the screen, even though the coal company sold the small chunks too. Most miners were unemployed during the summer months when the demand for heat decreased, reducing annual income substantially. In 1904, the price per ton paid was 50 cents. The average worker loaded 80 tons per month, roughly $40 in wages, less credit charges at the company store. Children often worked as door trappers, flagmen, mule drivers or janitors who cleaned the shower rooms.

Frank Dushak came to America when he was five years old and learned to speak four languages. He later wrote a memoir : *The first work I did in coal mine I door traper and flagman, mule drivers that was hawling coal wagons to the bottom of shaft whear it was liftet by kaysh to top of shaft and dumpet in cars. I was 13 years old when startet to work..I was paid 75 cts a day...I was burent by a gass explosion, their wher 5 of us burent in that gass explosion. I whas laed up fore 3 month so after I was abel to go to work again I begain to drive a mule...my sallry was $2 a day. Then after I dug coal. I was 16 years old and had a mans place ... so this is what experents I had in coal mining.*

Within 6 years, the Rillton mine produced over a half million tons of coal and employed 520 men and boys, many working up to 14 hours a day, never seeing daylight during the winter months. A lot of workers got injured, some even killed. No legal action was ever taken.

In spite of these dreary conditions in the mining community, a closeness among the workers developed as they watched out for the safety of one another. They spoke different languages but strived to speak English in order to share their experiences with their neighbors, unlike immigrants living in the cities of Pittsburgh, Cincinnati, Cleveland, Chicago, Philadelphia and New York where families grouped together in city blocks, holding onto language and customs of the old country. Even in small coal towns, people of different nationalities clustered together, had their own cultural gatherings and held native dances at lodges. For example, Herminie had an Italian lodge, a Polish lodge, a German Hall, a Slovenian Hall, 5 churches, a small community called Granishtown and a marching band.

Maintaining culture, tradition and heritage was important but it was less so in Rillton. In Rillton, there were no bands, no churches or lodges to reinforce ethnicity. The priority was getting along with the neighbors, regardless of heritage. Rillton immigrants settled in whatever houses offered room enough for their families, so long as they could afford it. Consequently, a two-family dwelling might house 12 Polish immigrants on one side and 12 Italians on the other, each family speaking a different language. But it didn't matter. They invested time and energy to communicate in English and yet adapt to the different lifestyles of their neighbors. It was the mixing of cultures that brought these families together and helped cement relationships for a very long time.

The families of Rillton, realizing the dangerous life within the mine, encouraged their kids to attend school and prepare for job opportunities elsewhere. Their idea of education was consistent with the objective of William Penn — every child would learn to read and write by age 12. It was the American way of life, a system very different from the feudalism of Eastern Europe but one that parents welcomed. In the case of white Europeans, unlike the blacks or native Indians, there was no class separation. For them, there was equal opportunity for education, occupation and housing. In America, it was possible to purchase a house, including land, without first completing military service. It was a question of money that came from hard work, albeit risky work.

But the dangerous conditions of the mine also took away opportunity, hope and dreams. When a miner was incapacitated because of a mining accident, the burden of the house rent fell on his sons. Otherwise, the family was evicted. Consequently, male students rarely attended school beyond the 10th grade. At age 16, most of them were working the mines. Not all mining accidents were recorded. In fact, none at all were recorded in 1905. In 1906, however, the Criterion Mine recorded the following:

Peter Flalko, age 28, single, Polish, Coal Loader (killed instantly by fall of slate in his room 5/28/1906).

Lawrence Grayiak, age 44, married, Coal Loader (foot crushed by fall of coal 6/2/1906).

Joseph Barbero, age 20, single, Italian, Mule Driver (killed instantly, squeezed between mine car and rib 10/5/1906).

RILLTON

John Yenko, age 40, married, Austrian, Coal Loader (killed instantly by fall of slate 8/29/1906).

Ruis Salvador, age 26, married, Italian, Coal Loader (foot crushed by fall of slate 10/22/1906).

In 1907, thirteen similar accidents were recorded; in 1908, seventeen accidents; and in 1910, eighteen accidents including 6 killed. Still, no lawsuits were ever filed.

Coal miners became increasingly agitated because of the working conditions and the method of pay. Since workers were paid by the ton, they received no compensation for "dead work" (laying track, shoring up tunnels, pumping out water and removing slate and clay). There was no credit for mining nut-sized lumps of coal and slack (very fine coal), both of which were deducted from the recorded tonnage. The coal companies strongly resisted any demands from the workers and particularly any attempt at unionization.

But union talks did begin in Keystone after the coal company suddenly reduced wages by 16 percent. On top of that, they demanded the workers pay for new safety lights and new forms of explosives. In early March 1910, some 400 miners signed up and paid dues to the UMWA. Keystone Coal immediately fired 100 workers for attending the meeting, at which point the rest of the miners walked off the job anyway. Word quickly got out and soon the miners' strike spread throughout the Irwin Basin. The Croatian Band of Keystone traveled to the surrounding mines in an attempt to gather support for a coal strike. Herminie joined the strike, then Lowber. Workers pitched tents after the coal company evicted them from their company-owned homes. Lowber became a tent city.

When the coal strikers marched to Rillton, they were accompanied by an Italian brass band with twelve members, some as young as 11 years old. They paraded up and down the mine. A man inside the mine yelled, "Come up above ground. There's a parade going on." Some of the men got behind the band and marched in a circle for awhile but later went back to work. None of the workers in Rillton joined the strike. But Mary Roper followed the band to Hahntown.

The strikers' march continued to Hahntown where many workers walked off the job immediately. More followed the next day. The 100 families evicted from their homes moved into tents on the upper part of the hill to the east. Other Hahntown families, who sympathized with the miners, hung large pots of soup over open fires to feed the children. Meanwhile, the coal companies set up fences and roadblocks to protect ingress and egress for replacement workers. Nearly all of these workers, some 270 of them, were recruited from eastern and southern Europe after the coal company offered free transportation from overseas. Of course, they never told the new immigrants that they would be employed as strikebreakers. If the workers tried to quit, the Iron Police prevented them from leaving, telling them they had to work off the cost of the transportation before resigning. If they still tried to leave, the police beat them. The new settlement on Adams Hill became known as "Scab Hill."

In the summer of 1910, a number of miner's wives were arrested for harassing the strikebreakers. Mary Roper, whom everyone called Mother Mary, encouraged the women to bring their babies and small children with them after being sentenced to jail in Greensburg. Most of them could not afford the $30 fine. Mother Mary instructed the prisoners to sing all night long and never stop, seeing that the jail was next door to the sheriff's home and very close to hotels and lodging houses in the area. After 5 days of sleepless nights, the townspeople demanded the judge order the women released. He did so immediately.

By mid-1911 the strike was over. Support from the UMWA ended due to the lack of strike relief funds. Most miners returned to work with no added benefits. About 400 of them were blacklisted and forced to seek employment outside of Pennsylvania.

18
SMOKY MOUNTAINS

Of the 1,600 Cherokee hiding in the mountains of North Carolina, many continued to live there for years without interference from the Tennessee militia. This included what was left of the small band of refugees who found their way to the Smoky's in May 1815. At age 17, Poki ran off to marry a young maiden from another clan. Later he persuaded the bride to re-settle with his own tribe in a valley near the Tuckasegee River. The tribe of 14 grew to 66 strong. Poki eventually became the head chief and had 3 children, 10 grandchildren and 7 great-grandchildren by the time he reached age 80. One day the youngest of his great-grandchildren came to his hut with aquestion: Did he know a squaw named Little Creek?

RILLTON

On their trip down the Ohio, Rilla and Josh encountered two storms. One produced gusty winds but little rain; the other pelted the boat with bullet-like raindrops that turned to hail. The storms were nothing like the one years earlier when raging waters driven by ferocious winds whisked Rilla's parents overboard at the mouth of the Tennessee. Rilla noticed a lot more wharfs along the Mississippi. There was coal for sale everywhere and it was very cheap. Josh piloted the boat with ease and learned to stay clear of the swells in the water from oversized barges. As they neared the land between the lakes, Rilla at first did not recognize the Tennessee River and they nearly missed the turn. It looked so very different from the raging mud waters she remembered. Now it was calm and displayed a deep, rich emerald color.

It took nearly two days to navigate the Tennessee upstream to the Great Smoky Mountains. Steep, rocky hills rising up on both sides of the river seemed to dwarf their tiny craft. There was not a sign of human life in this isolated area. The silence would have been eerie but for the occasional sound of a blackbird from the small marshes tucked between the gigantic boulders.

They docked the steamboat the first place they could, beside a flat rock protruding from the river's edge where the roots of a huge Black Oak clung to its side. Rilla spotted what looked like a footpath and remained on the boat while Josh surveyed the path. They followed the trail for about a mile and came to a wood shack with a horse tied to a post. Josh yelled out, "Hello there!" but got no response. He continued to call out as he and Rilla approached the entrance. After knocking, then pounding on the door, they decided the owner was not home and proceeded to get water from the rusty hand pump alongside the cabin. Then they heard the click of the rifle a few feet away and turned to see an old, bearded man wearing a weird hat and pointing a gun.

"Youns the owner of that there boat?" the old man asked. And with that question, the way the last word "boat" trailed off in a slight downward pitch and with the distinct nasal tone of the word "youns," Josh knew right off the man was from Pittsburgh.

The 86-year-old Rilla trailed behind the old farmer and Josh for seven miles up and down the mountain to the nearest Cherokee camp, bordering two rapid-flowing streams at the far end of a meadow high in the hills of the Smoky's. No one at the camp had ever heard of a "Poki." They went to the next camp, another three miles upstream to the left and came across a smaller Indian village with only four huts. The chief, who was very young, shy and apparently not interested in making eye contact, denied knowing anyone by that name but pointed in a direction further south along the stream, That was exactly the direction from which they had just come.

Four miles downstream, the old man from Pittsburgh decided he had enough of the wild goose chase and opted to head back home. Josh thought that was a good idea too. It was getting dark. By the time they made it back to the boat, it was nearly midnight. Josh, exhausted, sprawled out on the tiny mattress near the stern of the boat and fell asleep. Little Creek made some tea and studied the stars. *There must be a better way through these woods. It seems we're going around in circles.*

The next morning, a thick fog shrouded the river, making it difficult to see much of anything along the banks and certainly not the sign of a trail. And so they waited. Suddenly, out of the mist, a dugout canoe appeared before them. Two Indian braves stared at the steamboat as if they were studying it but said nothing and continued to paddle downstream. Rilla, now wearing a cowhide dress and a beaded headband, yelled out, "I am Little Creek. We are looking for Poki." But the canoe had disappeared into the mist and out of sight.

When the sun began to peek over the rocky cliffs and the fog began to lift, Josh steered the craft upstream, hugging the east bank. They passed by several streams and saw no trails. As the river narrowed and became uncomfortably shallow, they bumped into tree roots and summer flowers on both sides of the river. Josh did his best to keep the boat in the deepest part of the water, crawling ever so slowly forward. At this point the river looked more like a stream and so shallow that Josh suddenly shut down the engine to confer with Rilla. *How much longer can we navigate these impossible waters?*

186

They chugged along, passed two streams and then a third before coming to a muddy path along the river. They anchored, tied up the boat and walked the trail for about 15 minutes before running into 3 Indians. The lead scout signaled for Josh and Rilla to mount the 2 bareback ponies and follow them up the muddy trail to the high rocks. From there, the scouts led them down a very steep, winding path through more rocky boulders, across a bubbling mountain stream and into a canyon where they finally stopped at an old campsite.

A tall, slender man with a high forehead and gentle eyes appeared before them. It was Poki. He looked quite different from the 14-year-old kid whom Little Creek remembered some 70 years ago. His English had gotten worse, not better. But the smile and the way he pronounced her name, "Lil Creek," was the same.

The main camp, another mile directly east and just south of the Great Smoky Mountains was hidden beneath a rather strange-looking cliff. From a distance, it resembled the head of a wolf without the lower jaw. It reminded Poki of Ear Flop. The strange rock also made it much easier for him to find his way back to camp after spending time at the river. In his early years, he spent much time there, watching for boats, waiting to see if his sister Little Creek might be aboard one of them. And now, after all those years, she did come back, a thought that spun through his head over and over like a dream. Except the dream had finally come true. Somehow Poki felt reborn.

Poki made a point to have his great-granddaughter Tree Top join his talks with Little Creek, whom he now called "Ri-lah". Tree Top was designated the official interpreter. Poki loved hearing Rilla's stories about the land of Sewickley and her life on the farm. Rilla, in turn, was pleased to hear from Poki the tales of her Cherokee family. Not only had they escaped persecution by the Tennessee militia, but they also managed to live off the land in the tradition of their ancestors without menacing white settlers. This was possible in part because of the changing attitudes of the local citizens. They more or less conceded the rugged mountain terrain to the Indians after the North Carolina legislature declared the land a national park for the purposes of bringing deforestation to a halt. The threat of eviction from the U.S. government was ever present, however.

After several days at the Cherokee camp, rumors surfaced that Josh was starting to make eyes at Tree Top. Unlike the other great-grandkids, Tree Top spent considerable time around Poki's hut, making sure he didn't sleep in too late, making sure he wore the right outfit for the dance ceremonies and reprimanding him for smoking too many pipes. She was very motherly when it came to managing Poki's affairs. She thought he was way too disorganized and took it upon herself to straighten things out. The fact was, she spoke English better than anyone else in the camp and Poki needed her. He also genuinely liked her and was content to put up with her antics.

But while Tree Top at times treated her great-grandpa like an old dog unable to perform new tricks, she treated Josh more like a young puppy in need of encouragement. She showed Josh how to lace moccasins, bone fish and find the good hooks for fishing, how to use the atlatl and how best to plant beans, which was perfected by plunging the index finger into the soil down to the knuckle. Poki always used a stick. The finger was better, she insisted. Josh was fascinated with the girl — her eyes so daunting as her mouth was smiling. Her broken English was so serious, so direct yet comical because of the many grammatical errors.

Josh entertained the idea of remaining at the camp for the rest of his life but knew this idea was unlikely. He was gone for only 3 weeks but already missed his hometown. How ironic, he thought. He couldn't live in Pittsburgh because of his physical health, yet his feeling of emptiness left him wanting to go back to the smoky city.

One day he led Tree Top down the Little Tennessee to check on the steamship, which was protected in a small cove. Tree Top saw that the boat had no name and thought that was peculiar. "All white men have a name for boat, why not you?" she asked. Josh hadn't really given it a thought. Neither Tim McGrew, nor his Uncle Riley ever gave it a name and neither did he. The next day Josh and Tree Top went back to the boat with a clay pot of yellow dye and inscribed the name *CREEK RUNNER* on the hull in honor of Running Creek who gave up his life to find a better life for his people.

When the day came for Rilla to pass on to the Great Spirit, she opened a small tin box and handed Poki $600 cash. The money was to be used to preserve the history and culture of the Cherokee Nation as he saw fit. Poki thought a long time before deciding what to do with the money. Should he send all of the children to school to learn English and become citizens — maybe even politicians — and cast important votes in the legislature to assure the continued protection of the reservation? He wondered. And then one night he heard the howl of the Red Wolf from the mountains to the north. It was clear that the white settlers had not killed them off, as everyone had thought. *If the Red Wolf can come back, then why not the Cherokee?*

With Tree Top at his side, Poki made several trips to the University of North Carolina, the nation's oldest state university. He proposed educational courses to teach students the Cherokee language. The university administrators were simply not interested. However, the following year, a young professor argued the need for a music and dance instruction class, which would include, in part, Cherokee war dances. It was a start. Poki sent one of the tribe's best dancers, representing himself as the official War Chief. After a time, he won the hearts of many of the

European students who had never seen a real savage warrior. Years later the education department sponsored a Museum of the Cherokee Indian near the reservation, where courses in archeology, folklore, history, and linguistics were offered. Poki did well with his plan.

The marriage of Josh and Tree Top was a simple affair, nothing like the gala at Rilla's reception years earlier in Pennsylvania where a mix of booze and religion highlighted the day. Tree Top wore a fringed buckskin dress and a simple headband decorated with white and yellow feathers. Josh tried his best to dye his dark blue shirt white. It came out a dull grey, but no one really cared. In the spring of 1905, five years and nine months after Josh left Pittsburgh, he was on his way back home on the steamship he now owned with the $50 wedding gift from Rilla and Tree Top at his side. As the Creek Runner made its way north, Poki watched with tears in his eyes. He knew he would never see Tree Top again. He lived to age 90.

Josh converted the steamboat into a houseboat and docked it on the Youghiogheny near the Guffey mine where he sometimes hauled flats of coal downriver. In the very cold winter of 1910, the craft was landlocked for 3 months. Josh's allergies got worse from his constantly huddling around the coal-fired engine to keep warm at night. On a frosty winter morning Tree Top walked down the Yough to fetch coal from

RILLTON

Guffey and lugged two buckets full 2 miles back to the boat. There she found 37-year-old Josh lying flat on his back, dead from asphyxiation. The steamboat sat near the water's edge for several months. One day it was gone. And so was Tree Top. Someone said she probably took the boat downriver. Others said she was last seen roaming the woods near Guffey and just seemed to disappear.

19
LIFE OUTSIDE THE MINE

In spite of the coal strikes at other mines in 1910, there were no strikes at the mine in Rillton. In that year, the Criterion mine produced more than 500,000 tons of coal and employed over 500 men and boys. The population had reached its peak at roughly 2,000 residents.

A new trolley line was constructed alongside the Youghiogheny RR and ran from Irwin to Rillton. The trolley continued down Clay Pike to Herminie. Residents of Rillton could use the trolley to get to other places, like Greensburg or Pittsburgh. The trolley fare from Rillton to Herminie was 5 cents.

Charles E. Parr had built the company store next to the McGrew railroad station in 1905. Later, Trozzo opened a feed and supply store near Clay Pike.

RILLTON

A Baptist parsonage sat directly across the street. The MacDonalds from Guffey wanted to put up a hotel in place of the parsonage and ended up helping construct a new parsonage on Mars Hill. The parsonage was renamed Mars Hill Baptist parsonage. The name of the bar inside the MacDonald Hotel was called Bruno's.

For four months out of the year, children from Rillton walked about a mile south to Mars Hill School and met students from Keystone and Herminie.

In the summer months when kids were out of school, they would create their own games and find ways to keep busy. For fun, they would find metal cans, squash them and position them on the bottom of their shoes, then walk down the road and make as much noise as possible. They would watch the miners bring up the good coal, which was to be sold, and dispose of the bad coal that had to be dumped in the waste pile. Some kids waited for the arrival of the waste truck. Others ran as fast as they could once they saw the truck, for the waste pile always contained some good coal mixed in with the slate. It was practical for kids to pick out the good coal and take it home for heating later in the winter. Every kid did this.

Sometimes the kids would go down to the mines in the evening and heckle the night watchman, who took great delight in chasing the kids away from the mine. Another game was to run along the steep piles of waste at the slate dump and try to keep their feet from sinking into the fine slack. The trick was to keep the feet moving, scurry across the pile and not dilly-dally.

Every year, kids would dam up the creek with bags of muddy gravel and swim away the afternoon. Girls would jump rope or play hopscotch after drawing lines in the dirt with a stick. Boys played baseball in the road, using rubber balls and broomsticks.

With the coming of the mines, ashes from the boilers were plentiful and frequently used on snow-covered roads. Horse-drawn dump wagons allowed the ashes to fall on the roads through planks of wood connected to hinges. Once the snow melted, the roads were not quite as muddy, just a bit sootier. Occasionally a fire would develop at the slate dump by spontaneous combustion, for there was always a small amount of coal inadvertently mixed together with the slate. A terrible sulfur odor would permeate the air, sometimes for weeks.

Each week it seemed the mine would shut down because of a serious accident or other reasons, such as excess water. A long whistle let the miners know there was going to be work the next day. If it blew twice, there was no work that day. If the whistle blew after the mine was open, that meant someone got hurt in the mine. The kids would always run down to see what happened.

On payday, when the miners went to the company store to pay their debts, the children who tagged along would get a small brown bag of penny candy. Inside the store, there were groceries for sale in addition to miner's supplies, dresses, overalls, shoes, boots and other articles of clothing. Bushels of eggs, a 52-gallon barrel of pickles, a barrel of vinegar and a barrel of crackers greeted customers as they entered the store. Dried fish, sausages, hams and other meats hung from the ceiling. There were bins of coffee, tea, rice and beans. And jelly beans. Packaged goods were unheard of. People had to slice their own meat and bread.

Because of an act in legislature, there was a consolidation of the Sewickley school districts on July 15, 1911. The four previous districts — Mars Hill, Sulphur Springs, Youghiogheny and Sewickley Township — now became Sewickley Township School District. The school term was 8 months. Kids in junior and senior high school now had to walk or ride bikes 2 miles to Herminie instead of the one-mile hike to Mars Hill. However, for the younger students, a new grade school was constructed at the south end of Rillton. Kids from first through sixth grade needed to walk only a few blocks.

During the early years, lack of funds necessitated that schools be built with maximum room at minimum cost. Subsequently, the grade school at Rillton had two large rooms on the first floor and two on the second. In one of the rooms downstairs, a single teacher taught first and second grades, alternating instructions between them. For example, while the teacher instructed the second-graders, the first-graders practiced their writing skills or solved math problems from the previous session. Another teacher used the same alternating technique while teaching third and fourth graders.

There were roughly 25 students in each class. The subjects taught were reading, spelling, history, arithmetic, geography and penmanship. The teachers were hard on the children, which was typical in public schools. If the kids did something wrong, the teachers would hit them with paddles or rulers or box their ears. They spent a lot of time reading, memorizing and reciting. For writing materials, they used inkwells, pencils and white chalk. Although children were supposed to attend school until age 16, most kids in Rillton, like other coal towns, never finished the 8th grade.

School administrators were hard on the teachers as well. Here were the Rules for Teachers in 1912:

1. You will not marry during the term of your contract.

2. You are not to keep the company with men.

3. You must be home between the hours of 8 p.m. and 6 a.m. unless attending a school function.

4. You must not loiter in any of the stores in town.

5. You may not ride in a carriage or automobile unless he is your father or brother.

6. You may not smoke cigarettes.

7. You may not dress in bright colors.

8. You may under no circumstances dye your hair.

9. You must wear at least two petticoats.

10. Your dresses must not be any shorter than two inches above the ankle.

11. To keep the school room neat and clean, you must sweep the floor at least once daily, scrub the floor at least once a week with hot, soapy water, clean the blackboards at least once a day and start the fire at 7 a.m. so the room will be warm by 8 a.m.

Aside from education in the classroom, children learned to play together, respecting the strength and weaknesses and moral character of their classmates. More importantly, they established friendships that would not otherwise have existed if not for the daily meetings at school. Tony Moreno (Italian) and Randy Bulger (Hungarian) became good friends in the second grade. They dug small trenches in the backyard in an effort to divert fresh rainwater to their small pond and keep their minnows alive. They fished at Indian Lake, played marbles, built imaginary castles with wooden blocks and cooled off at the dug-out swimming hole in the Rillton Creek. The boys visited each other every day in the summer, so one of their mothers was always making lunch for two. Because of school, families came to know each other through the children.

In addition to the school, porches drew neighbors together like nothing else could. Each house had a porch and a rocking chair or two. Whenever someone walked by, the people on the porch would wave. Soon they were connecting faces with the houses. Whoever walked the most got to know the neighbors a lot sooner. Ted Fryer was one of those people, until he got his foot run over by a mine car in September 1910. Neighbors would stop by to find out how Fryer was getting along. Many had never spoken to him until after he was injured. Previously they just waved a "hello" from their porches.

Because of the high number of mining accidents, it was not unusual to see families move out of a company-owned house and witness an entirely new family moving in a week or two later. Still, the established residents would wave from their porches, a sign that the newcomers were welcome in their village.

The year 1911 brought a new social diversion, especially for the singles. John J. Bruno opened a bar in the MacDonald Hotel. It was long bar, made of mahogany with a brass rail and four spittoons. The work of a coal miner left him too tired at the end of the day to do much of anything. Now at least he could choose to relax at a saloon and bury his troubles in drink. When the bar first opened, men would stop by after work for a beer, or maybe a shot and a beer, and then go home. Some stayed a little longer, venting their frustrations of the day — the working conditions, the intolerant new foreman, inexperienced workers, the cost of goods at the company store and anything else that happened to stir up their day. But the whiskey was cheap and the short time spent at the bar was often therapeutic.

The unmarried men, however, wanted entertainment on weekends. For months they tried to convince Bruno to hire a band like the one in Guffey and hold dances on Saturday nights. When Bruno announced that the band was too expensive, a few musicians in Rillton got together, assembled their own band and agreed to play for tip money. For awhile, the band played polkas and waltzes, the same few songs over and over. Because of the repetitive, boring music, dancing was minimal.

But it was the beginning of ragtime and when the band started playing new songs, people from other towns headed to Rillton, usually by trolley. They strutted their way to the dance floor, performing the latest dances from the big cities — the cakewalk, the mazurka, the one-step and the foxtrot. Instead of trekking to Guffey, the single men in Rillton spent the entire night at Bruno's, learning the dances and lining up dates with the ladies.

By the time the coal strike ended in mid-1911, Bruno's was packed with people from all over the township. Meanwhile, the married men and women living in Rillton, not wanting to get linked up and perhaps falsely accused of intermingling with singles, used the trolley to find bars suitable for drinking and dancing in towns outside of Rillton. It was comical seeing Rillton people drinking the night away at a bar in Hahntown then heading back to Rillton while the Hahntown people were leaving the bar in Rillton to board the trolley headed back to Hahntown.

In a small town, rumors spread quickly. Occasionally, when dour events took place inside the bar — fist fights, throwing up, repeated cursing — fellow patrons would go out of their way to protect the wayward souls before word hit the street. Just as there was city culture, there developed in Rillton a thing called bar culture. It was okay to get tipsy but not okay to get drunk. If a worker got down and out, it was normal to endure his venting, which usually disappeared when someone bought him "one more drink." Seldom did anyone dance with somebody else's girlfriend, but if he did, it wasn't for very long and it wasn't very close ... unless the girl was from out of town. Not all rumors of course escaped detection, especially from Mrs. Robokowski.

Rita Robokowski was a small woman with a long face, pointed nose and ears that seemed to wiggle in the direction of conversation anywhere and everywhere. By the time any rumor got to her, it suddenly expanded with detail ad infinitum. She had the unceremonious talent of taking someone's small tale, throwing in a dose of garbage and then repackaging it into a new story of unadulterated bull. No one actually believed all that Mrs. Robokowski had to say, but the stories were so creative and so colorful, people were reluctant to ignore her

RILLTON

completely. When the coal company in Herminie brought in Negro strikebreakers, Mrs. Robokowski was the first to know about it, spreading rumors that they were fixing to come to Rillton. According to her latest rumor, a certain young man was to marry his fiancé within the month but instead ended up running off with an out of town girl he met in Bruno's bar and was never heard from again.

20

WAR AND PEACE

At the turn of the century, the great wave of immigration from central Europe to the US peaked in 1907, reaching more than 1 million new migrants. A significant number, nearly all of them coal workers, came from the Alsace-Lorraine area of Germany and ended up settling in western Pennsylvania.

On August 30, 1907, Barbara Elizabeth Zimmer and her sister Maria from Kleinrosseln, Germany boarded an ocean liner for the first time ever and traveled the open waters of the Atlantic Ocean. Maria was 16 years old, quiet and shy and not anything like her 14-year old sister, Barbara E.

Barbara was a bit vivacious, outspoken but generally entertaining. In spite of her broken English and limited ability to read the language, she had little problem making friends. By the second day, she had met nearly all of the ship's crew. The names fascinated her: Adrian, Pedro, Roberto, Julio. And they all seemed delighted to meet her. Whenever a crew member spotted Maria on deck alone, he would immediately ask the whereabouts of Miss Barbara.

Before long, Barbara was beginning to act as if the steamship *Compania* were her very own yacht. Each morning, she would wake up in the crowded steerage area of the ship where 500 or more passengers were packed in like cattle. Minutes later, she found her way to the main deck, relishing the cool breeze, smelling the salt spray and dreaming of a new life ahead in America. She had never experienced such day-dreams back in Kleinrosseln.

It took 9 days to cross the Atlantic from Liverpool to Ellis Island. The girls had $16 between them, more than enough to make their way to Greensburg, Pa. to see Father. Father Peter and his 17 year old son Sebastian had been working the coal mines in nearby Harrison City while mother Barbara was taking care of 2 yr old Margareta and 3 year old Anna.

The following year, Anna died from cholera. Peter blamed it on contaminated water and vowed to get out of the mine. He tried doing day jobs in Greensburg but could not earn a decent wage. He grew bitter. Family life became unbearable. By 1909, Peter took a voyage back to Germany and filed divorce papers.

Shortly afterwards, Maria and Barbara began working for a Greensburg laundry service while Sebastian worked as a flagman at one of the local mines. When mother Barbara announced that she intended to re-marry another miner named John Sauer, the older children made plans to move out of the house.

Peter and Barbara E lived together in Hempfield Twp. Maria got married and moved to Youngwood. A short time later, Barbara E moved in with Maria (who changed her named to Mary). The following year at age 20, Barbara delivered a child named William. Mary cared for the child while Barbara continued to work each day as a laundress and help pay for expenses.

John Sauer had emigrated to the US in 1906 and had worked in Penn Mines #1 and #5 with Peter Zimmer initially, but like many families, he had moved from one place to another. He ended up in Keystone. In 1910, nearly all of the workers went on strike. Once Keystone Coal started hiring scab labor, Sauer felt threatened and began working at the mine at Rillton. In Rillton, none of the miners went on strike.

In 1914, an outbreak of war in Europe had cut off the supply of labor from overseas at a time when the demand for coal was high. Coal companies began to rethink their position on the labor force. To offset the shortage of workers during the war, Westmoreland

Coal utilized more automation and increased wages. With higher wages and fewer mouths to feed, Sauer was finally able to save some money.

On September 17, 1915, John and Barbara Sauer bought 6 acres of land on the west side of Rillton. It was the last parcel, previously owned by Charles and Rilla Seymour.

Sauer built a farmhouse, a typical structure with a hollow clay foundation, wood siding, two brick chimneys and gable slate tile roof. There was no electric and no indoor plumbing. The farm had a chicken coup, a cornfield, an oversized vegetable garden and fruit trees everywhere. Before the war had ended, his fruit and vegetable stand had a steady stream of customers. And even after the war, when the food shortage problem had ended, Sauer continued to sell his surplus crops to the locals, who marveled at the oversized heads of cabbage and the delicious apples, pears, peaches and plums from his orchard.

Because of World War I, the legislature enacted the first military draft in 1917. The shortage of workers worsened. With all of the single men inducted into the armed forces, business plummeted at Bruno's bar. Bruno found it financially beneficial to shut down the bar during the workweek and take a mining job. The first American soldier killed in action was Private Thomas Enright from Pittsburgh, yet none of the inductees from Rillton lost lives. A total of 24 served in the military. Most of them returned to Rillton but were shocked to find their jobs no longer available.

It was a vast turnaround of events. The robust economy from WW I quickly ended once peace was declared. Industries all over the Pittsburgh area announced production cutbacks, layoffs and reduced wages. The labor force was seething with dissatisfaction. There were steel strikes, streetcar strikes and coal mining strikes, all demanding shorter hours and higher wages. Still there were no strikes in Rillton.

Since single workers had been more accident prone than the married workers, the coal company was reluctant to re-hire them. During the time they were out fighting the war, the labor force had become more efficient. Mining accidents fell. The townspeople heard fewer whistles each week. The miners, now wiser and more experienced, were encouraged. For them, it meant longer working hours and more production from fewer workers to offset the reduced wages. In 1919 the mine produced 398,000 tons of coal, was in operation 294 days and employed 307 men. There were only three accidents that year, all non-fatal. The number of residents in Rillton fell from 2,000 to around 1,200 but only a few complained. For most families, life was getting better.

The year 1919 marked the beginning of Prohibition. Bruno's bar was officially closed, though it remained unofficially open. Pittsburgh had a reputation as the drinkingest town in the West with more bars and saloons than any other comparable city. So it was no surprise that within a year the area was still regarded as the wettest spot in the United States. By 1920, more than 500 drinking establishments became speakeasies where whiskey was sold at $16 a quart. And the next year, there were more whiskey-selling nightclubs than ever before. Some 38,000 people were arrested, yet people went on drinking.

Most of the Rillton coal mining families did not sneak out to the saloons at night but had other sources of entertainment. Some stayed at home to play pianos, which sold like hotcakes during the war. They could go to Herminie and buy sheet music or listen to it in the "corner room" at Louis Averback's music store. Many listened to music from phonograph records or their Victorolas. A few families listened to broadcasts from the radio, though there wasn't much to listen to at that time — mostly farm news, church services and weather reports.

Porch talk with the neighbors was another source of entertainment. New rumors were spreading like wildfire, mostly from Mrs. Robokowski. Rumor had it that women in Guffey were sitting on their front porch rocking chairs, smoking tobacco in clay pipes. And some were even chewing snuff, which they pulled from their petticoats underneath their skirts. One woman looked part Indian. According to Mrs. Robokowski, the speakeasies up and down the three rivers of Pittsburgh were nothing more than cover-ups for mob activities, like gambling and prostitution. And last week, seedy-looking characters were seen going in and out of Bruno's Bar late at night.

Twenty-two year old Tony Napoli returned from the war in 1921. His job at the Criterion mine was no longer available, so Napoli was out of luck. The next day the young man looked for jobs in Herminie, Keystone, Lowber and other mines without success. It seemed no one was hiring.

In a last-ditch effort, he hopped a train from Guffey to Pittsburgh, walked the streets for several days and literally knocked on doors until he was exhausted. Hopelessness began to set in. One morning, he looked up and realized his life was as dark as the smoky city. He hated the smoke. He hated the world and he hated his life.

Napoli hitched a ride in a Packard truck back to the train station and asked the driver where he had learned to operate a vehicle. Before they reached the station, the driver showed Napoli how to drive for a fee of 25 cents. The next morning Napoli applied for work delivering ice, a job that paid 10 cents an hour. Drivers then could work as long as they liked. They were paid at the end of each day and were re-hired the next morning. For several weeks Napoli lived and worked out of the company truck, using his only pair of dungarees as a pillow while catching catnaps between runs. He learned to stop by the City Bakery to pick up a free piece of bread, to make pretzel soup from the pretzel crumbs mixed in water and to accept a free cup of coffee from a few gracious customers.

One day, on his third stop at the Corner Deli in the hillside area of Pittsburgh, a hefty man with brushy eyebrows named McNab pulled Napoli aside, scribbled a note, placed it in a plain envelope and said, "Take this to your boss right away." Napoli replied, "But sir, I've got to do my runs and I can't …"

McNab raised his eyebrows and barked, "Listen, you little Wop. Just do it. NOW!"

Napoli, shaken by McNab's thunderous voice, walked off as if he intended to comply immediately with the strange demand of the little fat man even though he actually intended to complete his run first. After all, the ice house was on the other side of town. But when he heard McNab say, "You hand him the message personal, understand? And don't you dare open that envelope," he changed his mind. Better to do as the man said. At least then, the matter would be behind him and he could then get on with the scheduled deliveries.

Back at the ice house, the cigar smoking Mr. Bigelow was too busy to see young Napoli. That is, until he learned of the urgent message. Bigelow ripped open the envelope and read the message: *Close the store. The Feds are on to us.*

At this point Bigelow ordered Napoli to unload the blocks of ice and to reload the truck with bottles of whiskey, which were hauled from the back of the store and hurriedly boxed and stacked haphazardly onto the truck along with kegs of beer. Napoli was ordered to run the cargo to Braddock, which was outside the jurisdiction of the new enforcement agent, John Pennington. Under Pennington, the raids on drinking places were frequent. He had padlocked many saloons, obtained convictions against the speakeasies and had arrested nearly 100,000 people for drunkenness since the late 20s. There were more than 10,000 stills in Allegheny County alone.

That day, Napoli narrowly escaped arrest by FBI agents who worked closely with Pennington in efforts to shut down the Bigelow Speakeasy. Bigelow himself was arrested but was released for lack of evidence. Meanwhile, Napoli was rewarded $50 for his bootlegging services by the owner of Red Tile Inn, another speakeasy located in a rat-infested area at the north end of Braddock. Napoli continued his bootlegging activities and by the next year, he had money to burn.

Pennington was infuriated and re-doubled his efforts to shut down as many speakeasies as he could. In the wee hours of the morning following the election, FBI agents waited for Napoli to arrive at the Bigelow Speakeasy before rushing in to make arrests, after which the practice was to machine-gun the bottles of whiskey lining the shelves along the wall.

Napoli had no idea the raid was instigated by law enforcement officers, as none of them wore police caps or uniforms, nor were any of the vehicles marked

— no insignias, no lights, no loudspeakers. And so he became panicky, floored the gas pedal and blew by a 1922 Plymouth coupe where two officers jumped off to the side before firing bullets into the back door of the truck. Napoli crashed the truck into the side of another unmarked vehicle, pushing it out of the way, and then headed down a dimly lit street on the south side of Pittsburgh. The chase was on.

Napoli found himself heading toward Braddock, perhaps from gut reaction. He tried hard to think but had no idea where else to go. When he reached the city limits of Pittsburgh, he realized he forgot to turn on his headlights, which worked to his advantage since the pursuing government agents had temporarily lost sight of the fleeing vehicle. By the time they picked up the trail, Napoli was headed across the Monongahela via the 22nd Street Bridge. Heavy fog from the river made it difficult to navigate at high speeds. Toward the end of the bridge, a white tail deer suddenly appeared in the middle of the road. Napoli braked hard. The truck spun clockwise, tipped over and slid into the bridge railing. There it rested half on and half off the bridge, teetering over a single steel cable stretched tightly between two steel posts. Kegs of beer rolled across the pavement as car lights began to pierce through the fog at the other end of the bridge.

Napoli found it impossible to open the door, as it was pressed firmly against the cable. He rolled down the passenger side window and jumped some 24 feet into the dark waters of the river below. He tried to swim and winced from the intense pain that shot through his left shoulder. Using his right arm, he paddled to the river's edge, clawed his way halfway up the bank, slid on the mud back into Monongahela, grabbed a tree root and hoisted himself to safety. His head pounded. He nearly collapsed from exhaustion. He lay still, waiting for something to happen. Exactly what that was, he had no clue.

The two agents in pursuit could have called on the local police to help in locating the runaway bootlegger, but given the impenetrable fog and their key interest in apprehending the big boys of the Bigelow operation, they opted to call off the search. Napoli limped his way back to his Braddock apartment. He wrapped his personal belongings in a blanket and tied the blanket to a stick. After stuffing $122 in his under shorts, he boarded the early morning train to Gratztown where he figured he'd catch the next train to Rillton.

When the train reached the Shaner Station en route to Gratztown, the conductor discovered a hobo asleep in an empty boxcar and quickly booted him off the train. Moments later, a tall man dressed in a suit ran toward the man, flashed his deputy badge and began interrogating the hobo intensely, an unusual event since hobos normally received no special attention whatsoever. It was then Napoli's mind snapped. It was a Federal agent, still looking for him. The agent had apprehended the wrong man.

RILLTON

Napoli shuffled through his blanket of stuffed items, placed a cap on his head and nonchalantly stepped off the train. He walked into the Hotel Shaner as if he were a guest, then exited silently through a rear door, climbed a steep hill and headed to the woods. Surely he could walk his way to Rillton, he thought. He just needed to find Guffey Road.

Napoli thought he was headed northeast but in fact was walking east over challenging terrain. Hungry and thirsty, he began to feel faint. Sweat dripped from his face. By the time he traversed the third hill, his feet hurt, his shoulder throbbed and he had a splitting headache. He cupped his hand in a small stream of water cascading down a ravine and gulped down several mouthfuls of the cool liquid. His clothes were saturated with sweat. He stunk. He was a mess.

On the top of the next hill, Napoli, now starving for food, came across a patch of raspberries and feasted on them ravenously. He did not see the foraging black bear at the other end of the patch until it stood up to sniff the air. Napoli stiffened and then fled down the hill from where he had just climbed. The bear followed. Napoli stumbled and fell forward, smashed his face into a tree trunk and lost consciousness immediately.

The young man awoke, lying flat on his back inside an odd-shaped room without windows. It was stuffy and dark except for the tiny rays of sunlight peeping through the cracks in the sidewall. He blinked, trying to adjust to the darkness. His torso was wrapped with a towel. Otherwise, he lay completely nude. His throat was bone dry, devoid of saliva. He tried to swallow but couldn't. He ran his tongue over his lower lip. It felt like sandpaper. His arms and legs felt like dead weight. He didn't try to move and lay there, looking up at the wood ceiling, wondering where on earth he could be. Having forgotten about his shoulder injury, Napoli reached for a container of water at his bedside, winced with pain, and then rolled over to grab it with his right hand. The bucket skidded across the nightstand — a wood crate — and banged onto the floor.

A thin but otherwise healthy looking woman appeared before him, kneeled down to touch his forehead and then walked out of the room with the empty bucket. Her hair was very straight and stretched down to the back of her knees. Moments later she was back with a fresh supply of water. The woman raised his head and held the cup while Napoli started gulping the water. Then she quickly pulled the cup away, shaking her head, no, before tilting the cup gently to allow Napoli to absorb small doses only.

Neither of them spoke, though Napoli was anxious to ask a hundred questions. The knot on his forehead at the time of his fall was the size of a baseball. Now, two days later, it was only slightly swollen but had turned to a red, purple and yellow wound from the edema. To show the seriousness of the injury, the woman reached for a mirror so Napoli could assess his own medical condition — a head contusion that could have killed him. A moment later the woman was gone again. Napoli didn't dare get up from his bed. For one thing, he was naked. For another, he could smell urine. He suddenly realized he had wet the bed, and the woman, whoever she was, had tried to control it with a towel wrap. How long had this been going on, he wondered?

Napoli studied his unshaven face and the ugly contusion that disguised his natural forehead. He tried to piece together the events that led to the accident but recalled little. The last thing her remembered was his being chased by a bear. A bear! He could have been torn to shreds. When the woman returned with a meal of cornbread and squash soup, Napoli sat up in his bed and did his best to bring the soup spoon to his mouth with his trembling hand, all the time watching the long-haired woman from the corner of his eye. His clothes had been washed and hung on wooden stakes driven between the wood boards of the wall. There was no electricity and no inside plumbing. A single candle lit the room. He saw the face of a slightly older woman whose skin was smooth and much younger in appearance. Though he had not eaten in two days, his stomach felt full after consuming one piece of the cornbread and a half bowl of soup. The woman encouraged him to finish the soup and, as he did so, he saw that she was wearing a wedding ring, not on her finger but around her neck.

By evening, having replenished his body with liquids, Napoli regained a little more strength. He managed to climb from his bunk and walk from the closet-sized room to the outdoors. The dwelling was not a square building but more tri-angular, tapering off to a sort of point at the far end. The structure was made of wood planks, painted black with a rusty tin roof on one side and a flat wood roof on the other. It was a shack, reasonably constructed, but still a shack. It rested in a ravine between two rigid hills near a fast-moving stream. The water splashing against the rocks echoed pleasant sounds, Napoli thought. Earlier in the day he could hear the sounds from his room. Napoli read the faded letters printed across an outside wall of the shack, *CREEK RUNNER*.

The next morning, Napoli woke up to the smell of cooked wheat germ and blackberries sitting on his night stand. The house cook was at it again, he mused. Who was this woman? He wolfed down the meal, climbed in his dungarees and hobbled to the porch, a 6' x 6' wooden platform sheltered by thatch. There he saw the mysterious long-haired woman sitting in her rocker, smoking a pipe and tossing berries to her 300-pound pet bear. She looked at Napoli and smiled. And then Napoli began asking her his long list of questions.

After 6 weeks of rehabilitation at the rustic cabin, Napoli felt it was time to leave for fear of overstaying his welcome. He paid $20 for his room and board, which was more than enough to cover the additional expenses incurred by Tree Top. After all, she had managed to live off the land for many years without cash, planting the usual corn, squash and beans and supplementing her diet with nuts and berries in the tradition of her ancestors. Rarely did she walk into town for goods. Once she went to Todd's Shoe Store in Guffey. On another trip she stopped at Rupert's dry goods store at the outskirts of Shaner where she could still exchange bushels of corn. Beyond that, she had little time or inspiration to shop, even if she had the money. No, money was not an issue.

The truth was that Napoli was fascinated with the woman but was not yet ready to make a commitment. His passionate feelings for her began to surface in the middle of their long talk that first night, which lasted until the wee hours of the morning when birds began their morning songs. The more time he spent with the 41-year- old, the more enticed he became. She was nearly twice his age. *Not my idea of a life-long partner*. Still, she was intriguing and Napoli looked forward to his nightly chats with her after dinner, a habit that deepened his interest in Tree Top's incredible past. Very rarely did she ask Napoli personal questions. She made him feel welcome and treated him not as a stranger out of the woods, but more like a brother.

One night, Napoli asked the woman why she smoked a pipe. Tree Top told him to pick up the pipe, and when he did, she said,

"The bowl is of the same red clay the Creator used to make the woman. Just as woman bears children and brings forth life, the bowl bears sacred tobacco and brings forth smoke. The stem is man and is from the plant family. Like a man, it supports the bowl, just like a man supports his family."

She showed Napoli how to place the sacred tobacco into the pipe with an ember from the fire so that it burned slowly. Then she told him,

"The smoke is the breath of the Creator. When you draw the smoke into your body, you will be cleansed and made whole. When the smoke leaves your mouth, it will rise to the Creator. All of your hopes and desires will be taken to him in the smoke. The truth in your soul will be shown to him when you smoke the pipe...If you are not true, do not smoke the pipe....

On their last night together, Napoli blurted out, "Come back to Rillton with me." Tree Top replied, "It is not my place." "But it was the place of your ancestors. And it was Rilla's place," Napoli argued. Tree Top said nothing but did have an interested look on her face, he thought. "It could be your place. Our place," he said. The silence that followed was awkward, if not deafening, to Napoli's ears, for silence was the one thing he did not want to hear. His offer was rejected, pure and simple. That was clear.

The next morning when Napoli gathered up his gear and said his goodbye, Tree Top stood at his side, saying nothing — no pleas, no questions, no emotion, no movement, except for her hair brushing against her face from the slight breeze.

Once Napoli reached the outskirts of Rillton and saw the dirt and dust hovering above the mine, he stopped dead in his tracks and wondered if that dreadful smoke would ever clear the air. A moment later, Napoli turned around and headed back to Guffey. When he got there, he told Tree Top he was ready to smoke her peace pipe.

21
THE DEPRESSION

In 1925 the mine in Rillton produced 10 percent less than it did in 1919 with fewer workers. Unemployment continued to grow from 1926 through 1929 even before the stock market crash in Oct., 1929. By 1930, when demand for coal fell by 50 percent, the work force was down to 125 men, only a fourth of what it was when the mine opened. Those that kept their jobs were forced to take large pay cuts. Instead of earning $100 per month, the pay was now $50. House rent remained at $25. Every penny earned or saved was precious. The dire predicament facing the average worker was not loss of money from the stock market but the loss of a job during hard economic times which began even before the crash.

RILLTON

It was possible for a family of five to budget their way out of the crises. Food prices were still affordable:

3 lb. pure lard	0.29
2 lb. boiling meat	0.25
1 lb. pork shoulder	0.13
4 cans red beans	0.25
4 cans pork and beans	0.25
1 peck potatoes	0.39
3 lb. ground meat	0.45
2 boxes shredded wheat	0.21
3 large bottles of milk	0.23
1 loaf of Vienna bread	0.05
2 lb. coffee	0.37

But for a family of 10 or 12, even after a steady diet of soup day after day, the debt owed to the company store could only get worse.

Major changes came at the end of the Roaring Twenties era. Railroad trains from Irwin stopped running in 1928. The mail was now hauled by trolley. Because of declining passengers, the trolley business was not doing well. Improvements to the Clay Pike highway led the way for more and more vehicular traffic along that route. To reduce costs, the trolley company began using one conductor instead of two. Then they eliminated the open-air trolley which had been a big hit for summer travelers. Still, they continued to lose money. In April 1931, the Irwin-Herminie Traction Company replaced the trolley with a large Studebaker bus but kept the same schedule. The last service out of Herminie was at midnight. The fare to Irwin increased to 25 cents.

During the Depression, men hopped trains from mine to mine, looking for a free meal. If clothing could not be handed down for someone else to use, women cut up the material into scraps to make quilts. Nothing was wasted, especially food. It was a time when people didn't feel entitled. They developed a taste for cheaper cuts of meat, perhaps sausage and scrapple (pork rinds and corn meal). They ate mostly from their gardens. Any dessert came from fruit trees. Birthday presents might not be handed out until the next Christmas. Some sold their furniture for pennies on the dollar and then sat on orange crates until someone could find a decent job. Before the election of 1932, families would gather around the radio listening to the speeches of Willkie and Roosevelt. People were looking for stabilization, something good to happen, anything to get out of the Depression.

Because folks all over town began planting their own vegetables, farmers were especially hit hard, including John Sauer. Food prices continued to fall to the point where it was no longer beneficial to harvest the excess crops. For a few pennies, customers were permitted to pick their own apples, berries, squash and corn. Still, Sauer ended up selling most of his chickens just to make ends meet.

RILLTON

Barbara E. Zimmer moved into the Sauer farmhouse with her 6 year old son William in 1919 for a short time. William attended Rillton School and stayed with the grandparents while Barbara lived and worked as a cook in a restaurant in downtown Greensburg. Thereafter, she worked as a butter girl, then as a waitress at a hotel until it shut down in 1929. She then got a job at the University Club in downtown Pittsburgh and later on became a hostess. By 1934, in spite of the depression, she was doing vey well. That year she boarded a ship to Havana, Cuba and vacationed for 2 weeks with her friends. The dreams she was having on the immigration ship *Camapnia* 27 years earlier were finally coming true.

But in 1929, things were tight. Bill Zimmer was forced to drop out of school before graduating. He made it through the 11th grade, then started washing windows in Irwin and later did odd jobs as a plumber and a pipe fitter in Jeanette. The combined income between Barbara and Bill was enough to keep the farm going.

Bill used to pal around with a kid named Mike Horvath. Mike dropped out of school at age 16 to work in the mines alongside his father, first in Rillton, then in Lowber, until both mines closed. While growing up in Rillton, they would walk the back roads and fields of Rillton, tramp through the creeks and look for wildlife. Mike was quite the hunter and would track down any game animal in sight. Bill hardly ever hunted except for shooting rabbits and pheasants and ridding groundhogs from the vegetable gardens at the Sauer farm. Towards the end of the Depression, Horvath landed a job as a mechanic in Adamsburg. After 3 months on his new job, Mike bought a car. Thereafter, the two pals spent Saturday nights hunting for single women.

Typically, Mike and Bill frequented such places as the Victoria-Italian Club of Rillton (which everyone called simply, the Italian Club), The Korner Bar in Hahntown, the American Legion in Irwin and the Moose Hall in Jeanette. At other times they would venture to the Keystone Bar or the Creighton Hotel, which later became Julie's Hotel in Herminie. One night, Mike suggested they stop at the Kooketz Tavern near Adamsburg. When they got there, the place was jammed packed with old men, playing pool and smoking cigars. However, they heard music and noticed young women entering the room on other side of the bar. They went over to investigate.

The music coming from the phonograph sounded wonderful, with songs like *42nd Street, Over The Rainbow, I'm Gonna Sit Right Down and Write Myself a Letter* and *Just a Gigolo.* They were enthralled with the music and laughter and dancing of the youngsters, all of which created a mood that seemed to melt away the blues of the Depression. They went back to the dance room the next week, and the week after that.

In the summer of 1939, Bill and Mike spent less time carousing bars and more time at the nondrinking side of the Kooketz Dance Hall. It was there that they met the three Parnell sisters. They were witty and sociable, though they didn't do much dancing. On the way home, Bill said he liked Fanny Parnell because she was as smart as a whip.

On the morning of Nov. 23, 1932, students from Sewickley Twp. School District took a field trip to the gravesite of Monacutucca's son[3] and placed a marker at the site to commemorate General Braddock's travels through Sewickley Twp.

On the same morning, a few days before Thanksgiving, George Parnell and his 16-year-old son Bud began cleaning up the entry to the main motor road. Two minutes later, a rock slide struck the trolley, killing George instantly. Bud Parnell escaped the tragedy, but because he was not an adult, he could no longer work the mine. And so the remaining nine members of the Parnell family were forced out of their home once again.

The Parnell's had already relocated three times in the last seven years. They simply outgrew the small house at Edna No. 1 mine. The children slept in bunk beds — four girls in one bedroom and four boys in the other. When another miner purchased their rental house, they moved to Edna No. 2 Mine, roughly two miles away, and rented a much larger, 3-bedroom

---

[3] It is located 1 mile from Rillton on Braddock Road

single family house with yards in the front and back. The oldest son Bud was nearly crippled from an auto accident at a very young age and could not work most jobs. But somehow he managed to work the mine alongside his father for 2 years, beginning at age 14, which meant additional income. Everyone seemed happy.

The unfortunate demise of George Parnell could not have come at a worse time. Economic strife during the Great Depression had hit a low point. More workers were being laid off. The unemployment rate hit 24.9 percent. Wages paid to those still hanging onto their jobs were reduced. Even school teachers' salaries were cut in half.

Widow Hulda Parnell found a small house to rent in nearby Arona for the next four years. Income was non-existent for several months, but as head of household, she qualified for a job as a seamstress in Jeanette under the new WPA Program, earning $1 a day.

Bud tried his best to find odd jobs, earning not wages but food and other household items for his services. One day he came home with a rocker and gave it to his older brother Earl as a birthday present. Everyone in the family used it. In the summer, the rocker sat on the front porch. In the winter, it was taken to the living room.

The oldest daughter Olive was married to a miner who was also killed in a mine. Olive took up a job at Grant's in Jeanette, bought a car and drove her mother to work each day.

In 1936, the family moved once again to an old grey farmhouse near the Edna No. 1 mine. Even though the boys dropped school by the 8th grade to find jobs, three younger sisters were bused to Harrold Middle School in Hempfield Twp. It was a good school with good teachers. Later on, Hulda encouraged the girls to attend high school, though Hempfield Twp. had no high school at that time. Students could choose to attend a surrounding school such as Jeanette, Greensburg or Norwin but they had to find their own transportation. The girls chose Norwin. Getting there was not easy.

In December 1938 Ruth Ann Parnell, whom everyone called Fanny, got up at 5 a.m., walked three miles up a narrow snow-covered road to catch the trolley from Adamsburg to Irwin. Twenty minutes later, she hopped off the trolley at Main Street and walked another four blocks to the Norwin High School. At 2 p.m. she raced through her homework. There was simply no time to do it at home. She boarded the trolley a little after 3 p.m. for the reverse trip and made it home just before the 5 p.m. dinner. After dinner, she helped with chores, listened to radio broadcasts with her family and plopped into bed. The next day, she did it all over again.

The school days at Norwin were challenging, not because of the long hours or the long trips or even the schoolwork. Fanny was in fact a straight A-student. She loved English class and especially Music class. One day she found herself tinkering on the piano at school, trying to reproduce the sound of a classical piano concerto she heard over the radio. The music teacher overheard the piano tinkling and rewarded Fanny with a free lesson.

A key problem for Fanny was the lack of friends at Norwin. But she did have old friends from Harrold Middle and one night they dragged her to a place called Jimmy Kooketz. Kooketz was a Harrold school bus driver during the day but also ran a tavern outside of the Edna No. 1 mine at night. He loved kids and cleared a space opposite the bar for them to dance on weekends. And so Fanny and her friends spent Saturday nights listening to the big band sounds at the Jimmy Kootetz dance hall. It was there that Fanny met her sweetheart shortly before World War II.

Rillton mine, which supported 520 workers in 1910, had only 125 workers by 1930. The mine finally shut down in 1938.

Miners scrambled to find jobs at mines outside of Rillton in order to take advantage of the opportunity. It wasn't easy. The Herminie mine had already shut down in 1937. The Lowber mine closed in 1938 and the Edna No. 1 mine in 1939. Work was available at Edna No. 2, but not until 1945. The Adams Mine in Hahntown also eventually offered jobs, but not until 1953. The fact remained that if residents wanted to remain in Rillton, they were obligated to find another line of work.

Frank Cheselske started a grocery in the basement of his home in 1939 about 100 feet from the old Company Store. Everyone called him Butch. After a few years, Butch added a regular store to the front of his home and cleared out a small space for parking. By the mid 1940s he was delivering groceries to people all over town, since many residents were without vehicles. By the early 50s, the store's regular customers were school children who would stop by after school to buy Blackjack gum, candy cigarettes, root beer barrels, wax lips, wax pop bottles, licorice sticks for a penny a piece, or else a Sugar Daddy, Necco wafers, Good and Plenty or a Dreamsicle for a nickel.

Trozzo's feed and supply store, originally opened in 1905, expanded operations after acquiring some of the tools from the old Charles E. Parr Store. Charles Trozzo, a WW I veteran, worked the store full time, along with his two sons. John Horvat started a welding business from his home. John J. Bruno tried to get back into liquor sales. Tony Shuster dropped out of high school to work with his uncle Frank in the construction business before being drafted into the Armed Services. Most workers, however, found employment in industrial cities in or near Pittsburgh, including foundries and glass factories located in Jeanette. They would hop the bus to Irwin and then board a streetcar to other cities. Only a few rode automobiles.

The great debate among politicians and scholars was whether FDR's New Deal really helped to end the Depression, a time when his policies greatly increased the role of the federal government. The government created a National Labor Relations Board, which encouraged increased wages and the growth of labor unions. This was supposed to increase consumer spending. However, most people hid the money under mattresses or tucked it away into savings, never really sure when the next shop, factory or foundry would shut down.

In late 1938, the economic recovery began to waggle upward again but many argued this was temporary, that WW II was what really brought the Depression to an end. For the most part, the argument held true for the people living in Rillton.

24

WORLD WAR II

After the Japanese struck Pearl Harbor, President Roosevelt delivered a war message to Congress. He began, "*Yesterday, December 7, 1941 — a date which will live in infamy — the United States of America was suddenly and deliberately attacked by naval and air forces of the Empire of Japan. Always will we remember the character of the onslaught against us ...*"

Twenty-four-year-old Mike Russin from Rillton signed up to join the Army immediately. Within a year, many others from Rillton signed up for military service, including Frank Anzur, Fred Augay, David Bazzo, Angelo Bazzo, Miller Ekovich, John and Nick Feals, David Anthony Horvat, Joseph Horvath, the four Mudrak boys (Andrew, Frank, Martin and Steven), Mike Kolesar, Frank Pekarsky,

Nick Perrino, Elton and Perry Plues, Frank Yurkovich, Frank Zappa and others.

Of the 825 people living in Rillton during World War II, 140 men and women marched off to war. The majority of entrants served after getting their draft notices which in some cases did not arrive until 1943 or 1944, well after American was deeply entrenched into the two separate theaters of war: Europe and the Pacific.

Increasing numbers of women worked in the factories to make up for shortages of labor. Children worked the farm fields, planting Victory Gardens to make up for food shortages. At night they hauled coal from the mines to heat the furnaces. A bucket of coal could provide heat for the entire night. It seemed that everyone was busy doing something in the war effort.

In the spring of 1942, the government began a food rationing system. It was complicated. War Ration Books were issued to each person of the family, even the very young. The books held stamps with assigned point values. A customer could only get one pound of coffee during a five-week period, for example. Besides coffee, rationed foods included sugar, butter, fat, beef, chicken, lamb, pork, hot dogs, canned fish, dried beans, baked beans, ketchup and prepared baby food. Ships that normally transported these items were being used in the massive war effort. Metal was needed for war material and couldn't be spared for canned goods. Butter was soon replaced with Oleo. Spam became popular. Everyone ate it.

Household cooks were constantly searching for food substitutes, new recipes or simple ideas to utilize more un-rationed food. Examples of un-rationed foods were eggs, fresh produce, fresh fish, bread, cereal, milk, spaghetti and macaroni, jams and jellies. The problem, though, was the frequent shortages of these items. There was a lot of hoarding, items sold in the black market and deals made under the table. Whenever a family came up with a few extra steaks, no one questioned it. Everyone at one time or other traded hoarded items for more coffee and other desired products with the neighbors down the street.

As soldiers were being trained for deployment across the seas to Europe and to the small islands of the Pacific in 1942, Bill Zimmer sat uncomfortably at his small rental house on Third Street in Irwin. Night after night, he wondered just when he would receive his draft notice in the mail. Other friends he knew in Rillton had already gotten their notices — Sam Yackovich, Robert Pekarsky, William Bruno, David Baughman. It was a matter of time. But it was also disconcerting. He had been married to Fanny Parnell for less than a year and they were expecting a child. He had plenty of work and money from the many overtime hours spent at the pipe foundry in Jeanette. But the **A** sticker on his car windshield severely restricted his gasoline purchases. He was allowed just enough gas to get him to and from his workplace with hardly any leftover to get to the grocer down the street, much less to the farmhouse in Rillton, which was now vacant, unoccupied and needed work. What should they do with the house?

The farmhouse in Rillton had received little attention since the passing of Barbara Sauer in December 1938. John Sauer tried his best to work the farm fields in the spring of 1941 but struggled with motivation. He was aging rapidly and no one was sure if he would make it through the winter. Sauer had already deeded the farm over to Barbara E on July 17, 1941, knowing that his days were numbered. On an early morning in July, 1942, Sauer died from a sudden heart attack on the front porch of the house he built in Rillton.

Barbara E, now the official owner of the property, was living and working in downtown Pittsburgh and was in no position to manage the property. There was no one left to maintain the old farmhouse except Bill. But Bill had neither the time nor enough gas to manage the property without help. The solution was to rent the house, in this case to a family in dire need of bedroom space. Meanwhile, the military service issue was still up in the air.

The U.S. Army became a global force within the space of three years. In 1939, the regular army numbered 188,000. With the outbreak of the war in Europe, there was a rapid increase in soldiers. By the time the Japanese attack came in late 1941, army personnel already totaled 1.68 million. Before the end of the war, it expanded to 8.29 million.

The full thrust of the European Theater of Operations did not come until December 1944 when 43 divisions were sent to the German front. William J. Zimmer got his draft notice into the U.S. Army on November 18, 1943, the same day as his 30th birthday. The following day he reported for duty, saying goodbye to his wife and two small children. Fanny prepared her mind for the worst as Bill prepared himself for the long trip to Indiantown Gap, Pa. as a part of the 28th Infantry Division.

The 28th Infantry was no slouchy operation. In fact it was the oldest division in the armed services, having been in existence since 1747 when Benjamin Franklin came up with the idea of a national guard. The army called it the Keystone Division, identified by a red keystone patch. The Germans, no strangers to the 28th, called them the Bloody Bucket Division, not just referring to the red keystone patch but an acknowledgement of the fury in which they fought during World War I.

After three months of intense training, Zimmer was sent to Camp Breckenridge, Ky for special training as a combat engineer. The focus of his Light Bridge unit was the quick building of bridges across treacherous mountain streams. It required additional training at Camp Forrest, Tn. for another four months and then some time at Camp

Shanks, N.Y. After nearly a full year of training exercises, Zimmer and his group of engineers embarked for overseas operations on Oct. 22, 1944.

Twenty-six years after the climax of World War I, the 28th Infantry Division from Pennsylvania was again riding through France, this time en route to the outskirts of Germany. When they rolled down the highways of France, the doughboys met cheering crowds jamming the roadsides. They were showered with fruit, wine and shouts of "Vive les Americains."

Their mission was to punch through the rugged German defenses known as the Seigfried Line inside the gloomy Hurtgen Forest. Even if there had been no defending Germans, traversing the forest would have been difficult. Entrenched with Nazis, the entry was doubly forbidding. There were 18,000 pillboxes (concrete bunkers) everywhere. Odds did not favor the 28th. After 5 days of quiet preparation, the troops were ready for the D-Day Operation on Nov. 2, 1944.

The Keystone men stormed through the snow-blanketed fields and hacked away at the Line for ten days, absorbing continual shelling from enemy fire. During the initial attack, the combat engineers acted as infantry, but soon they became intellectually challenged, even preoccupied, with the pillboxes. *How can we knock them out?*

By day 3 they tossed away the field manual and found new ways to destroy the emplacements using various techniques — plain fire, better use of TNT and a dozer blade to pile dirt over the super-structures. The 28th and the combat team made deep penetrations into what they now called Pillbox country. A month later, the tempo of severe, bitter fighting slowed to a crawl. When German radio declared the Red Buckets wiped out, the 28th began sounding off their new motto: *Roll On.*

On Dec. 16, the Germans pulled a surprise attack. Nine of its best divisions hammered away at the 28th with artillery and mortars that ripped into a 25-mile sector. The Keystone division was outnumbered, overrun and cut off but refused to stop fighting. The Germans struck again and again as the day wore on. Encircled, many of the doughboys fought and died in their places.

The survivors of the 28th snapped under the excessive pressure and pulled back on Dec. 22. But against the nine German divisions, the Bloody Bucket Division held so firmly that not only was the Wehrmacht (German Army) timetable for cutting off the Americans from the English Allies completely thrown off schedule but the entire mission was eventually aborted. Meanwhile, there remained a bulge in the newly drawn map of the Seigfried Line. The press was now calling it the *Battle of the Bulge.*

Each evening Ruth (Fanny) Zimmer listened to the overseas reports from Edward R. Murrow, who provided the latest updates on the battles of the Pacific and across Europe. Tension mounted each time she heard the word *bulge*. And the mere mention of the 28th Infantry Division sent her heart pounding. She could only deduce the number of casualties from the pictures painted in her head from Murrow's words. The death toll was seldom, if ever, talked about on radio or in the films that ran in local theaters. But she knew from the stories told by her family and neighbors that behind the scenes such battles could only result in severe casualties on both sides of the infamous Seigfried Line. Still, there was a sense of excitement that everyone was joining together against a common enemy, all making sacrifices that were expected. In a strange way, it was sometimes a joyful experience for her but a scary time as well.

To help get her mind off the war, Fanny spent her evenings listening to the big band music played on the radio. On Saturday afternoons she hauled her two young children to the matinee at the Town Theater in Irwin where they ran feature films like *Frankenstein, King Kong, Mr. Smith Goes to Washington, Wizard of Oz, Bambi, Since You Went Away, Mrs. Miniver* and the latest show, *This is The Army*. Fanny had two months to go before the delivery of her third child. In November 1944, she moved in with her mother, who was now back in Arona.

After being overrun by the unexpected blow of the Wehrmacht, American units began fleeing westward. At the same time combat engineers attached with the

101st Airborne (aka The Screaming Eagles) raced eastward via huge carrier trucks to defend against the capture of Bastogne. Civilians called out, "The Germans are coming that way," to which the engineers answered, "We know it. We're the welcoming committee."

During the latter stages of the conflict, the tactics employed by a handful of engineer battalions proved to be vital. The Kraut Command tried time and again to break through circular defense of the town but each time they were repulsed with heavy losses. During the siege, a Screaming Eagle remarked, "They've got us surrounded — the poor bastards." Knowing that the Germans were intent on finding a breakthrough point, engineers set up strategic weak points, purposefully allowing a few tanks to enter before counterattacking with tank destroyers and bazookas. The infantry following behind was cut to ribbons by Eagle soldiers. At least 148 tanks were knocked out before the battle ended on Dec. 27.

The Battle of the Bulge was the last major German offensive on the western front. In terms of casualties, it was the worst battle for American forces. Of the 500,000 men and women who fought there, the United States suffered 80,000 casualties. German losses were roughly the same, not including 100,000 taken as prisoners. The British lost 1,400.

25

THE POST WAR

On January 8, Hitler withdrew his forces from the Bulge. His final defeat in the war came a few months later. When the war with Germany ended officially on May 8, 1945, millions of people celebrated in the streets. But the celebration was short-lived. The rationing of food and clothing continued. Rubber, gasoline and leather goods were hard hit. Instead of wearing Buster Brown leather shoes, children were now wearing Red Ball canvas top shoes. Even after the surrender of Japan on August 15, 1945, rationing continued. But the world was at peace. Everyone in America seemed happy.

Because of rationing, many products were not purchased and the extra money was stashed away. Young couples started having babies again at an early age after steadily building up their savings during the war. In addition, public policy encouraged the raising of families. The new GI bill enabled many GIs to go to school at government expense, to purchase homes for as little as $1 down and to pay low interest rates on their loans. During the post-war boom, the demand for a home in the suburbs, a car, a refrigerator and a washing machine — all of the things imagined as a part of the American Dream — began to increase.

One of the problems that GIs faced upon their return to the United States was the availability of jobs. Not all of the GIs returning to Rillton looked for work in the local factories. America was on the move. There was a need for car salesmen, auto repairmen, appliance repairmen, telephone workers, truck drivers and deliverymen. Some of the veterans returned to their old businesses but others decided to start new ones.

Howard Bruno, combat engineer, started Bruno's Restaurant in 1947 on Irwin-Herminie Road. Nick and John Feals opened Feal's Garage in 1948 near Bruno's restaurant. Teddy Cheselske worked his father's grocery store where business started booming after the rationing had ended. Angelo Bazzo opened an ice cream shop. A milkshake cost 25 cents. Joe Kertis opened a barbershop. Haircuts cost 50 cents. T.C. Woomer operated a steel fabricating company in one of the old Westmoreland Coal Company buildings, manufacturing Eagle Jet Spreaders used to spread ashes and salt on roads during the winter months. Tony Shuster set up Shuster's Construction in

1950, bought the old slate dump and built a supply business. Later, the company specialized in pre-hung door units and ultimately sold the units worldwide.

On Christmas Eve in 1951, a house fire nearly destroyed the two-unit residential dwelling at the corner of Irwin-Herminie Road and Rillton Road. David Bazzo purchased the building in 1952 and started a real estate and insurance agency. A volunteer fire department building was not constructed until 1958.

After Bill Zimmer was discharged from active duty in November 1945, he met with a guy named Cervi who lined him up with a new job at the Fort Pitt Brewing Company in Jeanette. They needed a boiler man and Zimmer fit the position perfectly. Although the job description was boiler maintenance, Zimmer viewed it as an engineer's dream. He loved the work and habitually arrived on the job early each morning, tinkering on pipes, adjusting steam pressure valves, tapping on gauges and re-fitting connections that other workers hardly knew existed. At the end of the day, each kettle had to be perfectly clean; otherwise, Zimmer wasn't happy. Along with his new job came the dream of a new house, a dream that was out of reach for the moment but kept Bill's spirits alive. Initially Bill and Fanny rented a small asphalt-shingle house near the Edna No. 1 mine with no yard to speak of. It had a dirt driveway that ran alongside the dwelling to the front door, which was located at the rear of the house. Near the entrance was a small concrete porch with no railing. The 4 rooms inside were small, but the rent was low and there wasn't much furniture to go around anyway.

After a year of renting, Bill was getting antsy. Instead of buying a new home, he thought about building one near the old farmhouse in Rillton. But he changed his mind again and decided as a temporary measure to fix up the old farmhouse. Initially Ruth opposed the idea. She was reluctant to move into the house — any house — without electricity. She called on her brother George Parnell, Jr. to install the electric. The work was delayed for 6 months as the power company seemed to be in no hurry to run a power pole to the property.

Meanwhile, Bill worked on the heating. That too was delayed because the installation of radiators meant tearing into the plaster ceilings in order to run the required piping, much to the chagrin of the tenants. It took six trips and a borrowed truck to get enough salvaged piping from the brewery and six months of back-breaking labor to rough-plumb the project. Bill had to piece together iron platelets to assemble a coal furnace, cut through floors and ceilings, and route the steam pipes from the radiators to an old, scrapped boiler. It also took six cases of beer to maintain his positive attitude. Another month rolled by. Still, the job was not finished.

In the early spring, Zimmer came home from work and learned that the red-headed 7-year-old neighbor kid had pushed his 4-year-old boy from his tricycle and off the edge of the 3-foot high porch. He slumped down in a chair and declared it was time to move to Rillton, plumbing or no plumbing.

In April 1947, the Zimmer family bumped their way down the dusty road to Rillton in a '45 Plymouth coup. There were no seatbelts. The 3 kids stood up on the back seat to look out the front, rear and side windows along the way to their new home.

The gravel road into Rillton changed to dirt once they passed Butch's grocery store and headed up the hill. At the top of the hill, the road narrowed and descended straight down the other side, then meandered through a canopy of tall trees. The rutted road produced new rattling sounds from the car's frame but the woodlands were very scenic. There were no houses along this road except for a single block-foundation home extending 4 feet above ground. It was covered with a flat roof made of tar paper. A family of four resided inside. Two hundred yards beyond it stood the old, slightly dilapidated 2-story farmhouse amidst a sea of weeds. That was the new home. Bill parked the car close to some steps leading up an embankment and to a brick walkway, which was covered with weeds and nettles.

"Watch out for the nettles," Bill cautioned.

"What are nettles?" 5-year-old Barbara asked.

"They sting. So don't touch 'em!" he said.

The farmhouse, with its saggy, wooden front porch and loose tongue and groove siding was situated some 50 yards away and nearly halfway up yet another hill. Compared to the little rental house back in Adamsburg, though, it was a castle. "Well, kids, this is your new home," Bill said, beaming.

Inside, conditions were worse than the outside. The former tenants, jobless and 4 months behind on rent, allowed the home to deteriorate. "Renting to those people … a mistake," Bill muttered. The tenants apparently packed up and moved out in a hurry, leaving behind furniture and junk not worth keeping. There were paint spills on the kitchen floor, broken windows, and broken latches on the kitchen cabinet doors.

Bill opened one of the kitchen cupboards and Fanny screamed, "Snake!" Little 3-year-old Debbie screamed too. Whenever her Mum did something, she did it too. Bill very calmly placed a soiled towel over the 4 foot snake, picked up the rusty, tin pot and replied, "It's just a black snake." "Get it outside. OUTSIDE," Fanny demanded. Debbie screamed again. Bill carried the sheltered reptile to the back porch and dumped it in the tall weeds where it instantly disappeared into its natural environment. Four-year-old Tommy asked, "Why didn't you just kill it?" Bill gazed momentarily at the overgrown vegetation surrounding the porch, then looked at his son and replied, "Never kill a black snake."

Throughout her whole life, Fanny had never been a demanding person. Being next to the youngest of eight Parnell children, she spent the greater part of her life learning to share food, toys, holiday celebrations and whatever else was required for the sake of harmony within the family. Her clothes were, for the most part, hand-me-downs from other siblings. She had little girl fantasies, like attending a musical symphony or performing a piano solo in front of a theatre-filled audience or just going for a ride in Henry Ford's new convertible but did not take these thoughts seriously. Life in the patch would not allow it. Her days were filled with household chores, getting to school on time, making do with the war rations and re-adjusting to a temporary move to yet another small town until something better, or worse, came along. To her, life was a never-ending journey of compromises.

But now, after two months of trying to cope with the challenges of the old farmhouse in Rillton, she suddenly came to realize that the house would never be a temporary place to stay, rather a permanent homestead for years to come. On a quiet summer night in June, she abruptly sat up in bed and announced, "I want a commode." Bill said nothing. "And I want a bathroom tub… with hot water."

The commode was installed the very next weekend and was flushed by the kids all day long. It worked wonderfully. Before the commode was installed, everyone had to exit the cellar door, negotiate the wobbly brick steps, walk 30 paces up a slight hill to get to the outhouse which stunk to high heaven.

In the weeks ahead, Bill installed a commercial size water heater which required pipes of all sizes running in all directions along the ceilings of the three contiguous cellars. At least now there was hot water, if not a tub. Money for that would come a little later. Bill promised.

In the early spring, Bill planted a vegetable garden, his first one in years. He went all out, cutting down the overgrown weeds and nettles in front of the house with his scythe, then spading the rich clay soil with his only shovel. He cleared away the tall weeds around the fruit trees — 2 pear, 4 walnut, 4 apple, 1 peach, 1 plum, 1 cherry and a gooseberry bush. The vegetable garden, though small, was planted a little too close to the house and invited rabbits and groundhogs to conveniently find refuge under the porch. Despite the vermin, the summer harvest was surprisingly bountiful, especially the cabbages, radishes and beans. Tommy planted the beans by poking the soil with his index finger, then dropping a single bean in each hole. The beans were the best ever, Bill said. Next year the garden would be planted in the back of the house, he added.

One day Bill brought home a puppy. The previous owner said it was part German shepherd but would grow into a medium-sized dog. Its paws looked unusually large but everyone thought the dog was cute. Each month the dog grew by leaps and bounds. By the sixth month, not only did it already surpass the height of a medium-sized pooch, but it looked rather formidable, more like a wolf than a dog. The neighbors looked wary. Sometimes the dog was seen near Butches' when the kids bought candy. More often it was seen near the school.

Dutch followed the kids everywhere they went and had an incredible biological clock. He knew when the kids got out of school and would run to the school grounds moments before the dismissal bell rang. He'd walk from the shanty to the front porch each day, waiting for Bill to go to work. Dutch was quite a dog, even though he really did look like a wolf. The kids pretended he was Rin Tin Tin.

RILLTON

In the early summer, Tommy led Dutch on long exploration through the woods to the top of the ridge where the forest ended and a grassy field came into view. Beautiful pheasants fluttered. A red fox slipped into the tall grass. A large Pileated woodpecker hammered away at an old Elm. So wonderful was this adventure, the boy found it difficult to leave. As he headed back through the forest, he realized his dog had suddenly disappeared. Somewhat concerned, he ran home, only to see Dutch resting on the front porch, waiting for the boy to show up for dinner.

There was only one male instructor at the Rillton School in the late 40s. Built in 1917, Rillton School was an L-shaped, two-story wooden building painted white. First through fourth-grade students held classes on the first floor; fifth and sixth-grade students were on the second floor. A wrought iron fire escape stairway hung on the outer back wall near the corner of the L and had a torpedo-like iron weight that kept the stairway horizontal.

In the late summer of 1947, five-year-old Barbara Zimmer helped her mother pick out six new dresses at Grant's — five for school and one for church on Sunday. A week later she attended the first grade at school for the very first time. She walked down the dirt road about a quarter of a mile, then up a hill and down the other side to reach the school. Third-grader Eleanor Barbara Horvath, her closest neighbor and first real friend, walked with her and answered questions about what to do, what to say and what not to say, particularly in front of Mrs. Seneff.

Mrs. Seneff looked very much like the school marm depicted in comic books — short in stature, thin, a drawn-in face behind oval glasses and her hair in a bun. Very strict and never offering a smile, most kids cannot recall learning a single thing from her. She was always fussy about one thing or the other — tardiness, not paying attention, not speaking up. Not sitting up straight, of course, was paramount. That was every bit as important as reciting the Pledge of Allegiance. Mrs. Seneff grumbled about art class and wished the school administrators had never allowed finger painting. If a pupil got too messy, Mrs. Seneff would rant and rave for several minutes. Barbara would come home after school, convinced that the teacher didn't like her. Every kid thought that.

The next year was different. A new first-and-second-grade teacher named Mary Welty came to town. She too was short in stature but much younger. She had sparkling blue eyes and was full of energy. It was her first teaching job. On the first day of school, across the top of the blackboard she hand-wrote the alphabet, A to Z, in capital letters and then again with the scripted lowercase letters beneath. The third and fourth entries contained the printed letters.

Her handwriting was perfect. By the end of the semester, all but a few students had developed nearly perfect handwriting as well. Beyond being patient and understanding, she was as interested in her students' lives and daily activities as she was in teaching reading and writing. She loved teaching English, which was her major subject in college.

Miss Welty made everything fun. One day just before the afternoon classes began, she held an impromptu reading contest, scribbling two-syllable words across the blackboard. She asked first-graders to try sounding out the correct pronunciation. Now the students, used to reading simple words, like Dick, Jane, Puff and Spot, were suddenly faced with the word *husband*. Miss Welty was proud when Evy Nesbitt sounded out the correct answer. Many third-graders had trouble with that word, Miss Welty declared.

The kids made up a schoolyard game called Cops and Robbers. The Cops were the fifth and sixth-graders. The robbers, first through fourth-graders. It was the cop's job to run down as many robbers as possible and throw them in jail, which was behind an imaginary line under the fire escape. The only way to get out of jail was for another robber to touch the buzzer (i.e., the iron weight dangling from the elevated wrought iron stairway).

Given that the robbers outnumbered the cops by nearly four to one, their tactic was to assemble at the top of the hill, some 35 yards away, then rush down the hill en masse through the ring of defenses in order to get to the buzzer. The defense typically was a slip shot affair, the cops doing their best to lock arms in a semi-circle. The little robbers, wiggling around and between the long legs of the defending cops, would get through the pathetic defense just about every time. Some kid would touch the buzzer and make a *buzz* noise. Captives would flee in all directions. Some would get caught and thrown back in jail while some escapees would run around the building. Eventually, though, they would gather at the top of the hill and do it all over again.

One day after some careless boy smashed his head against the 50-pound buzzer, Miss Welty put an end to the Cops and Robbers game. But she provided enough alternate games on the playground to keep students active — dodge-ball, soccer (using a basketball) and baseball. It didn't matter that she only taught the first and second grade students. She invited older students to join the fun too. Sometimes she would umpire and at times even coach. She taught kids how to bunt a baseball.

Following a big snowstorm that struck in mid-January, Miss Welty showed the class how to make a skating path near the front door. By the end of lunch hour, it had become a solid sheet of ice. All of the kids yelled for Miss Welty to skate down the path. She did so, standing up all the way, better than most of the kids who fell flat on their rumps.

On May 1 (May Day) Miss Welty arranged to have the students vote for a May Queen and a May King. If a student got only a few votes, that student was appointed to the court. Everyone had to dress up for the ceremony which was held in the schoolyard on a bright, sunny day. Parents and photographers showed up. Pictures were printed in the local newspaper the next day.

One beautiful spring day, Miss Welty took her students on a long hike through the woods near the school. She talked about flowers and trees and anything else she thought they might like to hear. Very likely the true purpose of the trip was to erase the winter blues. But Miss Welty insisted that education outside the classroom was important.

At lunchtime, a school bell would clamor loud enough for the whole town to hear including Dutch a quarter of a mile away. The dog would bolt straight down the road at full speed to meet the kids before they reached the edge of the schoolyard on their way home to eat lunch. For Dutch, the drill had become so routine that he anticipated the timing of the ring and was able to get an early start. One day, moments after the bell sounded, Dutch stood at the front door as the children exited. They were terrorized. "It's a wolf!' some cried out and ran back inside for safety. As kids screamed, Debbie Zimmer tried to calm them down. "No, no, it's not a wolf. It's only Dutch." Moments later, Miss Welty went to the front door and vehemently ordered Dutch away from the building. Thereafter, the wolf-dog never treaded on school property.

Nicknames were common — Bugs, Si, Weed, Rip, Killer, Posey, Dodo. Ernest Anzur changed his name to Bucky. Mrs. Campoli always called her son Anthony in an effort to keep people from calling him Tony. But Anthony re-named himself Dago. Madeline Stitely was crowned May Queen. Everyone called her Taffy. When Miss Welty spoke to Robert Zimmer, he completely ignored her. She thought he had a hearing problem and conferred with his mother, who said, "Oh, he's not used to being called Robert. Everyone calls him Clipp." Thereafter, Miss Welty called Robert, "Clipp." Frank Stewart had red hair. They called him Red Grass, and after a time, simply, Grass.

During air raid drills students scrambled under their desks for safety. One day Grass became angry, not because of the inconvenience of crunching down under his desk. After all, taking time out for these drill exercises helped split up the day and was a sort of mini-recess. No, Grass was angry at Russia. In fact, he was furious. How could they threaten the school children like this after the United States helped them win the war? And when Miss Welty heard him vocalizing his displeasure, she led a classroom discussion about how that country was so very different from the United States. She talked about how the relations between these two emerging powers began to deteriorate as soon as the war came to a halt, the race among scientists to further develop the atomic bomb, the Cold War and the fears over the spread of communism. "Freedom will always win over communism," Grass stated firmly.

RILLTON

Miss Welty started another classroom discussion that focused on the names of small towns. Irwin got its name from a man named John Irwin; Hahntown from a man named Hohn; Gratztown from a Simon Gratz; Herminie from Mrs. Hermine White. Now the question was, how did Rillton get its name? No one in the class had a clue. Miss Welty thought the name might come from the creek running through town. A rill is the English word for a small stream. That could be the reason, she mused.

In the third grade, someone reported to Miss Welty the 2 boys wrestling in the ditch. The next day, she organized a wrestling contest. Anyone who wanted to wrestle could do so by signing his name to the list. Miss Welty drew a big circle in the yard, far away from the sewer ditch and acted as referee. Everyone figured Chuckie Karasek would win. Not only was he the biggest kid in class but a ruffian as well. Surprisingly, after rolling on the ground for two full minutes, it looked like Bugs Caldro had Karasek pinned. Miss Welty declared Bugs the winner on a fast three-count. Now, having won two matches in a row, Bugs was exhausted and struggled in his next match against the smallest kid in school. That match also ended on a fast count for the small kid, though no one heard the teacher actually do a count. Thereafter, the small kid was nicknamed Zip.

On the day after Labor Day in 1953 fifth-grader Russell Piovesan headed to school with a penknife in one pocket and 5 marbles in the other. By lunchtime, he had acquired 2 prize marbles from Pekarsky, 1 from Zip, 2 from Horvat and even 1 from Bugs. There was no question that Piovesan was good at marbles. He was even better at a game called "Momity Peg." Kids tried to flip a penknife from each finger, thumb, wrist, elbow and shoulder and

Weed   Miss Welty   Zip

then make it stick in the ground. A lot of kids carried penknives at that time. The loser of the game was obliged to make a small cut on his shin with the long blade of his personal penknife until he drew blood! Two days later many fifth-grade boys had shin cuts beneath their jeans. All except Piovesan.

One afternoon Miss Welty held a marble contest. She scratched a large circle in the dirt and placed marbles inside, crisscross fashion. Players knelt outside the circle and took turns trying to shoot a marble with enough force to knock one of the inner marbles outside of the circle, a distance of about 3 feet. Some of the kids wedged the shooting marble between the thumbnail and the middle part of the index finger. The better players, however, wedged it between the thumb knuckle and tip of the index finger, with the middle finger pressing against the tip of the thumb. Bugs used this technique and won first place. Piovesan came in second. Miss Welty sent pictures to the newspaper.

It was customary for Miss Welty to hand a mystery envelope to each pupil who passed her second-grade class. They were cautioned not to open the package until after graduating from high school. Otherwise, the surprise would be ruined. Years later students carefully opened the envelope to reveal the contents — old photos of their first-and second-year classes, old report cards, newspaper photos and an article of May Day, 1950. The students of Miss Welty never forgot her.

26
NEXT IN LINE

In spite of the post-war challenges, families were back together again rebuilding their lives and planning for the future as never before. Zimmer finally installed a bathtub. Now the kids could splash around in the bathroom tub instead of sitting cross-legged in the kitchen sink on Saturday nights. Neighbor Mike Horvath added another story and a half on top of the tar-papered foundation. His two daughters were overjoyed, thinking they had their own rooms until a third child came along. As the town boomed, so did the babies.

The parents of Rillton, like parents all over the United States, felt that education for children was a top priority. The focus led to great opportunities that enriched the lives of not just the kids but the parents too. Post-war parents raised a new and very different generation of children, children who never worked in coal mines. Nowadays, after doing a few household chores, they spent time doing homework or practicing musical lessons. On weekends they had time to read comic books like *Superman, Tarzan* and *Plastic Man,* watch cowboy shows on TV like *Tex Ritter* or make up their own cowboy and Indian games.

In the summer, kids swung on grape vines clinging to tall trees. They called them "monkey vines." They whittled saplings into arrows and bows, which at some point always seemed to snap when the string was drawn too tight. They tried to start fires with two pieces of flint or by rubbing sticks together, made kites from old bed sheets, stuck crabapples on the end of a stick and flung them as far into the air as they could. They stretched rubber bands from their thumbs, trying to kill flies, poked at tent worms in trees with long poles, played Jacks, Old Maid and Hop Scotch, caught frogs and crayfish and salamanders in the creek, rode down trees or spent time walking the woods or jumping the creek. Little girls picked daisy petals, wondering if he loved me or loved me not. They lay on their backs gazing at cumulous clouds overhead, day-dreaming about them and anything and everything. Post-war children spent a great deal of their time playing as well as learning.

Young Bobby Shuster used to play in the sand all day long, mixing different amounts of lime dust and water in his experiments to form new kinds of cement. Barry Horvat loved rifles and squirrel hunting and talked about his .30-06, which came out

30 "Yacht Six" when he said it. Chuckie Karasek wrapped balloons around the frame of his bike so they would rub against the spokes of front and rear wheels to sound like a motorbike. Si McCarthy lived halfway to Guffey but would walk to Rillton and play ice hockey on the frozen creek, using any tree branch that sort of looked like a hockey stick. Every kid at one time or other made a slingshot and fired crabapples from it or else hollowed out a weed stalk and blew choke cherries out the other end. And each summer, kids would dam up Rillton Creek with bags of sandy clay and create another swimming hole.

Whenever Ruth Zimmer made cinnamon rolls, using leftover bread dough, 7-year-old Julia Ann Horvath, despite being 200 yards away, would smell the sweet aroma and run over to her neighbor's kitchen to sample a fresh, warm treat. (At age 12 Julia Ann re-named herself Julieanne.) Fifty eight years later, Julieanne said, "Those rolls were like heaven to me." But the homemade pies were even better. The Zimmer kids would spend an entire morning in the briar patch picking blackberries to get a taste of sweet pie by evening. Part of the secret in pie-making was the dough. Every Mom used Crisco. A three-pound can cost 70 cents but would last all summer.

There was a short row of houses — all former coal company houses — located at the north end of Rillton along the creek. Although still a part of Rillton, technically the houses lay in North Huntington Township. The dividing line between the two townships went right through the middle of a two-family house. And so the Suglie family was ordered to pull their kids from Rillton School and send them to Norwin. Little Kenny Suglie, the fastest runner in school, suddenly disappeared from Rillton School after the third grade and never again played Rough and Tumble football.

Rough and Tumble was a game that resembled the Sack On A Mill game, except that it involved a football. The ball was hiked not through but around the legs as the center faced the scrimmage line sideways. Once the ball was hiked, everyone chased after it. Players would lateral the ball continuously until there was a fumble, at which point it was fair game to pile on top of other players until the ball came loose. Gary Sames was a puny kid, loved football and spent weeks trying to convert these R and T players into a regular football team in order to compete with the teams from other towns. In 1954, the Rillton team played Herminie and lost by 6 touchdowns. "Where was Suglie?" someone asked.

The football games, as well as the summer baseball and softball games, were played on a flattened area created from a bull-dozed section of the slate dump across from Trozzo's supply store. Exactly how the field got there was a mystery. One day, it just suddenly appeared. It quickly became a ball field as well as the Rillton playground. A few years later, the school threw in some playground equipment and a shelter. The rumor was that Frank Trozzo created the field. He was a quiet, solitary man with gentle eyes but hardly ever mingled with other people. He was usually seen at a distance, wearing an old straw hat while riding his tractor and clearing yet another nature trail for the kids, like the one behind the school, the one Miss Welty used for her nature trips. The little coal patch town of Rillton did at least have one philanthropist.

Eleanor Barbara Horvath was not so much a tomboy as she was a self-appointed leader of games. She got to say where the snow fort was built, how big and who could use it during snowball fights. In the summer, she put herself in charge of shack-building. Usually the shacks were made of tender saplings, which were easily cut with a pen knife or chopped with a hatchet. Only club members were permitted to help construct the shack. In order to become a club member, some kind of initiation was required. Her sister, Julia Ann, had to drink a full glass of "crick water". Forking over a nickel was another way of getting into the club. The important thing was to do whatever she instructed. One summer, the club decided to build a secret log cabin without telling Eleanor Barbara. It took all day to chop down one sizeable wild cherry tree, much less cut it into logs. The idea of course was dismissed. Even if the logs were cut, the insurmountable task of placing one heavy log on top of another was dubious. Nonetheless, the fallen tree caught the attention of Eleanor Barbara who became so enticed with learning the details of the secret plan that in exchange for this information she agreed to reveal the contents of a love letter written by a kid named Kirschner.

Not many of the girls were tomboys. Just as little boys imitated their fathers, the girls imitated their mothers, following in their footsteps and performing household duties. Typically, little girls wore dresses and buckled shoes to school, sat up straight, smiled warm smiles, were quiet, humble and reserved. They acted like little ladies. But they also believed in fairness and were sticklers when it came to right and wrong. Carol Bazzo threatened to sue a classmate for a quarter because he accidentally splattered ink from a desk inkwell on her sweater. She was serious. The little boy took it to heart and worried for days that he had done something wrong. He prayed to God for forgiveness. The lawsuit was never filed.

Both little boys and girls attended Sunday school, followed the instructions of their teachers, listened to their parents and generally tried to become good citizens. Except for the Quaker Church (which later became the Mars Hill Baptist Church) Rillton had no churches. Catholics attended mass at St. Edwards in Herminie. Protestants rode the bus to Irwin. Charles Pozniak (Posey) never understood why Jerry Montini could not, because of his religion, eat meat on Friday, but they respected each other's religious customs as well as their choices for President. Never mind that Eisenhower won the race over Adlai Stevenson. Everyone backed the President regardless. The only real arguments happened on the ball field after someone called a ball a strike.

Kids used to make their own Halloween costumes and go trick or treating without adult supervision. Before handing out candy, the homeowners would spend several minutes trying to guess who exactly was behind the mask. Then the kids would shed the masks and state their names. By the end of the evening, kids got to know the names and faces of the parents on the block. But by then, they were lucky to get beyond 10 houses before it was time to head home. Rarely did the kids soap car windows or throw corn at passing vehicles.

There were two really good areas for sled-riding: the main road into Rillton from the Bazzo Agency to the post office, about 200 yards straight down; and another steep road through the middle of town that crossed three streets and ended at the coal mine across the Rillton Creek. Sledding, for the most part, took place after dinner when it was dark. There were no traffic controls in town and very few street lights. Whenever a kid saw car lights, the word got out quickly and all sled activity came to a halt until the vehicle was out of sight.

In 1953, a little girl dressed in a white ruffled dress and wearing a shelled necklace walked to Rillton School from the hills of Guffey. She had a round face, dark eyes, red-brown skin and long black hair, which was twisted into two braids that dangled across her shoulders and extended to her waist. She sat silent in the fifth grade classroom and paid attention to every word of instruction from Mrs. Vanatt. On the third day of school, a class photo was taken. The little girl knelt in the front row and smiled as if she had not a care in the world. On the way home that day, she walked back toward Guffey, descended the hill past the Stewart residence and jumped mud puddles with the Zimmer kids along the way.

Barbara Zimmer was the first one to see the eight-foot serpent stretched across the road. At the time they had no idea it had been squashed by a vehicle but it did look as though it might be dead, or maybe just sleeping. Out of fear, Tommy picked up a red stone and threw it down hard at the snake. It winced slightly. It was still alive. He picked up another rock but before he hurled it, the little girl from Guffey grabbed his arm and said, "No. Never kill a black snake."

The kids glared at the reptile and were awed by its body, thick and muscular and as round as a silver dollar. It was a black Indigo, a slow-moving snake. Once it became clear that it had fallen victim to the fast moving tires of an anonymous vehicle, as it was squashed in two places, the girl from Guffey grabbed the mid-section of the beast as Tommy grabbed the tail end. In an instant they tossed the critter into the dense vegetation alongside the muddy road. When the Zimmer kids neared their home, they asked the little girl if she would like to stay awhile and then have their Dad drive her home later. She declined and said she had to get home right away.

The next morning, Tommy looked for the snake on his way to school but could not find it. Did it survive? That was the question. The little girl from Guffey never made it to school that day. In fact, she never came back to Rillton School again. Weeks later, Tommy thought about the girl. The last thing he remembered as she headed down that muddy road to Guffey was her long hair blowing in the wind, the shelled necklace, her white, ruffled dress ...and her boots. They looked like pieces of buckskin, laced together with rawhide. He remembered waving goodbye to her as she turned to look back. She raised her hand with closed fist and said *farewell*.

After the war, a huge surplus of potatoes was shipped to the public schools for consumption. The mothers in Rillton baked the potatoes overnight, then brought them to school the next day for lunch. Families were spending more time together, driving the countryside in their new cars and finding different places to go. They went to school picnics, church picnics, family reunions and army reunions. They visited the state parks, where women squeezed into their one-piece black bathing suits, which all looked exactly alike, and swam in the river. Women loaded up the picnic baskets, served lunch, did all of the preparations and clean up, then sat under shade trees and gossiped while the men drank beer, smoked toby cigars, played card games and horseshoes. Kids picked up a game of baseball, using a rubber ball or a mush ball since there was a shortage of baseball gloves and then played Hide and Seek and Hong Kong Kick the Can.

Families went to drive-in movies and watched *African Queen* and *Shane* and *Giant*, snacked on popcorn and fiddled with the speaker hung from the backseat window. They gathered around the Veterans Memorial site near the post office on Decoration Day (now called Memorial Day), wore red poppies and listened to the speeches of the war veterans. They waited for the firing of the rifles and Taps played by students learning the trumpet. They went to the Rillton Fair, watched the fireworks and walked home, disappointed that the few fizzles in the air were no better than last year.

Not everyone had a television set. Families would pile the kids into the car, drive 10 miles to the house of a nearby relative and watch *I Love Lucy, Jack Benny, Milton Berle, Red Skeleton, The Honeymooners* or *The Ed Sullivan Show.* These shows were, in part, the same the old vaudeville acts broadcast on live radio, but they were still entertaining. It was not unusual for two entire families to crowd the space of a single living room with their eyes glued to the television, laughing at one joke after another. Somehow, people felt bonded because of this simple experience.

The Italian Club became everybody's club. Weekend dances, Boy Scout meetings, spaghetti dinners and other social events were held on the main floor. The bar on the lower floor, the old speakeasy, served beer that came from local breweries — Fort Pitt, Duquesne, Iron City, Rolling Rock and Stoney's.

The Shusters had an extended family. Each year they held a summer picnic on a hillside, oftentimes used as a cow pasture at the north end of town. Great crowds of people, some not related to the Shusters, gathered there to feast on hot dogs and play summer games. Children dug for pennies hidden in piles of sawdust, ran wheelbarrow races and played Sack on a Mill. The picnic was open to anyone who wanted to drop by.

It seemed that the Zimmer family encountered one peculiar event after another in the early 50s. Until 1951, life was relatively peaceful and quiet except for Mrs. Wednick's cows. Each summer they would break through her fence, hoof their way down the hill and nibble the fresh green grass in the Zimmer front yard. Mrs. Wednick, a small-boned woman not more than five feet tall, could walk as fast as her cattle could run. Within 15 minutes the chase was on, her dark blue babushka flapping in the wind as she poked the cattle with her long stick until they got back up the hill. One day, after Bill complained about the cow manure, she replied, "Aaagh! It makes for da goot fertilizer."

Aside from the cattle intrusions, so peaceful were the summer afternoons, the kids could hear a vehicle coming a quarter of a mile away and tried to guess who was bumping down the rutted road. Horvath's Rambler clattered. Zimmer's Nash sedan sort of woofed. A truck hauling red dog from the township echoed loud thumps. Once the vehicle had passed and the dust settled, everything was quiet again.

But then in 1951, along came Smitty. That's what he called himself. He was dirty and grimy and wore the same smelly clothes day after day. After allegedly purchasing a piece of property in the thick woods almost directly across from the Zimmer house, Smitty began felling trees in order to clear a space for his small trailer. He lived there with his wife and a 2 year old child while trying to build a "real" house by himself. There was much pounding and hammering of nails well into the night in the early summer. When Bill Zimmer went over to ask what he was working on, Smitty replied, "The roof." And when Bill further asked how he intended to get the roof up onto the walls, once built, Smitty said he hadn't really thought about that. At dinner that evening, Bill concluded Smitty was nuts. In mid-August, Ruth invited Smitty's wife and child to the Rillton Fair to see the fireworks. Smitty threw a fit because his wife wore a nice dress. Before the year was out, the wife left Smitty. A week later, he put a gun to his head and committed suicide.

In the spring of 1952, Bill loaded up his saw-off shotgun to knock off the lettuce-eating rabbits that were hiding under the old chicken coop, otherwise known as the shanty. Tommy was instructed to walk around the left side and flush out the rabbits while Bill waited at the corner on the right side. When no rabbits appeared from the poking of a long stick under the shanty, the boy walked to the far side. And as he rounded the corner, suddenly one rabbit scooted out directly between the two hunters. Bill fired at the rodent and missed inches short of Tommy's foot. Mud splattered into his leg. Two bb's from the shot ricocheted into the back of the foot near the Achilles tendon. Later, Ruth dug them out with a needle. It was the last time the Zimmer boy went hunting.

In the summer of 1952, an 8-year-old kid named Kouts walked his rather large husky-looking dog past the Zimmer house. When Dutch barked at the other dog, Kouts instructed his dog to "sic 'em." Thereafter, the two dogs tumbled down the bank of nettles and briars and engaged in a fierce battle alongside the new red-dog road. Kouts was delighted, as his dog was on top of Dutch and seemed to be winning the fight. But a few moments later, the tide had turned. Now Dutch was on top, growling and snapping with a vengeance. The young boy panicked and foolishly tried to pull Dutch away from his dog, only to be bitten on the finger, not by Dutch but, ironically, by his own dog. Kouts ran home, crying for his dog to follow. Somehow the dog squirmed loose and took off running. A week later, the Kouts family spread rumors that the wolf dog at the Zimmer place attacked their boy and nearly tore off his finger.

RILLTON

In the summer of 1953, a man named Stryker started bulldozing the hillside across from the Shuster picnic grounds. Two weeks later, a house — a real house — was under construction. Bill worked on the plumbing. In exchange, Stryker bulldozed a new driveway to the Zimmer house. A month later, Stryker accidentally ran the dozer off the road. He tried to pull it up the steep bank with a steel cable tied to the back of a Chevy pickup, which reared up like a stallion. It did not budge the dozer. A few weeks later, Stryker bought a regular tractor but then traded that in for a motor boat. The next weekend he lay in a hospital with a severely lacerated foot from trying to start the outboard motor while standing on the propeller. He then traded in the boat for a mowing machine. It had a putt-putt sound unlike any other. Stryker loaned Bill the machine to cut a new ball field near the Horvath residence. It was a mistake. A small piece of woody brush flew from the blades and punctured Bill's left eye. That winter, Stryker traded the mower for an old dump truck and struck a deal to deliver coal at half price. As Stryker made the bend up the hill, the bed fell off the truck and the load of coal landed in the middle of the new driveway. No one was happy, especially the Zimmer kids. They were the ones who had to load the coal into buckets and haul it 60 yards up hill to the house all winter long.

War veteran Joe Antonich organized a Boy Scout troop in the fall of 1953. According to the rules, scouts had to be 11 years old to attend the meetings. A few 10-year-olds showed up in spite of the rule. Technically, the younger boys could not earn badges or regular awards but they did participate in every activity and were proud to earn the name of *Tenderfoot.* Of the 18 members of the troop, only four could afford the official Boy Scout uniform, and even then, the mothers of these kids bought only the shirts without the pants or the hats to match. Regardless, the little troop of Rillton scouts looked official marching in the 4th of July Parade in Herminie that year.

The following year, a high school drop-out called Jingles took over. No one knew his real name. Jingles spent a lot less time at the Italian Hall and a lot more in the woods. During an overnight camping trip, he sent the troop out with long spears cut from trees to hunt squirrel while he tended the fire. The night was pitch black. The young scouts had to yell to each other to find their way. Meanwhile, Jingles quietly followed the scouting party into the woods, sneaked up behind them and scared the daylights out of the few who were lagging. After the ploy, when the kids had finished rollicking in laughter, Jingles put on a show of scary faces. He would hold a flashlight under his chin and shine it up past his face, as he smiled a malicious grin and squinted his eyes. He looked like a Jack-O-Lantern. As he continued with this facial performance, there was a loud explosion that echoed through the forest. Jingles and the scouts rushed back to camp and noticed noodles dangling from the tree branches. The new scout leader had irresponsibly placed an unopened can of chicken noodle soup over the open flames of the fire.

Another trip involved fishing and camping near Barnes Lake Road. Jingles led a troop of six to a secret fishing pond. The scouts pulled in a number of Blue Gill with their new fishing poles (strings tied to the ends of sticks). After the haul, they hiked up the road ½ mile away to a one-room cabin, secured with a deadbolt lock. Jingles declared his key did not work and proceeded to break down the door, tearing the hinges away from the lock. They built a great campfire, consumed the freshly cooked fish and swallowed burnt marshmallows before bunking in the cabin. Early the next morning, there was a knock on the door. Jingles bounced up, slipped through the door and talked to the farmer before the kids were fully awake. They could hear Jingles talking non-stop, about how important it is for boy scouts to learn about fishing, blah, blah, blah. He said he figured it would be all right to use the vacant cabin and certainly he would repair the lock and so forth. A few minutes later Jingles came back into the cabin and informed the scouts that the owner simply dropped by to make sure everything was OK. He then told the troops to pack up; it was time to go. It was the troop's last camping trip with Jingles.

In 1954 Mike Horvath, who worked for Nash-Rambler, sold Bill a new Nash. Mike claimed it was better than Bill's 1952 model and way better than the old Studebaker, a vehicle that never made it over the muddy hills of Barnes Lake Road. A few months after the purchase, a red Oldsmobile whizzed down Oak Street in Rillton and plowed right into the side of the new Nash. After the responsible party's insurance company refused to pay for damages on the basis of an "unmarked intersection," Bill footed the invoice for the repairs.

Several months later, tragedy struck. In the wee hours of a cold morning in March 1955, a loud horn sounded and awakened the Zimmer family from their beds. Fanny looked into the nightstand mirror, saw flames and jumped out of bed, thinking the house was on fire. She looked out the window and screamed, "My God, the car's on fire!" Bill dug his feet into his slippers, rushed downstairs and swatted the flames with a towel, to no avail. Black smoke puffed its way to his lungs and he was forced to retreat inside and call the fire department. Meanwhile, orange flames and thick, black smoke shrouded the vehicle — the fenders, the doors, and the roof. There was no chance to save it. The Rillton volunteer fire department never determined an exact cause of the fire but surmised a cigar.

27
THE YEAR 1955

In 1955, Winston Churchill resigned as Prime Minister, Rocky Marciano retired from boxing, *The $64,000 Question, Mickey Mouse* and *Gunsmoke* premiered on TV, Disneyland opened in California and the AFL-CIO was formed. James Dean died. Steve Jobs was born. Dr. Salk from Pittsburgh introduced the polio vaccine. Arnold Palmer from Latrobe won the Canadian Open in his rookie season as a professional golfer.

If there was one particular year that represented the 1950s more than any other, it would have been 1955. Cars looked different, teens looked different, movies and television looked different, radios looked different and certainly the radio music was different. Color television sets were replacing black and white consoles. Kodak began selling color film for Brownie cameras. Vista vision, Cinerama and Cinemascope were introduced into movie theaters. Girls started wearing poodle skirts and saddle shoes, sometimes painting them pink and white. There were no more bins of rice, beans, tea, coffee or crackers in the stores. Everything was packaged. The packaging became more colorful. If nothing else, 1955 was a colorful year.

Ten years after the war ended, servicemen were still rejoicing the victories over Germany and Japan. Many of them would stop at the VFW on the way home from work. After toiling through their blue-collar jobs, they looked forward to the weekends to do as they pleased. With a five-day work week, increasing wages and no shortage of products, families bought modern kitchen appliances, television sets and bicycles for the kids. They bought bigger and shinier cars with more powerful engines. The black coup vehicles of the 1940s had all but disappeared by 1951. Hudson, DeSoto, Packard, The Henry J, and Studebaker slowly gave way to the Ford, Chrysler, Dodge, Oldsmobile, Buick, Pontiac and of course the Chevrolet, which became popular as the sponsor of The Dinah Shore Show beginning in 1951. The new cars came in bright colors — red, green, blue, yellow, pink, turquoise, peacock blue. And there were plenty of 2-tone colors.

The day after the car fire, Bill Zimmer drove home a new 2-tone 1955 Pontiac Chieftain, creamy white with a reddish-brown band painted down the middle of the hood to match the darker color toward the rear of the car. It had a Chief Pontiac hood ornament, whitewall tires, lots of chrome in the front, a wrap-around windshield and no pillar between the front and rear windows. The new style was fresh and quite appealing. "It looks like a convertible," Ruth remarked. "They call it a hard-top," Bill said proudly.

The big band sounds of Benny Goodman, Jimmy and Tommy Dorsey, Guy Lombardo, Glenn Miller and Duke Ellington had peaked during the war but continued to be played on the radio for years afterward. Beginning in the early 50s, more and more song artists previously associated with these bands became popular. Radio stations played fewer hits like *In The Mood, Tuxedo Junction, Chattanooga Choo Choo* and *Boogie Woogie Bugle Boy.* Instead the stations introduced pop songs, such as *Sentimental Journey, Mr. Sandman, Sincerely, Ragg Mopp, Hot Diggety, Harbor Lights, Music Music Music, Sugartime, Moments to Remember* and Dinah Shore's *Love and Marriage.* Polka bands became popular. Fun songs like *She's Too Fat For Me, Hop Dee Doo,* and *Lazy Mary* made their way to the radio. They matched the mood of the country. *Lazy Mary* was sung in Italian except for one or two verses in English.

> *Lazy Mary you better get up,*
> *She answered back "I am not able"*
> *Lazy Mary you better get up,*
> *We need the sheets for the table ...*

Bill Haley and the Comets released *Rock Around The Clock* in April 1954. By the summer of 1955, it rose high on the charts for 8 weeks. Alan Freed called it rock and roll music.

Pat Boone, purportedly a descendant of Daniel Boone, recorded the first No. 1 rock and roll hit, *Ain't That A Shame.* It was a Fats Domino song. He continued to introduce to the white market other R&B songs originally performed by African American artists - *Tutti Frutti, Long Tall Sally* and *At My Front Door (Crazy Little Mama)*, for example. He did well and young boys began wearing buckskin shoes just like Pat Boone. They called them White Bucks. Pat Boone, a faithful member of the Church of Christ and a devoted Christian, refused to give an onscreen kiss to co-star Shirley Jones during the filming of *April Love* because she was married in real life. People liked Pat Boone.

But Boone's rendition of the R&B songs was nothing like the sounds recorded by the original artists. The difference was that Boone sang the lyrics of the song, keeping pace with the rhythm and the beat of the music. Black artists were crying out a message, usually describing the pain or passion of love, unadulterated and loaded with African-American vernacular. When Little Richard pounded on the piano while singing *Tutti Frutti,* he voiced the drumbeat along with it, "Womp-bomp-a-loom-op-a-womp-bam-boom!" Pat Boone never got it. He himself admitted that he did not wish to do "Tutti Frutti" because "it didn't make sense" to him. The promoters of the song had to change the words "loose booty" to "aw rooty" so that the song came out *"Tutti Frutti, Aw Rooty!"* which was accepted among white audiences.

Little Richard's version of *Tutti Frutti* in 1955 gained popularity because of Pat Boone. His career took off. Each and every song was filled with lightning energy — *Long Tall Sally, Lucille, Rip It Up, The Girl Can't Help It, Slippin' and Slidin', Boney Moronie, Jenny Jenny, Good Golly Miss Molly, Keep A-Knockin'.* This was a whole new world of music. Interestingly, Pat Boone continued to rank high on the charts when he changed to a different style of music. His top hits in 1957, *Love Letters in The Sand* and *April Love*, could not have been performed successfully by artists like Little Richard.

Rock and roll music made good use of the electric guitar, piano and drums, along with saxophone and trumpet, while introducing variations in rhythm. Young teens would get together and sing "doo-wop" music. All they needed was a lead singer and a couple of others imitating anything that might sound like a musical instrument while trying to keep in harmony. The 1961 hit *Blue Moon* by the Marcels is a good example. After hearing the tune, one has to think hard: were there any musical instruments in that song or not? It didn't take long for white musicians to copy the style. There were small groups of both black and white kids standing on the street corners of

Pittsburgh, singing doo-wop *a capella.* After awhile, it was hard to tell by sound if the groups were black or white. The teens didn't care. Although the music was not warmly accepted by white adults, teens found it very compelling. It made them want to get up and dance.

Teenagers listened to these tunes not on a 50,000-watt radio station in Pittsburgh like KDKA, but on a 1,000-watt radio station called WAMO (an acronym for Allegheny, Monongahela, and Ohio). Everyone assumed the disc jockey was black since he played mostly R&B tunes from black musicians. He called himself the Daddio of the Radio and the Platter Pushin' Papa, and referred to his listening audience as "movers and groovers."

Porky Chedwick was one of 10 children of a steel-working father in Homestead, Pa. He was left crossed-eyed from a slingshot accident at age 8, which ultimately led to his inability to drive a car. He took on the job at WAMO as a sportscaster in 1948 but gradually expanded the music, which became more and more controversial. He was accused of corrupting the white youth of American once parents learned he was Caucasian. Meanwhile, because of his reputation, black musicians kept sending Porky new material, which pleased his fans. Chedwick never accepted payola, which was customary in those days, and was held in high praise by many artists, including Smokey Robinson, Little Anthony, Hank Ballard, Lou Christie,

RILLTON

The Marcels, The Skyliners, The Vogues and many others.

Bo Diddley, from Pittsburgh, said Porky Chedwick played records that no one else ever did. For Diddley, it was the beginning of a long and successful career. He presented a rhythm, Jamaican-style unlike any other, and drew great crowds of young people by performing at local high schools, Rainbow Gardens and other places around the city. In November 1955, he appeared on the Ed Sullivan Show and was supposed to sing *Sixteen Tons* but instead sang *Bo Diddley*. So infuriated was Sullivan that he claimed *Diddley* would not last in the business six months. (*Diddley* made it to the Rock and Roll Hall of Fame).

Some of the great songs of 1955 played on WAMO included *Speedo* and *Gloria* by the Cadillacs, *Sincerely, Please Send Me Someone to Love* and *Ten Commandments of Love* by the Moonglows, *Maybellene* by Chuck Berry and *Annie Had A Baby* by Hank Ballard. Ballard's song eventually was banned from air radio by the FCC, but until then Porky Chedwick played it almost daily along with Ballard's other song, *Annie's Aunt Fannie.* Other top rock and roll songs played on standard radio stations were making their way to the charts — *Earth Angel* by the Penguins, *Only You* by the Platters, *Dance With Me Henry* by Georgia Gibbs and a number of songs by the rising Elvis Presley. By 1956, ten of the 20 top hits were rock and roll recordings. Sometime during 1955, white buck shoes at school had disappeared. Clodhoppers with steel cleats came next, along with pegged pants, rolled-up shirt sleeves and black leather jackets (whoever could afford one). It was the year of the ducktail hairstyle. A year later, crewcuts were in style. Some called them flat tops. A lot had changed during 1955.

The source of rock and roll is a highly debated issue. Some argue that the term "rock and roll" arose from a song by Ike Turner called *Rocket 88,* a name borrowed from the new Oldsmobile Super 88 in 1954. On his way from Mississippi to Memphis, an amplifier fell off the top of the car — or was damaged by rain — and produced a fuzzy sound during the next performance. Turner liked the sound and went forward with his *Rocket 88 Boogie,* parts I and II. Some called the performance Rockin' 88. But for years railroad men had been using the term to describe the movement of trains across the tracks. Sailors used the term to describe their sails across the sea. In 1949, an album was recorded entitled *Rock and Roll Blues.* As far back as 1922, an artist named Trixie Smith sang *My Man Rocks With Me One Steady Roll.*

Since the early 1920s, records were sold on the 78 format and continued to be mass-produced until 1954. In 1955, a rivalry developed between Columbia Records and RCA Victor. Columbia sold 33 1/3 rpm LP (long-playing) records offering eight to 10 songs per side. RCA had issued a much smaller disc containing a single song per side and played at 45 rpm. They first became popular at the jukeboxes located inside of soda shops.

By the end of 1955, the common home record player offered a selection of three speeds (78, 45, 33 1/3). The players had a tall spindle that held several records, each one automatically dropped after the previous one had finished playing. There was also a combination cartridge adapted to the 45s with their larger holes. For new artists trying to make the charts with a hit record and for teens anxious to hear the next song of their choice, the 45 format became the better choice. At dances, a disc jockey would often change the disc after each song, though it was possible to stack several discs on the adaptor. Problem was, after awhile the records would get scratched.

Sewickley Area Joint High School held classes from grades 7 through 12 in the same building. When the 16 and 17 years olds began tuning into WAMO, so did the younger kids.

In the fall of 1955, a seventh-grader named Stevens walked down the hallway with an arm full of books while singing *Crazy Little Mama* on the way to his next class. In his bliss, he strayed to the middle of the hallway and regrettably into the path of an oncoming senior, a football lineman, who "colkonked" him. Books flew in all directions as Stevens landed on his backside. Thereafter, Stevens learned to walk along the sides of the hallways and avoid the center, which was reserved for upperclassmen.

For the Rillton young set, Herminie was the go-to place. It had a relatively flat street with a movie theater, a soda shop, a drug store that displayed the latest magazines and Sam's pool hall, which was open to teens for 10 cents a game. They could play a pinball machine for a nickel. The second floor had a wood floor and was used for either roller-skating or dancing on Friday and Saturday nights. Renting a pair of skates cost 20 cents, the same price as the ticket to the movie theater down the street. The cost to enter the dance was 40 cents. It was easy to get from one place to another because of the concrete sidewalk on the east side of the street. Come Saturday night, the walkway was filled with teenagers, headed one way or the other.

In October 1955, Barry, Si and Bugs thumbed a ride from Rillton to the Central Movie Theater in Herminie to watch the *Creature of the Black Lagoon*. The theater opened at 6 p.m. They stood in line, bought a ticket plus a candy bar, then hitch-hiked back home 2 hours later. Total cost: 25 cents. They went back a week later and saw *The Day The Earth Stood Still*. By the end of the year, they had seen a number of westerns like *Drum Beat* and *Red Mountain* and more sci-fi movies like *War of the Worlds* and *Them*. They were never late for the movie, never threatened or harassed by motorists and never spent more than a quarter per week. Meanwhile, rock and roll dances above Sam's Pool Hall were gaining popularity. Soon these moviegoers started attending the dances too.

During the winter, SHS held noontime sock hops at the high school gym. Everyone was required to remove their shoes to prevent scratching the hardwood floor, hence the term *sock hop*. Students started buying the 45 rpm records produced by local musicians, many of whom grew up in the Pittsburgh area, and played them at the noontime dances. Afterwards they exchanged records with their friends. Fats Domino became an overnight celebrity. His version of *Ain't That A Shame* was just the beginning. Within a year, he had 3 more hits — *My Blue Heaven*, *Blueberry Hill* and *Blue Monday* — and several more hits the year after that.

For Christmas, eighth-grader Barbara Zimmer got her wish — a new portable 45 record player with a cartridge and an automatic drop. She played *Earth Angel*, *Tutti Frutti*, *Speedo* and *Sixteen Tons* over and over again. By the next year, she had a boxful of records — *Splish Splash, Johnny B. Goode, Long Tall Sally, Sea Cruise, Kansas City, In The Still of The Night, Peggy Sue, Hound Dog, That'll Be The Day, Roll Over Beethoven, Why Do Fools Fall in Love, Yakety Yak* and many others. So did all of her friends.

The children of Rillton had suddenly turned into the next generation of young adults, enveloped by the simple, yet powerful force of rock and roll music.

When Bill Zimmer heard Gene Vincent's *Be Bop A-Lula,* he shook his head and said, "That kind of music will never last." So Barbara asked what kind of music he liked, and he responded, "The Mills Brothers." She stood there, scratching her head, trying to remember what songs they sang.

28
FOOTBALL FEVER

In 1955, the Steelers drafted a local boy named Johnny Unitas but then cut him during training camp. Unitas was forced to work construction jobs, though he still played sandlot football on weekends for $6 a game. The following year he was picked up by the Baltimore Colts and spent the next 18 years leading that team to two NFL championships and a Super Bowl. He appeared in 10 Pro Bowl games and was the NFL MVP eight times.

Western Pennsylvania had a reputation for producing great football players. Besides Unitas, there was George Blanda, Ernie Davis, Joe Namath, Dan Marino, Joe Montana, Jim Kelly, Tony Dorsett, Mercury Morris, Randy White, Mike Ditka and many more. All of them grew up near Pittsburgh yet ended up playing for other teams.

It is ironic that even though the birth of Pro football took place in Pittsburgh[4], the city did not have an NFL franchise until 1933 for various reasons — the war, the depression, start-up costs and Pennsylvania Blue Laws preventing the team from playing on Sundays. Once Pittsburgh got a team, it took another 40 years just to make the playoffs. Year after year they struggled, posting one losing season after another.

But things changed in the 1950s, not because of the number of wins but an adjustment in attitude. It began with Ernie Stautner. Players all around the league felt he was the toughest defensive tackle ever to play the game. His tackling was more than brutal. It was punishing. Other players on the team responded with gang tackling unlike they had seen before. Opponents dreaded playing in Pittsburgh because of the physical pounding that affronted them. It seemed that the whole city of Pittsburgh adopted the idea of playing tough, hard-nosed football, regardless of the outcome. Stautner was the only Steeler ever to have his jersey officially retired (No. 70) by the Steeler organization. During an interview, he commented, "We finally got to where we didn't give a damn for anybody and we didn't have the material but we knew that somebody was going to have to pay. The tradition

---

[4] The Allegheny Athletic Association defeated the Pittsburgh Athletic Club on Nov. 12, 1892. Pudge Helfelfinger was paid $500 to play in that game.

of the Pittsburgh Steelers is rock 'em sock 'em football, and we're proud of that."

Hard-nosed football became the dominant theme in high schools all over western Pennsylvania. Sewickley High was no exception. It was a small school with a small field, small players and a small coach.

John C. Bruno stood only 5'4" tall but had a big heart, big ideas and a big nose for smelling out football players. Within his 36-year coaching career, he posted several undefeated seasons, not an easy thing to master given that Sewickley was one of the smallest schools around. In the early 50s, he led the team to two straight undefeated seasons, but because of the Gardner point system was not awarded a playoff spot. In 1953, SHS beat McDonald 13-7 for the WPIAL Class B title.

In 1955, because of the Gardner point system, Bruno's bid for a playoff birth was rejected even though his team was undefeated. Frustrated with the system, Bruno arranged to have his team play not other B teams but A teams from opposing schools that had two to three times as many students to choose from. Although some of the A teams refused to play the Sewickley Bisons, others agreed. Roughly half of the new football schedule included A teams. By 1960, this little school played strictly A teams, and even a AA team. SHS not only got into the playoffs but won the WPIAL Class A championship that year, 14-7 against Beaver.

Of the 38 coal mines in Sewickley Twp., only three had hired African Americans — Herminie, Lowber and Scott Haven. They were brought in as strike breakers, beginning in 1910. When the mines shut down, most of the families left. A few remained in Hermine and Scott Haven but none in Lowber. There were only a few African Americans in each class at Sewickley, roughly 1.5 percent of the student population. Between 1956 and 1960, only two black males participated in varsity sports. Both were harassed from time to time because of the color of their skin, but they were accepted and even admired by most of the SHS students, generally speaking.

One of the black athletes was Noble Milton, who not only was a tough, solid running back, but a good student. He won the spelling bee contest, the Citizenship Award and a scholarship to the University of Pittsburgh.

The other black student athlete was Gary Bartlett. Bartlett loved to dance and loved to run. In 1957, he performed a tap dance in front of the student body during a Spring Variety Show. Then he went out for track.

But the track team, which was coached by Bruno, consisted of nothing but football players who were more or less mandated to run track in order to stay in shape for next year's football season. Backfield players were required to run sprints and relays.

RILLTON

Linemen ran long distance or did the shot put. Due to lack of equipment, there were no pole-vaulting, high-jumping or javelin events. The 440-yard run was a joke since there was no oval track. Beginning near the end zone, the athletes had to run down the side of the football field, make a 90-degree turn left at the fence post, run another 60 yards or so, then turn left again and head back the other way.

Bartlett, who had very fast feet, was good at making these turns and would come in first place just about every time. However, at the regular track meets — and there were only two scheduled each season, one warm-up meet at Jeanette and the annual county meet at Hempfield Twp — Bartlett never won or even placed. No one else from Sewickley won any events either, so it didn't really matter. But the football team was in shape. And that was the main objective.

The following year, Bartlett, who lived near Hempfield Twp, picked up a new dance called the Slop from his black friends. He shared it with his white friends at Sewickley. It became the latest dance craze overnight. Jimmy Adams, who had a knack for dancing, roller-skating and gymnastics, learned it immediately and wowed everyone at the Saturday night dances. Others followed — Barry Horvat, Jerry Montini and Fuzzy McGrew. At football camp, Bartlett spent half the night teaching players how to Slop to the tune of *Wake up Little Suzi*e.

After Arnold Palmer won the Masters Tournament in 1958, the golf membership at the strictly Jewish Baldoc Hills Country Club outside of Irwin nearly doubled. There was a shortage of caddies. The caddy master encouraged existing caddies to bring new friends to the course for caddy lessons. Several kids from Rillton, ages 14 to 16, hitch-hiked rides to the country club to cash in on the job offer.

Typically, a caddy earned $1.50 per bag for nine holes, including tip. On weekends, caddies were likely to double-bag two consecutive rounds (36 holes) and earn $12 for the day, which was good money. Donuts at the caddy shack cost a nickel. A 16-ounce bottle of soda cost ten cents. Naturally, the experience of caddying aroused interest in young boys taking up the game of golf. It seemed that once the Little League days were behind them, the same kids that used to pick up a game of baseball in 1955 were now hitting golf balls across the Trozzo field with a golf club. By the next year, the caddies were playing golf on local public courses.

For three years, the Horvath and Zimmer kids rode the bus to the Evangelical and Reformed Church in Irwin to attend Sunday school, followed by church services beginning at 11 a.m.. Usually they didn't get back home until 12:30 p.m.. By the time Tommy hitch-hiked a ride to Baldoc, there was only enough time left in the day to caddy one round of golf, so he would come home with $6 in his pocket. In order to double his income, he would need to skip church. Surprisingly, his mother agreed to the plan.

The next week, he caught the first bus home after Sunday school at 10:50 a.m., raced inside to change clothes and headed for the golf course via Clay Pike and Barnes Lake Road. He got lucky. He arrived at the course by noon, just in time before his caddy number (101) was called. One day, when he encountered difficulty thumbing a ride, he missed his number by a mile. They had just called Kwee's number. They nicknamed him Kwee because of his speech impediment. His number was 303. He pronounced it "kwee oh kwee." It was the last number on the list. But at the end of the day, Tommy had still managed to double-bag two rounds and earn the $12.

Robert Pekarsky needed another $5 to acquire a set of used, steel-shafted clubs from Richie Gurdjian, so he offered to sell Tommy his old wood-shafted clubs for exactly $5. The sale included a driver and a 3-wood (both painted sliver), a 7-iron, a 9-iron and putter. They practiced hitting the 9-iron in the Zimmer front yard which was now a good 60 yards long, thanks to Stryker's new mowing machine.

Even though the networks had televised the Sam Snead golf matches for two years, Bill Zimmer, like every other parent in Rillton, shrugged off the idea that golf was a sport. After all, why would anyone want to hit a ball and then go chase it? But three weeks later, Bill picked up a golf club and tried to hit a ball across the yard into the tin can sunken into the ground.

But no sport in Rillton could compete with the town's passion for football. In late July, when dead heat smothered the atmosphere, a certain smell — the smell of football — infiltrated the air on the Trozzo field. A full month before football camp, eager players trying to make the Sewickley football team peddled their bikes to the practice field, did calisthenics in unison, ran a trail through the old coal mine and around Indian Lake. Then they headed back to the Trozzo field to complete their workout, running wind sprints up the steep hill at the east end of the field. As usual, coach Bruno, who resided at the top of the hill overlooking the field, would take a ride in his car to see who was working out. Bruno didn't miss much when it came to piecing together a football team.

Football camp in 1958 was no picnic. Training began on August 18 and lasted for 10 days. Though the nights were very cool in the mountains near Indiana, Pa., the dog days of August were extremely hot, the air heavy and still. Football practices started at 9 a.m. and 2 p.m. each day. Each session began with laps around the practice field, followed by 15 minutes of calisthenics, then sprints before a series of drills. There was little time for standing around. Continuous movement was the order of the day — every day — and was designed to whip the players into shape. Linemen pushed dummies and padded sleds up and down the grassy turf halfway through the morning before pushing against each other. Three teams of running backs would run the same play over and over before running a different one. They would run full speed to an imaginary hole, run 3or 4 more steps beyond that point, then jog to the backfield where they would line up and race through the drill again.

Dry mouth was always a problem. By mid-morning during the first session, players reached for lemons tucked behind the webbing inside their helmets in order to quench their thirst. Out-of-shape players breathed more heavily than the others, but no one escaped the heat. Sweat poured from their brows and soaked right through their shoulder pads, jerseys and pants, as if they had stepped out of a steaming hot shower. This would occur roughly at 10:30 a.m. when there was still another hour to go before lunch.

If the morning heat was unbearable, the afternoon was nearly impossible. Ninety-degree heat feels like 120 degrees inside a football helmet. Some players passed out. Some got sick from the heat, some by accidentally swallowing a wad of chewing tobacco. Players still standing would snicker. So would some of the coaches. Watching others grovel in the heat was part of the fun at football camp.

At night, the sophomores were harassed by upperclassmen. They were often forced to take cold showers, sleep on wet bunks, gulp down large spoonfuls of mustard, do duck walks or extra pushups.

Some were whipped on the bare butt with a broom. After several practice sessions, the scrimmages which began on a grassy field soon turned to a dust bowl from the cleated shoes plowing up the soil. The sophomores took an additional beating, for they had to defend against the bigger, stronger upper class linemen and running backs who were executing offensive plays. Bruno never called a pass play. It was always a run, usually up the middle or off tackle. Sophomores would get pounded again and again as they tried to tackle the ball carrier with blockers out front. Oftentimes after the play, they would end up face down in the dirt. The dirt on their faces would then turn partly muddy from the profuse sweating, a scene that could have been used in a sci-fi movie.

After the first week, Bruno's team scrimmaged against the Indiana High School team and got romped. Bruno was livid. When his favorite play up the middle failed to gain any ground, he threw his play sheet down, walked over to the center, pulled up and down on the face guard, slapped the side of the kid's helmet and growled, "Where's your head?" Then he said, loud enough for both teams to hear, "Run the same play again. This time, block!" On the second attempt, the team gained one yard. Bruno's chin jutted but he remained silent for the rest of the scrimmage. But when they got back to camp, he had plenty to say.

The next day of training camp was a backbreaker. Two-on-one blocking drills extended well into the hot afternoon. Grunts and groans and bellows sounded out as bodies collided into each other with fury. Helmets smashed against other helmets. Chinstraps flew off. Clouds of dust puffed as bodies were pounded to the ground. Elbows were scraped raw, knuckles were bashed, knees were twisted. There were split lips and bloody noses. At the end of the day, the upperclassmen were too exhausted to harass the sophomores. They lay in bed at nighttime motionless, listening to the hoot owls before crashing for the night.

On the 9th day, the Indiana team came to camp for a second scrimmage. Bruno mandated that his defense give up no more than two yards on any given play. He also insisted the offensive team run the same four plays over and over. Said Bruno, "Every time we run a play, I want you to col-konk somebody!" At the end of the day, Indiana did manage to run one play for a four-yard gain. Most of the others, however, went for no gain. Their players were so physically beat that the Indiana coach called off the last series of plays, pulled his players from the field and sent them back to their lockers. For Bruno, it was the best moment in camp. For the Sewickley players, the best thing about football camp was the ride back home after 10 days of hell.

The parents, teachers, janitors, school bus drivers, local citizens and businesses in Sewickley Twp were great supporters of the Bison football team. They talked about the team on a daily basis, contributed money to the booster club, made bets in bars, idolized the coach and his brand of hard-nosed football, knew the names of the players and read the newspaper stories, recounting the exciting plays after each game. On Friday nights, fans raced to the stands to find a good seat. The place was packed. Young boys brought footballs to toss around behind the bleachers at halftime. Between watching the team run plays and cheering the crowd, the cheerleaders seldom had a moment's rest.

Following the games on Friday night, Herminie jumped. Students flocked to the downtown streets and headed right to Sam's, which was now called the Rec (or as many said, the Wreck) either to play pool or attend the dance upstairs. One night an older, pudgy-faced man with a strange-looking eye climbed the stairs at the Wreck and set up a microphone at the far end of the room. No one knew who he was. But when he began playing his 45 rpm records, there was no doubt that this man was the official Daddio of the Radio. He was masterful, methodically arranging the floor speakers, flipping the right record to get the right sound and the right mood. The result was a combination of power and magic that echoed halfway down Main Street. Porky Chedwick made rock and roll music come alive. The Wreck became the hot spot of the whole area. Students from Hempfield Twp, Jeanette and West Newton rode in cars to Herminie for action. Never were they disappointed.

RILLTON

In the spring of 1959, on the last day of school, Grass decided to run down the Rillton Creek to see where it would go. His friend Zip joined him. The journey began at the Rillton Bridge where they started hopping the smooth rocks as they made their way downstream. Within a half hour, their shoes were soaking wet. They splashed forward, flushing out a pheasant, quite a number of crayfish and salamanders and a sizeable reddish-brown water snake that scurried down a hole along the muddy bank.

A few hundred yards beyond the Horvat property, everything turned quiet but for the sound of a few cardinals. Mesmerized by the solitude and the feel of the cool, clear water sliding past their feet, they sat down on a rock and spent a few minutes emptying their shoes of sand and rock. The air was sweet-smelling from the Mayflowers and the Sugar Maples lined up along the banks. A young, spotted Robin hid in the shade of a tall tree. A half mile later, there was no sign of civilization. Grass spotted a shiny trinket, which turned out to be a small arrowhead wedged in the gravel beneath the shallow water. An instant later, from the corner of his eye, Zip noticed a small patch of lime green grass along a small rill trickling into the creek. He climbed the bank, ran his hand across the soft grass and marveled at its radiant glow. Then he heard a strange sound.

"Did you say something?" he asked Grass, who replied, "I didn't say anything." Zip thought he heard someone talking. They listened again but heard nothing. Eager to get to his destination, Grass said, "Let's go." But as they rose up to leave, Zip heard the sound again. "Did you hear that?" he exclaimed. "Hear what?" Grass said. Zip answered, "That sound from the water hitting the rocks. It was coming from the rocks. Something like … air wall or air well." Grass shrugged his shoulders and made a face that indicated they might be getting crazy. Then he turned and splashed his way downstream once again, frightening a pair of mourning doves, a frog and several other critters.

To make better progress, they began hopping across the small ponds and using the sandy banks when practical. They crossed under Dick Station Rd., passed a huge farm field to the right and two U-shaped bends in the creek that seemed to lead them around in circles. After crossing Lowber Road, they reached the Little Sewickley and followed it for another half-mile to the Big Sewickley, which Grass thought was the Youghiogheny River. As soon as they reached the water's edge, the young creek runners stopped dead in their tracks, for the entire creek was rusty-red in color and emitted a distasteful odor.

Disappointed, they turned around and walked home with sore feet that lasted for three days. That night as Zip lay in his bed, the trickling water sound resurfaced in his head: farewell. Farewell! The word he heard was *farewell*.

RILLTON

Sewickley Township, named after the Indian word *Seweekly,* was once a land of many sugar maples which lined the banks of the Little Sewickley Creek. The original Indians, the Shawnee, enjoyed good relations with the early white settlers, who called the place Sewickley Old Town. There, they set up several mills to convert maple tree sap into syrup. While grading for the new Rillton-Sutersville Road in 1962, workers discovered arrowheads, trinkets and even Indian skeletons. Some historians tried to visualize what life was like along the Sewickley creeks prior to 1900. But the 40 years of coal mining operations made it difficult to piece together a meaningful history.

Lowber Mine shut down in 1938. Twelve years later, a large discharge of acid drained from the main portal and polluted the Sewickley Creek with more than a ton of iron contamination per day. Roughly 64 years later, a company called Iron Oxide Recovery proposed to eliminate the pollution by reclaiming 1,500 tons of waste iron sludge from the old mine site, then selling it to a pigment producer in Virginia. During the process, Sewickley Creek Watershed Association set up a new water system designed to optimize the iron oxide recovery process. The new water system, called the Lowber System, is targeted to collect three quarters of a ton of iron solids every 5 to 10 years. It is the first self-sustaining mine drainage treatment system in the world.

29

CRUISING

Rock and roll dancing originally consisted of two kinds of dances — a fast dance, which everyone called the jitterbug, and a slow dance with various combinations of the two-step, sometimes including a pivot. Both dances required contact dancing with a partner. Some of the young dancers glided easily across the dance floor. Like Coon. Coon developed a great pivot. It was especially noticeable when he danced with a cheerleader named Gloria Ricci. Others found dancing difficult, even humiliating, so they stood around watching others, listening to the music, trying to have a good time.

The salvation for these wallflowers came with the Slop, a non-contact dance that could be performed solo. Other solo dances followed — the mashed potato, the twist and the pony. Come Friday night, a lot more teens performed solo dances at the Wreck. But then a new fad developed — borrowing Dad's car to go cruisin'.

During the 60s, the US experienced its longest uninterrupted period of economic expansion in history. Unemployment was a mere 5.5 %. Congress initiated a plan to lower taxes. John F. Kennedy, the new President, envisioned a new frontier. Parents and teachers envisioned more kids going to college. Once the baby boomers were old enough to drive, some families bought a second car. Several students bought their own cars and more times than not would haul friends around so long as they helped pay for gas. Each town had its own hot spot. For the young adults at Sewickley and West Newton it was either Main Street in Herminie or a place called Barney's.

Barney's was a tiny drive-in restaurant that served mainly hamburgers and milkshakes. It was located halfway between West Newton and Herminie on an otherwise isolated two-lane highway in the boondocks. Why Barney's became a hot spot is conjecture, possibly because the one-mile stretch of road in front of the place made an ideal spot for the kids to race their cars, screech their tires and peel out in the presence of other teens.

Cars entering Barney's would typically do a complete circle around the building before finding a place to park. Some would continue circling just for the fun of it. Music from WAMO blared through car radios. Smokey Robinson's new hit song *Shop Around* seemed appropriately named for cruising around the restaurant. Teens checked each other out through their car windows. No passenger escaped detection. Weed drove '56 Mercury convertible; Dago, a '52 Ford Fairlane; Foxy, a '56 Chevy; and Lips, a '55 Olds 88 with super gear. One day, a bunch of kids piled into the Olds to test the super gear. It sounded and acted much like second gear. But Lips was proud he got to drive his Dad's car.

In 1957 workers at the Ft. Pitt Brewing Company went on strike and never returned. The company simply closed up shop and went out of business. Bill Zimmer found another engineering job at Duquesne Brewery, Pittsburgh, within a week and earned more money than ever before. When the time came to trade in his '58 Rambler for a new car, he held onto it as a second vehicle to ride to and from work. Meanwhile, Barbara, who now had a driver's license, used the brand new 1960 Pontiac for church, school functions and cruising with her friends Judy, Ursie and Mary Ann on Friday nights. Whenever Bill asked about Barbara's Friday night plans he'd always get the same answer from her: "The Wreck, then out to Barney's."

To help students save money for college, history teacher Joe Andreo helped line up summer jobs at Westmoreland County Club where he worked as a part-time bartender. Much like Baldoc Hills, this was a private club. Members were all Jewish but the workers were not. The general manager was from England, the chefs and maitre d from France, except for the head chef who was from Germany. The head hostess was from Kentucky. The bus boys were mostly high school students. Communication was not good but the pay was. The students earned upwards of $40 a week and saved most of it. A small portion ended up at Barney's for hamburgers.

For years, the budget for sports-related activities at SHS was so limited that nearly all of it was spent on football equipment. A few dollars went to pay for basketball, baseball and track equipment. Whatever was left over was used for gymnasium items such as volleyballs or nets or cheerleading outfits. No money was allocated for girls' sports. When Bruno, who was the athletic director and sole purchaser of such equipment, was granted a 10 percent increase in the 1960 budget, he spent all of it on new football uniforms and headgear. When his new purchases arrived, he turned to one of his assistants and with a rare smile remarked, "Now we're cruising."

The summer of 1960 was unusually hot. Hurricane Donna, a category 4 storm, swept the Florida Keys and wreaked havoc across the Lower Peninsula. So hot was the first day at Deer Head, the new football camp, Bruno changed the practice hours beginning at 6:30 a.m. and later in the afternoon at 4:00 p.m., which was a first. He had a strong team, very experienced and eager to prove itself. Some of the players defied the heat, exclaiming, "What doesn't kill us can only make us stronger." They were very outspoken and borderline cocky.

On the 6th day of practice, upperclassmen began to whine, not because of the heat but because of the unnecessary delay in scrimmaging against the sophomores, a tradition at football camp. The whining continued. At first Bruno ignored them, but by the next day, after Snooky pressed the issue even further, Bruno changed his mind. Said the coach, "Okay boys, you want a scrimmage. You got one. ….I want the right side of the line on this side of the football and the left side on the other." When the left offensive line swung around and looked into the faces of the right offensive line and realized how much bigger the opposition was, they gulped. "But what about the sophomores?" Arlotta protested. The coach answered, "Never mind about the sophomores. I want to see who my football team is. I want to see this half of the team break through the line. I want to see this half stop 'em. No end runs and no passes. Now go to it."

With the line up on the field, there were only 3 places to run the ball — between center and guard, guard and tackle, tackle and end. After a few plays, Bruno blew hard on his whistle, accused the players of blocking and tackling like sissies and said he wanted to see somebody knocked on their can. "I see pushing and hugging. I want blocking and tackling. I wanna see you col-konk somebody. I wanna see who's tough. Before this day is over, I wanna see BLOOD!"

The scrimmage resumed at 5:15 p.m.. Hitting became more intense, as offensive linemen lunged forward and tried to crack a hole in the defensive line. The stubborn defense turned defiant, then aggressive, then angry as they crashed forward, trying to knock the offensive line backward. Now nose to nose, helmet to helmet, offensive tackle Bob Stolick (Stock) gritted his teeth and strained with all his might to unload on the pesky opposition. Shoulder pads collided into one another with fury, helmets smashed together and sounded like lightning. Linebacker Karasek lunged into the gap between two offensive linemen and cracked the helmet of halfback Bill Hunter. Hunter refused to go down, standing on his feet to the end of the play. On the next play, the defense smacked Hunter again, driving him backwards and sideways and trying their best to cause a fumble. But Hunter, as usual, held onto the football. The defense questioned, will he ever fumble that football? (A few days later, everyone called him *Willie*, short for Will-he.)

Now angrier than ever, the defense was out to get, not just Hunter, but anyone else who dared carry the ball. Gang tackling intensified. Bodies pounded the turf like thunder, causing great clouds of dirt to puff from under stacked bodies and fill the air like smog in LA. Pekarsky groaned while limping back to the huddled but denied feeling pain. Fuzzy McGrew, pounded to the ground and flat on his back, bounced up with renewed determination, in spite of hopping on one leg. When Lipniskis (Lips) took a moment to rest on one knee, Bruno yelled out, "Let's go boys. This is the real McCoy!"

The scrimmage, which had evolved into a willful, wanton, reckless abandon effort to body destroy the opposition, lasted much longer than the scheduled 45 minutes. The assistant coaches, fearing unnecessary injuries to key players, kept looking at Bruno, signaling for at least a heat break, if not an end to the struggle. But Bruno was so engrossed in the contest of wills that he allowed the battle to continue for another 37 minutes and not a moment before he noticed blood pouring from the shins and elbows and knuckles and faces from nearly half of the players.

At 6:37 p.m., bruised, battered, limping and now bleeding, the team scrimmage came to a halt. The head coach from the New Brighton camp a quarter of a mile over the hill heard the commotion at Camp Deer Head, walked to the top of the hill and witnessed the last 10 minutes of the Sewickley skirmish. When it ended, he walked down to Bruno and announced he was forfeiting the scrimmage with his team, which had been previously scheduled for the very next day. "My boys are just not ready for this," he said.

The Sewickley Bisons rolled through the season that year going undefeated and winning in the playoff championship game. Most of the teams they faced never scored a single point. Bruno was overjoyed, not just because he'd won another championship and no doubt the best one ever. His B team had jut won the class A title!

It was one of the few years in his coaching history that he spent actually coaching the team instead of devoting hours to recruiting players. In years past, he would buy jewelry for the cheerleaders as payola for talking their boyfriends into playing football. This year was different. Plenty of players from the largest senior class in the school's history tried out for the team, so bribery wasn't necessary. For weeks, everyone talked about the championship game. An assistant coach remarked, "Bruno was right when he said, 'Now we're cruising!' "

In 1971, following the coach's death, the community donated $10,000 to improve the old football field where John Bruno led his football team to so many victories during his 36-year career. A bronze plaque was placed at the far end of the field in his honor.

30
THE CHANGE

Following the war, the people of Rillton passed though a time of peace and prosperity. There was a window of time (1950-1965) that dramatically changed the town for the better. In the late 1940s, only a few vehicles traveled the dusty roads through town. Most of them were painted black, had black tires and were bubble-like in appearance. Mostly everyone walked — to the store, the post office, the school, the Italian Club, the bus stop on Irwin-Herminie road.

By 1955, half the kids rode bicycles, spent more time in school, played musical instruments or participated in sports. Some worked odd jobs, trying to save money for college. Brand new brightly colored cars sped up and down the streets, sporting whitewall tires, wraparound

windshields and huge fins jetting out from the rear
fenders. When the drivers complained of mud and
potholes, trucks from the township came down the
roads spreading "red dog" hauled in from the coke
ovens in Lowber.

As jobs became more plentiful,
homeowners sealed up old chimneys and replaced
coal-fired stoves with furnaces, scrub boards with
washing machines, outhouses with indoor
commodes. They installed hot water tanks for
baths on Saturday night, purchased new ranges
with ovens and replaced iceboxes with
refrigerators. While many appliances could be
bought on credit, most people paid cash. It was a
learned habit from the harsh days of the
Depression. Families did things together.
They took the bus to church in Irwin or Herminie
on Sundays, had picnics on summer weekends,
went to drive-in movies and spent vacations with
relatives. It was the age when TV took off. During
the day, moms watched soap operas and quiz
shows. On weekends there was a rash of half-hour
cowboy shows for kids — *Tom Mix, Gene Autry,
Hopalong Cassidy, Roy Rogers, Lash Larue, Cisco
Kid, Wild Bill Hickok, Sky King, Lone Ranger*. The
children loved these shows and idolized the movie
actors who conveyed the same messages of right
and wrong taught to them by their parents,
teachers and the news media.

Neighbors got involved in the community. This was a time when 8-year-old girls could play in the woods all day long and not be molested, when young boys could hitchhike from town to town and never worry about kidnapping. Children obeyed their elders, trusted their neighbors, believed the soldiers in the military would protect them, held their hands over their hearts during the pledge of allegiance, respected the flag and stood by their President. The one big fear arose when Russia developed its own atomic bomb in 1949. Kids hid under their desks during air raid drills at school.

Swing bands that dominated the music on the radio in the late 40s were slowly disappearing. A new style of music cropped up in the mid-50s, rock and roll. It was rooted from rhythm and blues, jazz, gospel and country music. Much of the music was geared to 16 and 17-year-olds (*Puppy Love, Sweet Little Sixteen* and *Sixteen Candles,* for example). So compelling were the words and rhythm to these songs that everyone wanted to be age 16, including seventh-and-eighth-grade students. The same kids that learned reading, writing and arithmetic at Rillton School were suddenly reelin' and rockin' in downtown Herminie on Friday nights just a few short years later.

RILLTON

Post-high school education was a popular topic of discussion in 1961. Rillton parents, who before could only dream of sending their kids to college, now had their chance. But could they afford it? Because of the football team's success on the field, recruiters from college football campuses all over the United States swarmed the Sewickley High School building like flies, seeking talented players. Three players from Rillton took advantage of these "football scholarships" and went on to complete 4 years of college. Several other players on Bruno's team did the same. Such opportunity was unheard of in the previous decades.

A significant number of male and female students earned academic scholarships that year as well. Roughly half of the girls who volunteered as candy stripers entered the school of nursing. The majority of males and females found local jobs, settled down and looked to get married soon after graduating high school. A bunch of students entered military service. It was the beginning of the Vietnam War and the draft was reinstituted. There was a big push for young recruits to sign up for service under a program called the Buddy Deal, where buddies would end up being stationed together. It worked. Si, Weed and Dago all joined the Marines as buddies.

After graduation, Barry Horvat decided to throw a dance party. He spent the entire day cleaning out an old garage along Mars Hill Road and then borrowed a stack of 45s from his friends, including *My Guy* by Mary Wells. His girlfriend Marcy Farmer loved that song.

The kids at the party feasted on potato chips, pretzels and coca cola and rehashed the good old days — when the creek froze and they played ice hockey with dead tree branches shaped into primitive clubs; when they stocked small sunfish in dug-out ponds along the creek and tried to fend off water snakes with a .22 caliber rifle; when Weed nearly chopped off his foot at boy scout camp after Jingles handed him an axe; and when Mr. Decker threatened to throw a student in his seventh-grade math class from a third-story window. But mostly they danced. Dust and dirt from the old garage floor flew everywhere. During the song *Mr. Postman*, a passing motorist stopped his vehicle and asked if there was a fire. Si replied, "It was just Barry doing the Slop." They didn't know it then, but for many inside that crowded garage, it was the last good rock and roll party for years to come. Everyone later realized that friends go their separate ways after high school, shoving off to college or following dreams to places like Florida or California.

In the summer of 1961, a man named Leo, who ran a hamburger restaurant in Herminie, tried to open a drive-in restaurant near Indian Lake, similar to Barney's. It went out of business a year later. Teens still preferred Barney's, which was packed almost every night. Crabapple Lake swimming pool opened for the first time in Herminie. All around Pittsburgh, popular singers performed at high schools. Chubby Checker did his Twist, Bo Diddley pulsated a unique sound of music from his square guitar and the Isley Brothers brought down the house with their new song *Shout.* The usual entrance fee for these events was 50 cents. A few years later, ticket prices rose to $5.

When Linda Rupert threw a house party in the winter of 1961, Mag Ruzza, on her first semester break from college, taught everyone a new dance called the Frug. Like the Twist and the Pony, it was a good freestyle dance, though it didn't last very long. Neither did other solo dances that followed it — the Fly, the Swim, the Shimmy, the Jerk, the Monkey, the Funky Chicken and others. The dances were little more than upper body and arm movements, each dance seeming to imitate the other. They were superficial dances, many of which were broadcast live from Dick Clark's American Bandstand starting in the early sixties. As the new dance craze era moved forward, rock and roll fast dancing temporarily took a backseat.

Until the mid-sixties, talk of the Vietnam War in Rillton was sporadic. LBJ seldom held press conferences. What viewers picked up from the news on TV were bits and pieces of a confusing struggle, which was not really a war as they knew it. They thought it was another attempt by Russia and now Red China to spread communism. The evening news reports were straight-forward, limited to 30 minutes and did not include an in-depth, enigmatic analysis of such events. Our military was doing what it had to do to stop the spread of communism, people thought. If bombs needed to be dropped on the commies in targeted areas of North Vietnam, then so be it.

Wives in Rillton talked about their kids in college or the ones in the military, the new bottled eggs from the A&P store in Irwin (10 or 20 eggs could be poured from bottles without breaking the yolks) and the crazy weather. For two straight years bad droughts hit the area. Howell's dam nearly dried up, forcing the township to run a back-up water line from Indian Lake. Then, heavy rains flooded the streets of Pittsburgh, the worst flood in 10 years. They talked about Angelo Bazzo closing the ice cream shop and buying out the Trozzo store and the new road from Mars Hill all the way to Sutersville, which increased the traffic whizzing by Rillton School. "They should post a speed limit," said Mrs. Sikora.

Conversation of the men at both the Italian Club and the VFW centered mostly around sports. They followed the Olympic Games, watched Bob Hayes run the 100 meters in 10 seconds flat and rooted for the United States to beat the other teams, especially the Russians, in pole vaulting and other events. Bill Zimmer complained about the new Occupation Tax slapped on the poor workers in Pittsburgh, but no one seemed to care about that. The Vets were still angry at Khrushchev for trying to sneak missiles into Cuba. And when China detonated their first atomic bomb in 1964, it flared up new arguments about the arms race. At least Rillton had the protection of the Nike site up the road. There was talk about utilizing the old Youghiogheny RR Lindencross tunnel near Hahntown for shelter in the event of a nuclear attack.

And then news of the war got uglier. Bombs targeted for infiltrators from North Vietnam instead killed innocent civilians. Photo journalists caught all of this on camera and televised the images on the evening news — blood splattered on the streets, children crying, student demonstrators displaying mixed messages of hate and peace signs in front of the cameras. Captured American pilots were being paraded in the streets of Hanoi in front of jeering crowds. U.S. troop levels increased to 389,000 with 5,000 combat deaths. At the same time, 90,000 South Vietnamese soldiers had deserted their own army. Now people were getting antsy. They wanted something done about the war.

Everything had changed by 1966. The great civil rights movement, which flared up in the south, pitted peaceful marchers against German shepherd dogs. Martin Luther King, Jr. claimed the Vietnam conflict was hindering progress in the civil rights movement. Hollywood celebrities like Jane Fonda and the Smothers Brothers comedians supported an anti-war movement as well as athletes. Cassius Clay, a hero when he defeated Sonny Liston in 1964, became Muhammad Ali a year later and refused to be indoctrinated into the army. The Black Panther Party, founded in 1966, encouraged its members to carry guns and maintain a street mentality. Two American Olympic medalists gave the black power salute with their black armbands during the playing of the National Anthem. Rioting occurred in black ghettos during the hot summers in Watts (1965 through 1970) and in Newark (1967). Beatles and other singers let their hair grow much longer. Elvis said it was "unruly." Martin Luther King gave his famous "I have a Dream" speech but was shot and killed two years later. So was Bobby Kennedy. Rock and roll music turned into "hard rock." Lead singers yelled angry lyrics into microphones plugged into oversized loud speakers while electric guitars and synthesizers screamed in the background. It was an era of political assassinations, war protests, defiance of the establishment, sloppy dress, unshaven faces, long hair and liberal ideas that challenged all rational behavior by everyone over age 30.

RILLTON

In trying to maintain his popularity while addressing the war and other polarized issues, President Johnson took a middle of the road position. General Westmoreland had asked for 209,000 additional troops to fight the Viet Cong. Johnson authorized 45,000. War protesters cringed. WW II vets fumed. It seemed that LBJ could do nothing right.

In July 1966, by decree of law, Sewickley High was forced to merge with West Newton and South Huntington high schools. There was friction between the schools, the pupils, the parents and school board members. Hardly anyone was happy. It took 10 years to get it all straightened out. The great football era at Sewickley ended when John C. Bruno stopped coaching. Four years later he passed away at age 58.

At the VFW, WW II vets were talking about the conflict on a daily basis. Great arguments emerged. "Maybe they should just nuke 'em," said some. "But what about China? They got bombs, too," was the counter-argument. They denounced the civil rights marches. Most thought they were uncalled for and questioned why the 3 murdered civil rights marchers went down South to stir up trouble in the first place. But after few beers, the conversation always came back to sports. In the first NFC-ACF Championship game for the NFL title in January 1967, the Packers beat the KC Chiefs by a score of 35-10. Everyone knew Vince Lombardi's Pack would beat the daylights out of "that other team."

It was as troublesome for war vets to fully explain the Vietnam debacle as it was for the college students to fully come to grips with the war's necessity. What the students saw on campuses across America was a growing scorn from Liberal Arts professors, increased resistance to the draft and a growing disrespect of the local police tactics used to control mostly peaceful demonstrations. But they weren't alone in their vacillation. In time, half the country came to renounce the war, which didn't end until 1975. Draft-dodgers were pardoned and the country began slowly drifting back toward the center from the extreme edges of politics. In Rillton, there was always an unwavering, heartfelt commitment to support the troops no matter what. But still lingering in the minds of many was the intellectual challenging question: was it acceptable to draft young recruits to fight an ideological war, such as Vietnam, one that did not, at least on the surface, involve our national security?

Beginning in the early 60s, rock and roll music slid in all directions First came the British invasion — The Beatles, Rolling Stones and later on The Animals, The Kinks, The Who and Herman's Hermits. They called it British rock. Out of

RILLTON

California came surf music from the Beach Boys. Heavy metal rock became popular as well as the rhythm and blues Motown sound out of Detroit, which included The Four Tops, The Temptations, The Supremes and Marvin Gaye. There was garage rock, when youngsters started rehearsing songs out of their garages, like the Kingsmen and Paul Revere and the Raiders. There was pop rock, folk rock, hard rock, soft rock, psychedelic rock, progressive rock (with full orchestras in the background), jazz rock (Chicago), country rock and, later on, punk rock and new wave (Devo and Police). By the mid-sixties, everyone simply called it "rock." The new rock music raced through the airwaves from coast to coast like a great winter storm. Somewhere beneath the white noise lay the simple sounds of doo-wop playing on radios still tuned into the WAMO station in Pittsburgh.

When Zip came home for his 10-year high school reunion, his friend Dago telephoned to "shoot the shit." Dago was now living in one-half of the double-family house opposite his parents at the north end of Rillton. By the time they finished a second round of beers, Mrs. Campoli cooked up a batch of spaghetti, something she always did when Zip came home from college. And now she was back at it again, this time for a high school reunion.

"Mama, there you go, always cooking for this guy, like some kinda goombah!" said Dago.

"That's my Anthony. Always with the teasing. You know he's just kidding, right?" glancing at Zip. "Of course he knows. You think I would insult my friend?" Dago answered before Zip could speak.

Just then, 76 year old Tony Campoli, still ailing from the coal mining accident of 50 years ago, hobbled into the kitchen using a cane. He stood only 5'2" tall and looked rather frail but was a delightful man, full of vigor and wit and always ready to talk about life, even if the topic was something as mundane as the weather.

"Your Dad still planting cabbages? You know, he always did outdo me on dat," he began, encircling his arms, rounding out the size of an imaginary cabbage head. "But I out did him on everything else!" "Once, my Dad tried to make red wine from grapes like you. It tasted like vinegar. He never tried to make wine after that," Zip replied. "He never told me that," Tony said, shaking his head. "No, he never told me." He laughed uncontrollably. "Next time I see him, U'ma gonna rub it in his face." And then he laughed even harder.

During the Sewickley reunion of 1971, the Moose hall in Herminie was filled with newlyweds trying to introduce their spouses while at the same time trying to rediscover the lives of their old schoolmates. Some of them hadn't seen in each other in 10 years, even though many lived only a few miles apart. Gart bad-mouthed the new Yough High School. "When you slice the football budget in half, no wonder you end up with a lousy team," he grumbled. Most alumni, however, reminisced about the old school days — Mr. Pritts in English class cracking his paddle against his wooden leg, like a rattlesnake warning its victims; the Saturday night dances that Bruno hated because they scratched up the gym floor; the broken floorboard at Sam's roller skating rink that caused kids to stumble into the wall; and the time Sam threatened to throw Porky Chedwick out of his building because he brought in Negro singers.

Interestingly, no one discussed Vietnam. Classmates did share some gloomy stories though. Frank Mayo, a class clown, the one who nicknamed Tom Lord *The Good Lord Tom*, the one who looked at the world with cynicism and drove teachers half nuts with his classroom antics, suffered through months of unbearable headaches and ended his life by committing suicide, they said with a gun; Francis Gedman was killed in action; Fuzzy McGrew lost his life in a bar fight after returning from the war; and John C. Bruno, the coach whom everyone in Sewickley Township admired, passed away earlier that year.

But there were up-lifting stories too. Classmates remembered how Kay Kolesha used to walk up and down the halls of Sewickley on crutches in the 7th grade. Everyone thought she had polio. At the reunion, she dispelled the rumor. Turns out, she fell off a horse and broke her leg. It had nothing to do with polio.

Grass had an unusual story to tell but figured no one would believe it except Zip.

Grass: Remember the day we ran the crick and you heard voices coming out of the little stream past Barry's house?

Zip: Not really.

Grass: Then a few days later you told me it sounded like *farewell.*

Zip: Yes...I do remember.

Grass: I heard it two weeks ago when I walked the new trail around Indian Lake.

Zip: Heard what?

Grass: You know, the voice from the woman.

Zip: A woman? You think it was a woman?

Grass: Definitely a woman. She said *farewell running creek*.

Zip: ...Farewell...running creek? That makes no sense to me.

Grass: You're right. It makes no sense. Just thought I'd pass it along.

With that, the two kids who ran the Little Sewickley Creek 12 years prior shrugged their shoulders, walked off and never spoke of the matter again.

What bonds students in the days of their early education goes beyond the familiar faces that show up at school each day. It is the shared experiences and the chain of friendships that develop along the way. For most graduates in the class of 1961, the bonds ran uncommonly deep. Whenever the time came for a reunion, adrenalin raced through their veins. Graduates as far away as the west coast and Florida made special plans, committing to find a way back to Sewickley Township just to spend a few short hours with old friends.

Like most high school reunions, Sewickley's 10th began with a crowd of young men and women playing the role of grownups in front of their old friends whom they last remembered as kids. By the middle of the evening, when the hair came down and the neckties came off, the same people were hugging and teasing one another like grammar school children. And as the evening came to an end, ideas of all sorts popped up for the next reunion. Something was missing. What was it?

"We should lug out the old 45 rock and roll records and have a sock hop," Faith suggested. Others agreed. After all, what is a reunion without oldies? Thereafter, each and every reunion whaled out oldies but goodies, not the ones from

American Bandstand, nor the ones from California, nor Woodstock, but the doo-wop tunes straight from the heart and soul of Porky Chedwick.

Sewickley High closed its doors in 1976. Half the building was demolished and the other half was converted into a recreation center. The loss of the building, however, would not erase the memories that linger in the minds of the hundreds of formers students who relive their youthful days at the reunions.

Rillton School was torn down about the same time as SHS. Residents were saddened, and rightly so, for that building represented the cornerstone of activity during the 1950s. When the kids stopped attending school there, the town's social structure began to shut down, for it was the kids who knocked on doors at Halloween and made the widows feel a little less lonely. The kids were the ones who bought candy and soda pop and ice cream and kept the stores in Rillton open for business. The kids gave Mr. Trozzo an incentive to mow the grass in the ball field and kept the Moms busy cooking spaghetti dinners in order to raise money for the Boy Scout troop so they could march down the street and wear their shirts and badges on Decoration Day. And it was the kids who brought life to the Italian Club when they played songs from their rented musical instruments in front of a group of tearful mothers.

After the school closed, students started boarding a yellow bus at the old Company Store en route to schools outside of Rillton. They were dropped off at the same place later in the day. A few years later, the bus drivers dropped kids off at their front doorsteps, where their Moms or older siblings would cart them around in the second family vehicle to places outside of Rillton, such as movie theaters, shopping centers and activities at their new schools. Football players would ride cars to Herminie, do workouts at Crabapple Park, then jump in the swimming pool. In the process, money was being spent outside of the village. Bicycles sat in garages, hardly even used. Kid traffic in Rillton came to a near halt.

When ice cream sales bottomed out, Bazzo hoped to recapture the sales by purchasing Trozzo's feed and supply store across the road from the ball field. Unfortunately, the kids who were expectedly driven to the store because of thirst or hunger for ice cream weren't using the field anymore. Men's softball leagues still used the field but they were beer drinkers, not soda drinkers. Trozzo sold the store to Lemon's Market in 1972. A few years later, Lemon's Market closed for good. Stores went out of business, not because of any economic downturn or failed government program but because the market for these items were driven by kids.

Infrastructure in Rillton had always been on shaky ground. Initially, there was a mass transit system with trains running from Irwin to Gratztown and points beyond as early as 1904. This was followed by a trolley service until 1928, and finally bus service that lasted until the late 1960s. Meanwhile, Rillton's muddy roads were covered with ashes, then red dog. Asphalt paving didn't arrive until the mid 1950's. After all, it took years for people to save enough money to buy their rented houses, let alone pay more taxes to cover road maintenance. But once the roads were fully improved and vehicular traffic took over, bus service came to an end. Anyone without a vehicle would need to bum a ride.

The old company houses were solidly built. Properly maintained, many had lasted more than 100 years. Initially the houses had no indoor plumbing. During heavy rains, outhouses overflowed and contaminated the cisterns and water wells. In the late 1940's, the township ran fresh water lines to these homes from Howell's Dam, backed up by Indian Lake. Homes were improved with indoor plumbing but the waste water ran to underground septic tanks and absorption fields, which overflowed into the Pennsylvania clay soil which doesn't percolate very well. For years the waste water mixed with rain surface water and seeped into the small rills feeding the Rillton creek. It took a hundred years before the township finally installed sanitary sewer lines in town.

Several of the old company houses in town had depreciated beyond repair. Some were torn down and replaced with mobile homes, which is often the case with other coal towns in the area. Due to the absence of zoning ordinances, other parcels were converted to commercial use, a dilemma that discourages people from building new houses inside the village. Most developers have constructed housing communities in areas outside of Rillton. In spite of this anomaly, most villagers have kept their yards free of unsightly debris, trimmed their shrubbery and planted flowers and vegetables as their ancestors would have done in years past. Part of Rillton had not lost its flavor.

Like most other coal towns, Rillton never had enough commercial businesses to support a Chamber of Commerce or any plan to make the common areas more attractive. Once the Rillton School closed, more businesses shut down - the Joe Kertis Barber shop, Bazzo's Insurance agency and the Italian Club, to name a few. War Vets and their wives used to maintain a small plot of land around the Veteran's Memorial, which was set up in front of the old post office. Everyone coming into town could see and admire it. But it was relocated alongside the VFW building and is now hidden from view. Since the mid 1960's Rillton's identity as well as its infrastructure had been dismantled. Presently, there are no unique landmarks to distinguish this town from dozens of others just like it.

But for the children who happened to grow up there in the right window of time, when the war had just ended, when social life was buzzing at places like the Italian Club, Trozzo's ball field, the Shuster picnic grounds, the Memorial Day parades and the Rillton schoolyard – when the town was at its peak – for them, never was there a better time to learn about the world and experience what are now only distant memories of a town called Rillton.